Alvin Lincoln Snow

**Tales told in a country store and accompanying verse**

Alvin Lincoln Snow

**Tales told in a country store and accompanying verse**

ISBN/EAN: 9783337137441

Printed in Europe, USA, Canada, Australia, Japan

Cover: Foto ©Andreas Hilbeck / pixelio.de

More available books at **www.hansebooks.com**

# TALES

TOLD IN A

# COUNTRY STORE

AND

# ACCOMPANYING VERSE

———

BY

## REV. ALVIN LINCOLN SNOW

———

CRESTON, IOWA:
THE SNOW PUBLISHING FIRM
1898

# List of Poems.

# Salutation.

This life of ours is like a crowded street,
　Through which we pass but once.　We cannot turn,
　Retrace our steps, however we may yearn:
On must we press, though with reluctant feet:
Yet as we go we may drop words replete
　With lofty fancies that within us burn—
　Thoughts that may cheer some mortal 'mid earth's stern
Realities—such I would fain repeat.
Hail, gentle reader!　I will call thee friend,
　Although mine eyes have never seen thy face,
　　Although thy hand hath never clasped mine own.
"Of making many books there is no end:"
　Yet hope I this of mine may find a place
　　Within thy heart—awake responsive tone.

Alvin L. Snow.

# Tales Told in a Country Store.

## REMINISCENCES

OF A

## RUSTIC SUMMER VACATION.

# Tales Told in a Country Store.

———

In a portion of country I now know quite well,
  Not extremely remote from a flourishing town,
Whose location and name scarce 'twere worth while to tell,
1.    Is a small country store, weather-beaten and brown.
Near by, two roads cross, and a guide-board is placed,
  The way-faring traveler's route to make plain.
By truant boys' jack-knives and shot-guns defaced,
  It stands like a martyr in sun and in rain.

Most beautiful farms this quaint building surround;
  Broad meadows and vast fields devoted to corn.
What herds of sheep, cattle and horses abound!
2.    O, city youth! curl not your proud lip in scorn!
The denizens live by the sweat of the brow;
  Though not eager to grasp for "the latest thing out."
There are, among those who there follow the plow,
  Many minds that your "cultured set" vainly would flout.

'Tis a mixed population;--not mixed in the sense
  In which we that term so expressive oft use;
They are not from all parts of the world so immense,
3.    Nor yet are they people of various hues.
The citizens there hail from near and from far—
  From the South. from the North, from the West, from the
    East;
From every state that is bless'd with a star
  In our flag's constellation there seems one at least.

The city-bred person exclaims, "O, how dull!
    No soirees, concerts, lectures—why, what a dead place!"
But oft 'tis relief to have e'en a brief lull
4.    In the bustle and whirl of life's maddening race.
And that is the reason I fled from the crowd,
    And rambled down thither to sojourn awhile,
Away from the stilted, the formal, the proud,—
    Away from the tyrannous edicts of Style.

In short space of time I the fact understood,
    That that little store was the centre of all
Attraction and int'rest in that neighborhood—
5.    At least for the male portion—young, old, short, tall.
One after another, when day's toil was o'er,
    The farmers would come—some would ride, some would walk.
For groc'ries or mail,—for post-office and store
In one were combined—then they'd linger and talk.

In Winter and Summer this custom prevailed
    Alike—with this diff'rence, not striking nor great:
In Winter, the concourse that met seldom failed
6.    To average larger, and linger more late.
'Tis a strange thing, but true; to their fields men would go—
    Labor hard from the rise to the set of the sun,
And, however a-weary in toil they might grow,
    To the store wend their way when the day's tasks were done.

Now, if men were as constant in going to church
    As the denizens there in that calm country place
In frequenting the *store*—then how many a search
7.    Would   the   pastors be spared for lost sheep—strays from
            grace!
If men can be prompt for *one* purpose, then why
    Can they not for *another?*   If people can walk,
Say two or three miles, hot or cold, wet or dry,
    To swap yarns, can they not for a good Gospel talk?

How can men who are weary as weary can be
    Hitch up and drive out, just to be *entertained,*
Then when summoned to *worship* put up the bold plea,
8.    "Too tired?"—I want this conundrum explained.

# Tales Told in a Country Store.

Why do men who get up ev'ry day of the week,
    Except Sunday, at five—men supposed to be *live*—
Fail to rise till too late the Lord's temple to seek?
    At what sort of conclusion ought one to arrive?

But you say I am preaching. I did not intend
    To do so at all—I meant simply to tell
What transpired down yonder. These lines I have penned
9.    Some eyes there may see, but—perhaps it were well.
This digression excuse. I will instantly stop,
    And turn without pause to the matter in hand.
But no pardon I crave for the *lesson* I drop;
    I would it were pondered throughout the whole land.

At the store, upon barrels and boxes and kegs—
    Whatever afforded a ghost of a seat—
Men would take up their stations and, crossing their legs,
10.    The day's sundry doings con o'er and repeat.
The Government's action formed ground for a part
    Of discussion as well as each local affair;
The latest discov'ries in Science and Art
    Oft came in for no mere insignificant share.

When they had recounted to each one's content,
    The news of the day, of the country and place,
And gen'ral discussion its force had well spent,
11.    A silence profound oft would reign for a space.
But presently some one a tale would begin,
    Suggested quite often by something just said;—
Some-times having origin wholly within
    The fanciful realm of the tale-teller's head.

"Twas a free-for-all lyceum—not so in name,
    But in fact and effect— oft in profit as well.
Scarce a session was held that was dull, flat or tame,
12.    Whatsoever the unenrolled members befell.
With a song the assembly informal oft closed,
    In which all would join—but full often the song
Was a solo the singer himself had composed:
    A sort of *finale*, dismissing the throng.

Now, I am no loafer; I never have been;
　　And I hold to pass time in *mere lounging* is worse
　O, worse far than useless—'tis positive sin.
13.　　What well used were a blessing, ill-used is a curse.
　　But whoever might have an occasion to go
　　　To that common resort on a beautiful eve,
　　Would be struck with the quaint entertainment I know,
　　　And loth as was I the unique scene to leave.


　　And now, as I call up to mind the delight
　　　And enchantment I felt in that lone country store,
　　On hearing those brawny soil-tillers recite
14.　　In their own simple language their artless tales o'er,
　　I am moved to recall and relate what I can
　　　Of the stories thus heard—not avouching their truth
　　With a hope they may cheer the worn, world-weary man,
　　　And furnish diversion for age and for youth.

"WHEN WHO SHOULD TAP MY KITCHEN DOOR?—
WHO BUT A 'POOR' OL' TRAMP?"

*See page 15.*

# Chapter 1.

---

---

When I went, that first eve, to the little brown store,
　　I went for my mail, and for nothing beside.
Speaking frankly, I longed for my fireside once more:
1.　　And earth seemed uncommonly dreary and wide.
As I from my boarding-place sauntered away,
　　A half-homesick feeling arose in my heart;
I thought of my dear ones, and fancied that they
　　Were thinking of me.—We are seldom apart.

I expected a good lengthy missive from home,
　　To tell me of all that was happening there.
Having granted my thoughts full permission to roam,
2.　　I found myself soon at my goal unaware.
As I entered, and cast my first glance at the crowd,
　　Repulsive it seemed. I felt bored and annoyed
By the Babel of voices, then boist'rous and loud.
　　Of aught that could charm seemed the place wholly void.

At once I resolved very soon to return;
　　But as just then a bystander called for some stamps.
I gazed round again, in attempt to discern
3.　　Any face I might know.—They were speaking of tramps.
Having glanced through my letter—that treasure had come—
　　And feeling my lonesomeness partly dismissed
By its contents so precious, and somewhat less glum,
　　Temptation to linger I scarce could resist.

One had just read aloud, while the rest all gave heed,
    Of a case of a "specimen," somewhere in Maine.
Representing himself in the sorriest need,
4.    He applied at a farm-house for food—not in vain.
"Stay there," said the lady, quite kindly,—"Stay there,
    In the porch; and I shortly will bring you some food."
A sandwich and tea she made haste to prepare;
    In this fellow's *menu*, these, 'twould seem, were tabooed.

The sandwich he promptly returned in her face,
    With the tea saturated her gown clean and neat;
And then, with a most diabolic grimace,
5.    Smashed the prized china cup on the floor at her feet.
Then with language disdainful--a mocking adieu—
    Slightly bowed, turned and leisurely rambled away.
Apropos of this episode, each had some new
    And original thing on the subject to say.

One by one, those assembled recounted some bit
    Of experience had with this wandering class,
Interlarding accounts with grim humor and wit,
6.    Such as e'en in most brilliant assemblies would pass.
One told of a stranger like this whom he fed,
    One evening--with warmest and tend'rest regard.
At morn he discovered the cheese, ham and bread
    In Christmas-style hung on a tree in his yard.

One remembered a straggler who claimed to be starved,
    And appeared at his kitchen for something to eat.
Bread and butter he furnished—some ham, too, he carved—
7.    And constructed a lunch that could hardly be beat.
But in passing the hog-pen soon after, he saw
    The occupants hastening something to munch
Curiosity prompting him nearer to draw,
    Some fragments he found of that well-prepared lunch.

Then one of the group--a tall, angular man—
    By whom, till that time, few remarks had been made,
With vehemence startling, said: "Shoot the hull clan!
8.    I'll tell ye a tale to lay yourn in the shade."

So, shifting his quid, and at once taking aim
    At the wooden spittoon—which he missed, by the way—
Uncrossing his legs and adjusting his frame,
    He proceeded to voice what he purposed to say:—

        " 'Twas late one evenin', work was o'er,
1.      The air was chill an' damp,
        When who should tap my kitchen door?—
        Who but a poor ol' tramp?

        He spun a very piteous yarn
11.    O' hunger, cold an' damp,
        An' wished to sleep within my barn,
        And get a bite—the tramp!

        Such wand'rers then 'were scarce to view
111.   Down *our* way—seldom seen;
        Their visits were like angels'—few,
        An' ruther far between.

        My wife she called 'em "pesky scamps."
IV.    I thought her biased then;
        *I* rarely called 'em even tramps,
        But poor way-farin' men.

        I fancied 'em a class abused
V.      Alike by great an' small,
        Misjudged, ill treated an' misused
        By high an' low an' all.

        An' so, as I beheld his form
VI.    Amid the shadders dim,
        A feelin' tender, soft an' warm
        Rose in my breast fur him.

        I said, 'Come in, poor wand'rin' lad!'
VII.   I then my table spread,
        Regrettin' sorely that I had
        Fur him no clean, soft bed.

Brown bread an' butter, pork an' beans,
VIII.    Substantial food an' good,
    I brought (reflectin' *I* had means
      To gain a livelihood.)

An' then I brought on cake an' pie,
IX.    An' some delicious fruit.
    My wife she eyed the scene awry,
      But kep' discreetly mute.

He gracefully sat down to sup,
X.    Responsive to my nod,
    An' bowed as if a-off'rin' up
      His silent thanks to God.

Laws! how he handled fork an' knife.
XI.    As if he ne'er had seen
    A good square meal in all his life!
      An' yet he wasn't lean—

But big an' burly, hale and stout,
XII.    With plump an' rosy cheek.
    (My symp'thy was too much drawn out
      To notice his physique.)

Sakes! how he ate an' ate an' ate,
XIII.    As if he ne'er would stop!
    My pity fur him was so great
      The big tears had to drop.

The cups o' coffee that he drank!
XIV.    The stuff he stowed away!
    His spirits rose as victuals sank,
      An' he was glad an' gay.

When he was done, he chatted long
XV.    'Bout places where he'd been,
    In lonely haunt, in rushin' throng
      But ne'er in paths o' sin.

To me minutely he explained
XVI.   How he had lost his pile;
       Fur somehow Fortune never deigned
           Upon him long to smile.

He had been once a millionaire,
XVII.   An' traveled o'er the earth;
        But since that he'd known want an' care—
            An' what kind acts was worth.

He'd visited with duke and prince,
XVIII.   Had dined with queens an' kings.
         Great int'rest did my boys evince
             In all these marv'lous things.

The incidents he glibly told
XIX.   Seemed each a fairy tale,
       An' from his fluent lips they rolled
           As if they'd never fail.

But when the ol' clock chimed out ten,
XX.   He checked himself an' yawned.
      A kind o' spell seemed broken then,
          As if by magic wand.

My children all had held their breath;
XXI.   My wife had ceased to sew;
       An' ev'rything was still as death,
           When he arose to go.

He said he guessed that he'd retire.
XXII.   To take much-needed rest.
        His smooth politeness you'd admire
            In any high-bred guest.

I then expressed my great regret,
XXIII.   That, as my house was small,
         I had no spare room.   This he met
             With, 'Never mind at all.'

My kindness he'd remember oft.

XXIV.    When Luck, the fickle dame,
Should lift him once again aloft,
    He'd want to know my name.

I gave him that, an' he withdrew,

XXV.    Down in my barn to camp,
Singin' a song — to me 'twas new—
    'I'm but a poor ol' tramp.'

My children's visual orbs once more

XXVI.    Resumed their nat'ral size;
An', all preliminaries o'er,
    In sleep we closed our eyes.

'Twas midnight. I should jedge. — or nigh—

XXVII.    When from sweet dreams I woke.
Great Scott! What roarin' rent the sky!
    The air was full o' smoke!

I rushed out with my night-clo'es on,

XXVIII.    (The air was chill an' damp)
To find my barn was nearly gone.
    Gone was the poor ol' tramp.

I shivered at a distance safe.

XXIX.    The lurid scene to scan.
An' how I longed to see that waif —
    That poor way-farin' man.

Naught could I do but gaze an' sigh

XXX.    As long as I desired.
'Twas but a few brief days since my
    Insurance had expired.

You never saw a bluer soul—

XXXI.    On that you may depend—
The flames a-ragin' past control—
    I watchin' 'em ascend!

My neighbors come like birds in flocks;
XXXII.    They were a helpless crew.
I stood a-shakin' in my socks,
    As if I nothin' knew.

They spoke consolin'ly, like this:—
XXXIII.    'Pshaw, man! you're richer yet
Than thousands! Things will go amiss!
    Don't lose yer grip! Don't fret!'

'Most ev'ry proverb, dull or bright,
XXXIV.    From Adam's day to ours,
Was quoted to me that sad night,
    To save my mental powers.

Excited people come by loads
XXXV.    Fur miles an' miles, I ween;
We heard 'em tearin' 'long the roads,
    A-rushin' to the scene.

'Twas vain! The ruthless element
XXXVI.    Still claimed the right o' way,
An' run until its force was spent:
    Its progress naught could stay.

The splendid bran-new phaeton
XXXVII.    I'd bought the day afore,
To please my wife an' little son —
    Alas, it was no more!

My farm-machin'ry — ev'rything
XXXVIII.    Wherewith I tilled the soil—
Lay in a shed which formed a wing,
    It was the fire-king's spoil!

My cows an' hosses an' my sheep,
XXXIX.    My hay an' all my corn,—
All lay in one black smokin' heap,
    When dawned the light o' morn!

Where was the hero o' the night—
XXXX.     My new-found friend so true?
The sheriff tracked him in his flight:
      But soon he lost the clue.

I vowed he'd tried to shield the knave,
XXXXI.     An' that I'd hunt myself;
But soon opined I'd better save
      My trouble, time an' pelf.

Some said 'twould be like huntin' in
XXXXII.     A mow or stack o' hay,
To find a needle or a pin.
      The world is wide, said they.

An' though I ached to see his face,
XXXXIII.     An' ask him to explain,
I voted it a wild-goose chase,
      An' calmed my anxious brain.

As I was rummagin' around
XXXXIV.     The conflagration's mass,
A remnant o' a pipe I found—
      My visitor's, alas!

His very tones I recollect,
XXXXV.     When 'I don't smoke' he said.
He had a habit I suspect,
      O' smokin' when a-bed.

I often wonder where he roves,
XXXXVI.     That lazy prince o' liars,—
Devourin' honest people's loaves—
      An' startin' extra fires.

'Sadder an' wiser?'—Well, I guess!
XXXXVII.     Sadder, to say the least!
I vow my wisdom is no less,
      An' p'r'aps my stock's increased.

They say we're ne'er too old to learn.
xxxxviii.   There's knowledge not in schools.
Exper'ence is a master stern,
   An' teaches all 'cept fools.

As onward through this life we go,
xxxxix.   We find out more an' more;
The more we live the more we know,
   Upon this earthly shore.

I used to reckon charity
l.   O' all the virtues chief;
But prudence, though a rarity.
   Now leads—in my belief.

All men are architec's o' fate;
li.   So I have somewheres read,
If each man does his luck create,
   How keerful should we tread!

Way-farin' men now jog along.
lii.   I let 'em all pursue
Their weary way; I'm big an' strong:
   My words are short an' few.

I say to sech a would-be guest:—
liii.   'Find quarters furder on.'
An' ne'er am I content to rest
   Until I *know* he's gone.

I keep a gun an' dog.  The brute
liv.   Escorts 'em to the gate,
With look an' manner resolute;
   An' they don't linger late.

I have no malice in my heart,
lv.   But deep down in my soul,
There's joy at seein' 'em depart,
   Where'er may be their goal:—

LVI.
Fur somehow, since that evenin' when
    I housed him from the damp,
I have not felt as I felt then
    Toward the poor ol' tramp."

While the story went on, all was still in the store;
    One could plainly have heard the proverbial pin.
But as soon as the speaker's narration was o'er,
9.    A confusion of voices ensued—quite a din.
The hubbub soon ceased, and discussion arose,
    In regard to some logical, feasible plan
Whereby our long-suffering land might dispose
    Of this bug-bear, this humbug, this "traveling man."

One suggested that none be permitted by law
    With no money at all on the highway to roam.
One remarked, with a wink, that, if rightly he saw,
10.    Such a rule would confine present comp'ny at home.
'Twas suggested by one that each pilgrim be made
    To disclose a sworn record of all his past life.
The facetious man said if such law were obeyed,
    Some he knew would keep close to their children and wife.

But more serious arguments quickly displaced
    The ones that were given in lightness and jest.
Some were worthy our Capitol's halls to have graced,
11.    And ably were rendered, with vigor and zest.
But whether or not a sure plan they discerned
    For abating the nuisance, I cannot now state.
I looked at my watch. It was late. I returned
    To the place of my sojourn at rather brisk gait.

That night I had some most remarkable dreams,
    As sleep-won at last in my chamber I lay.
My mind conjured up the most marvellous schemes
12.    For frightening unwelcome callers away.
To my own home transported, I stood at the door,
    When attacked by a stranger of profligate stamp.
Fiercely struggling, I triumphed! I woke—on the floor,
    With a badly-smashed chair and an over turned lamp!

**22**

"IN A MINUTE, SOME WILD REVOLUTIONS SHE MADE."

*See page 25.*

# Chapter 2.

I wondered, while leisurely strolling along
    Tow'rd the store, what the paramount topic would be,
For talk and discussion, that night in the throng,—
1.    Marvelled whether or not it would interest me.
A hint of tobacco-smoke lurked in the breeze,
    As I drew near the door, which was slightly ajar.
With chair tilted, legs crossed, hands clasping both knees,
    The proprietor sat with a half-spent cigar.

"You're early; or, rather, I guess the crowd's late.
    Beg your pardon," he said, in his brisk, cheery style.
"I think you've some mail; yes, there is, sure as fate!
2.    Have a glimpse at the *Daily?* Sit down; rest awhile."
With some hesitation, I seated myself;
    But just for a moment—so then I believed.
He fell to arranging some goods on a shelf,
    And I to perusing what I had received.

So absorbed was my mind with its task—so engrossed—
    I scarce heeded aught that was passing around;
But at length, glancing up from a page of the *Post,*
3.    Myself in a good-sized assemblage I found.
Incited by impulse and pre-formed resolve,
    I arose to my feet and prepared to depart;
But ere action could out of purpose evolve,
    Curiosity chained me with magical art.

"Have you heard of the would-be elopement?" one said.
    A full chorus of voices responded, "Why, no!"
"Yes, indeed!—down at Hinkman's. Lil wanted to wed,
4.    But the ol' folks they told the young feller to go.
Well, he went,—an' fair Lilian she went with him, too.
    They 'loped, an' her daddy loped after 'em both
On his high-mettled racer, with wondrous ado,
    With many a threat, an' with many an oath.

Fur the State line the couple a bee-line had struck,
　　An' were makin' good headway—they had an hour's start—
　.When they met with a piece of uncommon ill luck,
5.　　An' were rudely an' ruthlessly sundered apart.
They were on the 'home-stretch'--from the line 'bout a mile—
　　An' in sight o' the preacher's, when Lily desired
That he'd slack up his hosses a wee, little while:
　　Out o' danger they seemed, an' the beasts 'peared so tired.

Well, he did.　'Twas a mighty mistake.　Lookin' back—
　　Peekin' over his shoulder—the ol' man he saw
Like a blood-thirsty hound comin' hard on their track:
6.　　Neck an' neck at his side rode a knight o' the law.
A strikin' and marvellous scene then ensued!
　　Then follered the wildest, *excitingest* chase
That *ever* in them parts or *any* was viewed—
　　The runaways kep' a good lead in the race.

Yes, he had fine nags.　But in 'passin' a clump
　　O' trees by the road, comin' round with a sweep,
The right for'ard wheel struck a gnarly ol' stump,
7.　　An' left 'em forthwith.　They a-lit in a heap.
*He* came to himself in a room o' the jail;
　　*She* came to herself in her own room at home.
I wonder if this is the end o' the tale,
　　Or whether again they'll endeavor to roam.

Now, if *I* had a daughter that wanted a man
　　*That* bad, I believe I'd just let 'em pursue
To its end an' fulfillment their nice little plan,
8.　　An' not interfere with their sweet game.—Would *you?*"
This to *me* was addressed.　I was nearly struck dumb,
　　But soon managed to say my resistance I'd gauge
In great part by conditions—especially some—
　　The youth's prospects and habits—the girl's tastes and age.

Then up spoke a man with a thin, freckled face:—
　　"Elopements are plenty, too common, that's sure;
An' often they lead to distress an' disgrace.
9.　　The problem is, *how the great mania to cure.*

But waivin' that question, it's wonderful strange
   How so many smart schemes fur sech business fall through.
When *almost* successful—presto! there's a change!
   Is it chance?  No, 'tis Providence—that is *my* view.

An incident happened down close to a place
   Where I formerly lived—in the country below—
The funniest episode—*very* queer case—
10.   It occurred—well, I guess about six year ago.
A young girl detarmined ag'in the advice
   An' will o' her parents to marry a scamp.
She, bright 'nough but green, thought o' course he was nice;
   But he was as wuthless as any low tramp.

The ol' folks a trip to the city had planned;
   At morn to depart an' at eve to return.
The young sprout he found out the lay o' the land,
11.   An' got her persuaded their wishes to spurn.
So they made out their program.  They'd get on the train
   At Gates, by the wagon-route five mile away;
An' to save observation, an' some time to gain,
   They'd take a short cut;—through a pastur' it lay.

Well, all went as merry as merry could be,—
   Yes—'as merry's a marriage-bell', some one has said,
When he, as if struck with hysterical glee,
12.   Turnin' one or two somersaults, stood on his head.
She screamed as ef murdered; an', glancin' about,
   Saw a big ram a-backin' to git a fresh start;
But stood as if glued in her tracks.  There's no doubt
   That she then lost her *head* as she'd late lost her *heart*.

In a minute, some wild revolutions she made,
   An', 'slightly disfiggered, but still in the ring,'
Once again faced the foe, who no mercy displayed,—
13..   Unsparin as any ol' barbarous king!
Her lover, recovered somewhat from the shock
   Of his recent performance, arose in some wrath,
. An' speechlessly motioned her tow'rd a huge rock
   That ascended in grandeur not far from the path.

Ensconced on its top, they could smile on their foe;
   But ere they could reach the Gibraltar they sought,
Both kissed terra-firma 'bout six times or so,
14.    Performin' feats seldom in circuses wrought.
On the boulder at last, out o' harm's way they sat.
   But the smile that they smiled was a sorrerful one.
Coat in strings; ditto gown; each was minus a hat;
   An' the tear-drops were prone with the blood-drops to run.

Well, they smiled on their foe—ef a-showin' the teeth
   Is smilin". With int'rest he answered their smile,
As he paced back an' forth on the hard ground beneath
15.    In true soldier fashion—reel sentinel style.
The sun in the western horizon sunk low,
   An' sadly they watched it as fas' it slipped down.
They longed to depart, but their guard wouldn't go;
   An' soon would the ol' folks be back from the town!

The ol' folks returned. She was missed. A quick search
   Was at once made by neighbors. The mis'rable pair
Were found an' removed from their comfortless perch.
16.    She was promptly restored to her parents' fond care.
He was given due notice an' time to depart,
   An' the very nex' day bade the region adieu;—
With all wounds neatly dressed—'cept the wounds o' his heart—
   He departed fur verdanter fields—pastures new."

There fell a brief silence. A man tall and thin,
   With a thin and sharp voice, next proceeded to say
That *he* knew a case that seemed closely akin
17.   To the cases described—quite as comic as they.
His falsetto tones drew attention from all;
   Ev'ry eye in the room turned the speaker to scan.
With slight nasal accent and singular drawl,
   He delivered his story. As follows it ran:—

      "Twas a youth o' sixty summers
         Loved a maiden o' sixteen;
      Suitors were not welcome comers—
1.        Parents wished no weddin'-scene.
      So, as Fate refused to ope
      Any other door of hope,
      They decided they'd elope.

In a farm-house lived the maiden;
   Her adorer dwelt in town;
Oft with sweet-meats amply laden,

II.      In great style he would come down:
An' the damsel loitered nigh,
As his chariot-wheels rolled by,—
O, the twain were wondrous sly!

So they put their heads together,
   An' arranged a purty scheme;
All seemed fav'rin'—e'en the weather—

III.     The fulfillin' o' their dream!
Sudden frosts the flowers nip;
Sudden tempests wreck the ship;
Many a slip 'twixt cup an' lip!

Was it chance?—They had been sittin'
   Underneath an apple-tree;
Far above 'em birds seemed flittin','

IV.     While they planned that night to flee.
So they *guessed*;—they little *knew*.
He had said, 'I'll come for you
Ere the night-express is due.'

Was it chance?—A climbin' brother
   Heard the plan fur her escape;
An' his fancies, somehow 'r other,

V.     Took a sort o' hum'rous shape.
When the golden sun had set,
An' the dews the earth had wet,
In the yard he loosed his pet.

What a difference in viewin'
   All things lies 'twixt age an' youth!
What a diff'rence in pursuin'

VI.     Purposes an' plans, in truth!
Had the ol' folks been aware
O' what *he* knew, then an' there
*They'd 'a' laid a diff'rent* snare.

Billy's record was embellished;
   But he had the usual faults
O' the goat-tribe. Much he relished

VII.    Makin' folks turn somersaults.
 Strangers allus roused his hate.
 His young master, all elate,
 Crep' behind a bush to wait.

 Night was dark, an' rain was dribblin',—
  Not a star was to be seen.
 All was silent, save the nibblin'
VIII. O' his goat-ship on the green.
 Hark!—A nearer-drawin' sound
 Causes the youth's heart to bound!
 Strainin' eyes, he peers around.

 Soon he thinks he sees, though faintly,
  Some one stealin' up the path;
 An' with feelin's far from saintly,
IX. Hears his Billy's snort o' wrath!
 Suddenly there is a shout—
 Wail o' sorrow long drawn out!—
 Ah, there is no room fur doubt!

 Now he sees a dark form flyin'
  Down the pathway to the gate,
 An' is sure his pet is vyin'
X. With its more than rapid rate!
 Caller stoops (delay is rash!)
 Fur the gate-latch:—like a flash,
 Nimble foe o'ertakes him!—Crash! ! ! ! ! !

 * * * * * * * *

 Sleek ol' Billy's seen to hover
  Often round the village green,
 But that ardent ancient lover
XI. In these parts no more is seen.
 Fur the news o' his late call
 An' abrupt departur'—all—
 Got afloat—his cup was gall!

 'Twas a source o' fun an' laughter,—
  'Specially among the young;

**28**

An' not long he lingered after,
XII. To be slaughtered by the tongue.
Those who fain had been the girl's
Suitors—fellers with soft curls
Flung it at him—impish churls!

Some gave mock congratulations:
 Asked about 'his bonny bride,'
An' about his preparations
XIII. For a weddin'-tour beside;—
Asked with soberness o' face—
Which was no result o' grace—
'Bout 'their future dwellin'-place.'

This he bore with Moses' meekness.
 Thinkin' it could not last long,—
Soon would die o' age an' weakness:
XIV. But his fore-casts were all wrong.
Still the young ones grinned an' leered,
Still the old ones sneered an' jeered,
Wheresoever he appeared.

As a crown to all his trouble,
 Climax, acme o' his shame,
Makin' his annoyance double,
V. To his gate one night there came
Boys in swarms, in troops, in clans,
Bearin' cow-bells, oyster-cans,
Guns an' sticks an' ol' tin pans.

All his patience an' endurance
 One big death blow then received.
Then he lost his strong assurance:
XVI. O' conceit he was bereaved.
'Twas the sad concludin' stage;
'Twas the 'Finis'-labeled page.
Naught could his chagrin assuage.

So he stated that his brother
 Was most perilously ill,
An' he took a train fur other

**29**

XVII.         Parts, far, far from Westerville.
      Maiden tarried with her mother,
      Managed soon her grief to smother,—
      Now is solaced by another."

---

# Chapter 3.

---

DILAPIDATED JONES, AND OTHER AIR-TRAVELLERS.

---

That evening I turned, on receiving my mail,
   To look at a stranger who entered the door.
That visage! so wrinkled! so hollow! so pale!
1.    Its like I had never set eyes on before!
A dry, withered, misshapen piece of mankind,
   Minus arm—minus leg—plus a rickety crutch—
Hump-back—broken nose—deep-red scars—one eye blind—
   This is only an outline—accept it as such.

He applied for his mail with a quavering voice,
   And upon its receipt, without pause hobbled out.
At his speedy departure, I could but rejoice.
2.    For the sight was distressful, as no one can doubt.
I accosted a farmer who just then arrived:—
   "Who is that?"   "Why," he said, with surprise in his tones,
"Don't you know? —That's the man who claims Fate has deprived
   Him o' all life's best things—that's Dilap'dated Jones.

A very appropriate sobriquet, too!
   I said to myself: then I ventured to ask:—
"What shattered him?   What did the poor creature do?
3.    Enlighten me, pray, if 'tis no mighty task.
Did he delve far, far down in the bowels of earth,
   Turning out the black fuel, or bright-shining ore?
Did he work in a powder mill?—Waiving all mirth—
   Jests an' pleasantries all—tell me now, I implore!"

"HE 'LOWED HE'D BETTER DROP."

*See page 34.*

"Well, 'tis no lengthy tale," said the farmer. at length.
   "He might yit be as healthy an' hearty as we.
An Apoller in looks, a Goliar in strength
4.   Ef he'd only ben wise as he now 'pears to be.
But, jes' like some others, he wanted to *soar*.
   The earth was too low fur 'im—nothin' too high.
The days o' his proud aspirations are o'er:
   He says he is merely a-waitin' to die.

I'll tell ye the story o' how he got fixed
   As our eyes now behold 'im;—I 'lowed you'd ben told.
They say that prosperity 'n' 'versity, mixed,
5.   Make the sum o' this life with its scenes manerfold.
That he's had his share o' the latter he'll swear
   In a court-room,—or any place under the skies:
He'll also declare that Dame Luck's ben unfair
   In regard to the former.   It chanced on this wise:

      Jones used ter be an airynaut,
         Went sailin' through the air,
      'Twixt earth an' sun an' moon.
      In what they call a b'loon,
i.         Which goes where birds don't dare.
      But he's give up the business
         O' ærial exploration,
      Becaze o' diffyculties
         That attend sky-navigation.

      I reckerlect his last ascent;
         'Twas Independence Day;
      He rose as ef on wings,
      An' sped tow'rds Heav'nly things,
ii.         Away—away—away.
      But he's give up the business,
         O' ærial exploration,
      Becaze o' diffyculties
         That attend sky-navigation.

      Up shot his air-ship till it seemed
         The smallest o' all specks.

Enchanted an' amazed,
The people up'ard gazed
    Until they strained their necks.
But he's give up the business
    O' ærial exploration,
Becaze o' diffyculties
    That attend sky-navigation.

Then he kem down an' hung awhile,
    Suspended in mid-air;
You've seen hawks watch fur game?
His motion seemed the same,
    As he was hov'rin' there.
But he's give up the business
    O' ærial exploration,
Becaze o' diffyculties
    That attend sky-navigation.

Ere long, 'way off in the northwest,
    A cloud rose with a frown;
With mutterin's o' wrath,
It threatened Jones's path,
    An' so he started down.
But he's give up the business
    O' ærial exploration,
Becaze o' diffyculties
    That attend sky-navigation.

Descendin' straight as any spear,
    He struck a blast o' air;
An', chancin' off his guard,
The wind it hit 'im hard—
    Whisked him he skurse knew where.
But he's give up the business
    O' ærial exploration,
Becaze o' diffyculties
    That attend sky-navigation.

It swirled, twirled, whirled him—hurled him 'long.
    Quite feather-like, o'er earth;

Each minute, as it passed,
He reckoned was his last,
VII.      An' wished he'd ne'er had birth.
But he's give up the business
    O' ærial exploration,
Becaze o' diffyculties
    That attend sky-navigation.

He 'lowed he'd better rise a bit,
    An' heaved some ballast out;
The sand-bag (Heav'n knows how)
Struck some lone widder's cow—
VIII.      Killed her (the cow) past doubt.
But he's gave up the business
    O' ærial exploration,
Becaze o' diffyculties
    That attend sky-navigation.

He soared again, then like a fiend
    On maddest mischief bent,
With force—momentum dire—
Pounced on a tall church-spire;—
IX.      It reeled, an' down it went.
But he's give up the business
    O' ærial exploration,
Becaze o' diffyculties
    That attend sky-navigation.

Dismayed, he cast his anchor out;—
    The thing unroofed a mill,
Then chanced a pond to skim,
Where small boys took a swim.
X.      Their cries give Jones a chill.
But he's give up the business
    O' ærial exploration,
Becaze o' diffyculties
    That attend sky-navigation.

Le ' 's see! what *did* he drive at next?
    A lightnin'-blasted pine!

His egg-shell craft was wrecked
Forthwith—what could he 'xpect?—
XI.          But Jones he grabbed a line.
But he's give up the business
    O' ærial exploration,
Becaze o' diffyculties
    That attend sky-navigation.

He sprung, hung, swung an' clung fur life,
    While his dismantled ship,
A-flittin' o'er shocked crowds,
Went up to meet the clouds,
XII.          Then took another dip.
But he's give up the business
    O' ærial exploration,
Becaze o' diffyculties
    That attend sky-navigation.

Soon,—as his strength was failin' fast,
    And as he couldn't stop,
Nor choose a landin' soft,
Nor keep from goin' 'loft,—
XIII.          He 'lowed he'd better drop.
But he's give up the business
    O' ærial exploration,
Becaze o' diffyculties
    That attend sky-navigation.

He lighted like a ton o' brick!
    It broke 'bout half his bones.
Nex' day (age forty then)
He *looked* three-score-and-ten.
XIV.          A used-up man was Jones!
But he's give up the business
    O' ærial exploration,
Becaze o' diffyculties
    That attend sky-navigation.

The doctors took an' patched him up
    Accordin' to their plan,

But soon the fact was plain
That they essayed in vain
  To make him a whole man.
But he's give up the business
  O' ærial exploration,
Becaze o' diffyculties
  That attend sky-navigation.

XV.

He says exper'ence makes one wise:
  He's ben a fool he owns.
He's taken his last sail.
Now, sir, you know the tale
  O' D'lapidated Jones.
Yes, he's give up the business,
  O' ærial exploration,
Becaze o' diffyculties
  That attend sky-navigation.

XVI.

With no sign o' perturbation,
Not a tear o' lamentation,
Jes' a sigh o' resignation,
He has made his abdication.
An' descended from his station
As the Champion o' Creation—
Marvel o' this generation
In that wonderful vocation,
That hair-raisin' occupation.

XVII.

With his fam'ly's approbation,
An' the cordial admiration
O' each sensible relation
Who with constant trepidation
Watched each reckless demonstration,
Carin' naught for each ovation,
He has made this abjuration,
With a vow o' confirmation
Which shall have no abrogation.

XVIII.

O' ærial navigation,
Super-mundane exploration,

Now he speaks in deprecation,
An' without dissimula tion,
XIX.     Says it's an abomination;—
Which is railin' accusation,
So some cranks make affirmation,
Holdin' sky-ward transportation
Worthy o' all men's laudation.

Oft he says in conversation,
That although sech navigation—
Sech uncertain exploration—
May afford some recreation,
XX.     An' a heap o' specerlation
To a fine imagination,
When exists no indication,
Not the slightest intimation
O' ærial mutation—
    Remarks in solemn tones.
There's lots an' lots o' danger.
To which he is no stranger,
In bein' a sky-ranger.
He'd rather be a granger.
A low Jew money-changer,
Or dog in some one's manger,
    Is happier far, says Jones."

By the time my informant's narration had ceased,
   I was not the sole listener.   Full half a score
Stood or sat grouped around us.  The number increased.
6.  Till the usual crowd filled the little brown store.
The theme of the evening was drawn from the tale
   Of that mis-hap of Jones's so wondrously dire.
Tales many were told; some a bit flat and stale,
   Others thrilling and fresh—full of fancy and fire.

One discoursed of a couple who'd planned to be wed
   In a monster-balloon, in the fields of mid-air,
To their parents' displeasure, abhorrence and dread.
7.  They were surely a most disobedient pair.
They made search all around—low and high, far and wide,
   For a clergyman reckless enough to comply

With their hearts' wish.   At last one through pity complied,
   And they started away on their trip to the sky.


Well, the words had been spoken that joined them as one,
   Far, far above earth, in the vault overhead.
Their descent was already in safety begun;
8.   All dreams of disaster had faded and fled.
But somehow or other, the car gave a lurch,
   And bridegroom and bride were at once downward hurled.
Ironical Fate!   At the door of the church
   Where they *should* have been wed, their dead forms touched
      the world.


One told of a sky-rover who for long years
   In successfulness soared through Heav'n's wondrous domain
With no cause for grief, no occasion for fears,
9.   Till he lighted in front of a "limited" train.
That that was his last trip 'tis needless to say.
   They found a few shreds of him—part of his hat—
A scrap of his coat;—half a furlong away,
   His gold ticker—mashed inconceivably flat.


Another one told of a man who had gone
   On ærial trips—say five hundred or more—
Unscathed, till one day he descended upon
10.   A sky-scraping church-steeple—his journeys were o'er.
The balloon was impaled.   The sharp spire ran up through
   The entire flimsy structure, protruding above.
On its point—like a worm on a hook—in full view
   Writhed the æronaut.—Who such recitals can love?


I could bear it no longer.   My bed-time drew nigh,
   And, departing, I sought my *pro-tempore* home,
Wond'ring whether men safely would yet range the sky,
11.   Or by law be confined on earth's bosom to roam.
That night, in my slumbers, I sailed o'er the moon
   In air-ship extremely—astoundingly vast!
That voyage was my first journey in a balloon,
   (A dream-one at that) I daresay 'twas my last.

# Chapter 4.

---

---

The evening was stormy and dark—O, so dark!
   But, taking a lantern, I went to the store.
"Why, how are you, Noah?   How's all in the Ark?"
1.   Said the jolly proprietor, laughing all o'er.
"That's just what I came to discover," I said.
   "I've a letter here—eh?"—He replied, "You're quite right!"
I opened the missive, and eagerly read
   Such a message as only true Love could indite.

I fancied at first, with a slight glow of pride,
   That I was the only one who through the storm
Had ventured; but, glancing around, I descried,
2.   In shadowy corner, a stout, burly form.
"Hello!" said a ringing voice.   "Thought yerself brave,
   Like as not, pokin', 'long through the wet to come here!
The rain may pelt down, an' the elements rave;
   I'm as good as the next man, each day o' the year."

'Twas Thompson, the peddler, whom ev'ry one knew
   In the country around.   With good nature he beamed.
Whatever might happen, he never got blue;
3.   Ev'ry mortal's best friend and consoler he seemed.
Hail-fellow well met on an evening like this!
   I said to myself, and sat down by his side.
An item of news he was scarce known to miss,
   And freely dispensed what he knew far and wide.

38

". . . . . SAL WAS DRESSED HER VERY BEST,
ALL FRAGRANT WITH COLOGNE, SIR."

*See page 42.*

"What's new?" I enquired.   He replied, with a smile:—
  "O, I guess nothin' much."   Then of things common-place,
Like crops, markets, weather, talked glibly awhile,
4.   As the wind howled without, and the rain poured apace.
Then  a  thought  seemed  to  strike him:—"O, say! have you heard
  How Si. Simpkin's William got caught in a trap
Uncle Si. set for varmints?   What!—never a word?—
  Well, Billy was one o' the wust frightened chaps.


Way it happened was this:—he'd been out round the bluff.
  To see Hookey's gal—he's in love there, you see,
An' the hour bein' late, an' the road bein' rough,
5.   He took the short cut by the ol' 'Haunted Tree.'
He was down in the holler, a gun-shot from home,
  When somethin' give way with a turrible snap!
Where the boys all insist that spooks frequently roam,
  He found himself fast in the jaws o' that trap.


All night he yelled vainly, 'Help!' 'Fire!' 'Murder!'—all
  That is gen'ly most potent mankind to arouse.
At morn the ol' man heard his agonized call,
6.   As he sat in the barn-yard, a-milkin' the cows.
The leg that was caught was broke half way between
  The knee an' the ankle.   The doctors who set
The limb were afeard fur a while o' gangrene.
  I saw him to-day—he's in no danger yet."


Here he paused, as if having a mind to refrain
  From further remarks, seeming dreaming.   Without
Pattered, spattered and clattered and chattered the rain,
7.   With mutter and sputter in gutter and spout.
"That reminds me," at length he resumed, with queer smile.
  "How one time I trapped—not for pelts, nor for pelf!
You want to know?   Well, we can't go fur a while;
  I don't much mind tellin' a joke on myself:—

# Tales Told in a Country Store.

"No purtier gal than Norton's Sal
I.
    E'er donned a cloak or bonnet;
An ef I'd ben a poet, sir,
    I would 'a' writ a sonnet

As full o' grand an' glowin' words,
II.
    O' burnin' adoration,
As any that ol' Petrarch penned
    In his infatuation.

But, as it was, I jest made love
III.
    In clumsy boyish fashion,
A-hesertatin' all along
    To manerfest my passion.

However, ev'rything went smooth,
IV.
    In spite o' each new-comer,
Until a city chap came round
    To fool away the Summer.

He wore a shinin' stove-pipe hat,
V.
    An' deemed a cane was handy,
An' flung on sech tremenjus style,
    We fellers called him "Dandy."

He seemed to hev, sir, from the start,
VI.
    What money he c'u'd handle;
An' soon the gals around him flew,
    Like moths around a candle.

He seemed the idol o' the sex;
VII.
    An I become alarmed, sir,
An' fearful that with his fine looks
    An' ways Sal would be charmed, sir.

I soon found out that, unbeknown
VIII.
    To me, he'd called on Sally—
*My* Sal, the queen o' all the fair,
    The Beauty o' the Valley.

# Tales Told in a Country Store.

IX.
O, I was mad, sir, you'll not doubt—
　　Mad as I *could* be—yes, sir,
The terr'ble feelin's that I felt
　　I've no words to express, sir.

X.
Well, once hitched on, he hung around;
　　An' I kep' out o' sight, sir,
Till I could work some stratergem
　　To put my foe to flight, sir.

XI.
I medertated day an' night;
　　An' soon I was a-layin'
Plans fur a trick that seemed as slick
　　As that he'd ben a-playin'.

XII.
Well, sir, there was a strip o' wood
　　That run 'twixt farmer Norton's
An' where that fine bird had his nest—
　　Ol' Hezekiah Morton's:—

XIII.
An' through this mile-wide timber-belt
　　A path led, 'long which Dandy
On Sunday evenin's made his way,
　　Loaded with flow'rs an' candy.

XIV.
There was a bear-trap lyin' 'round
　　An ol' an' rusty thing, sir,
I scoured it up an' 'iled it up,
　　An' got it so's 'twould spring, sir:—

XV.
I took it to that neck o' woods,
　　As gay as any cricket,
An' on one lovely Sabbath eve
　　I dragged it from the thicket;—

XVI.
With skill an' care, I set it where
　　I knowed he'd come along, sir,
An' kivered it with leaves an' sech—
　　So's he'd see nothin' wrong, sir,—

41

XVII.
An' then I turned an' skipped across,
By my ol' route, to Norton's,
Sure that he wouldn't, *couldn't* come—
That dapper chap from Morton's.

XVIII.
I chuckled as I hastened on;
Myself I flattered greatly;
I saw my rival baffled weep—
Myself a victor stately.

XIX.
"All things are fair in love and war."
This proverb is no new one,
Ignorin' scruples, I essayed
To make it seem a true one.

XX.
What does *he* care fur truth an' right?
Fur aught but love an' beauty?
I ground my teeth, an' laughed to scorn
The still small voice o' Duty.

XXI.
Well, Sal was dressed her very best,
All fragrant with cologne, sir,
An' pride an' independence seemed
Commingled in each tone, sir.

XXII.
I chatted some, or *tried* to chat;
There seemed no use o' talkin':
Her mind seemed fixed; my thoughts were
mixed;
'Tell you, I felt like walkin'.

XXIII.
But still I stayed. She fidgeted,
An' sort o' intimated
That all was o'er forevermore
Betwixt us; yet I waited.

XXIV.
I strove to waken mem'ries old;
Her manner seemed less distant;
I thought the victory half won,
An' Fate my sure assistant.

XXV.

Three quarters o' an hour had passed,
    As near as I could tell, sir,
When through the open window come
    A sharp, blood-curdlin' yell, sir.

XXVI.

I 'sot an' said, quite unconcerned,
    An' solemn-like as preachin':—
'Can there be panthers prowlin' round?
    I 'lowed I heerd one screechin'.'

XXVII.

'Panthers!' Sal gasped; an' I could see,
    So white her fair face turned, sir,
She was alarmed. I thought *I* knowed
    Why she was so concerned, sir.

XXVIII.

Soon rose another cry as shrill
    As any wild beast's yelp, sir;
Then one that seemed extremely like
    A human call for help, sir.

XXIX.

Sal cried:—'O, some one's bein' eat!
    Quick, Sam! take Father's rifle,
An' save him! Quick! Why don't you *go?*
    *Don't* stop to fool or trifle!'

XXX.

'O, I guess none's wuss off than skeered,'
    I said; 'twas unexpected!—
This rescue-job:—'twould hardly do
    To go as she directed.

XXXI.

I hesertated, hemmed an' hawed,
    An' kind o' blushed an' stammered.
I reckon—hardly know jest what;
    An' still *he* bawled an' clamored!

XXXII.

'Coward!' she hissed, an' snatched the
      gun,
    An' sprung out like a deer, sir;
An' guided by them piercin' shrieks,
    She soon knowed where to steer, sir.

43

XXXIII.

An' I?—I stood dazed-like awhile;
Then suthin' seemed to wake me.
I struck fur home another way,
Fas' as my limbs could take me.

XXXIV.

You see, when I begun the game, .
I hadn't calkerlated
The pain he'd feel, an' how he'd *squeal.*—
My projec' was ill-fated.

\*     \*     \*     \*     \*

XXXV.

Well, sir, he got her, after all—
Folks say it was a pity—
An' fur awhile, in splendid style,
They flourished in the city.

XXXVI.

They had a big palatial house,
An' lived on cake an' brandy;
But 'las fur all her high-toned airs,
An' 'las fur precious Dandy.

XXXVII.

He monkeyed with the Board o' Trade;
An' all his father's savin's
Went in the twinkle o' an eye—
Jes' like a pile o' shavin's!

XXXVIII.

He strove misfortune's cup to drown
In countless cups o' liquor;
But all his efforts only made
His woes—an' tongue—the thicker.

XXXIX.

He drove a coal-cart fur a year,
An', ever sinkin' lower,
Seemed like a weed clear gone to seed,
A-waitin fur the mower.

XXXX.

He took a pistol, one sad day,
An' sent his brains a-flyin.
An' Sal?—She takes in washin' now—
The fact there's no denyin'."

# Tales Told in a Country Store.

Still the rain madly poured and the bass thunder roared!
  The proprietor opened a moment the door.
Gleamed the lightning's red sword!   By its flash we explored
8.    With our eyes the drenched landscape—now well flooded o'er!
Still the storm kept its rate—made no sign to abate!
  "Well, well," said the peddler, "we'll take what is sent!
Though the hour is late, we can naught do but wait;
  So, biding our time, let's be patient, content."

"Very well; entertain us, and patient we'll be.
  Shell out some more news; tell a story or twain;
An' from cankerin' care an' from murmurin' free,
9.    We'll do as in Boston they do—let it rain."
This came from the post-master.   "Tell us," said I,
  "About how that train came so near being wrecked,
Up country—where was it?—At Hapley?—Or Guy?
  The details, no doubt you can well recollect.

Who delivered the warning so timely that saved
  All that train-load of lives?   Has his name been disclosed?
On a high shaft of granite it ought to be graved,
10.   To the gaze of uncounted admirers  exposed."
"So say I!  Let us hear it!"   The store-keeper cried,
  "Our friend here, the poet, will put it in verse—
Will you not?"   "Yes, indeed!" I quite promptly replied.
  Thus urged, he proceeded his tale to rehearse:—

          "You want to hear the story?
            I've told it time on time!
          You wish me to repeat it?
1.          You'll frame it into rhyme?
          You think 'twould grace a poem?
            I'll tell it, then, once more.
          I'm partial to rhyme—its music an' chime—
            I'll gladly tell it o'er.

          The hero was Bank's Blakey,
            A wondrous chap to ride
          A-hoss-back o'er the country,
11.         An' through the wood-lands wide!

He'll gallop off at mornin'—
    Sweep like the wind away—
An' seldom return till evenin' lights burn
    With bright an' heartsome ray.

He took, in one excursion,
    The road that by the track
Runs down tow'rd Hapley Station,
III.    An' said he'd soon be back;
But, as the day was charmin',
    The high-way smooth an' good,
He kep' on an' on, until he had gone
    To edge o' Lost Man's Wood.

There, as he pulled the bridle,
    In act to wheel about,
He saw a sight that stopped him,
IV.    An' made him fairly shout!
The railway bridge—a trestle—
    Had been consumed by fire!
There yawned 'mid the track a chasm deep,
        black—
    Destruction was entire!"

A warnin' mus' be given
    At Hapley—town beyond;
Too deep the stream fur fordin',
V.    But he would not despond.
The lurid pyres o' Sunset
    Was blazin' in the West;
In one hour he knew the reg'lar was due.
    So he mus' do his best!

At once he tied his pony,
    An' raked an' racked his brain
Fur some safe plan o' crossin',
VI.    But ev'ry one seemed vain.
At last the lariat seizin,'
    Which he fur sport oft bore,
He lassoed a stump that stood in a clump
    O' trees on t'other shore.

Well, how the youngster managed
    I don't quite understand,
But by that raw-hide cable
vii.  He worked himself to land.
He skipped then fur the Station—
    Five miles ef more than one—
As ef he had wings, like sprites an' sech
        things!
Ah, he is great to run!

He made it— no time left, though!
    Jest as he hove in sight
O' Hapley, in the distance
viii.  He saw the engine's light!
They signalled her an' stopped her,
    An' so the 'xpress wa'n't wrecked.
No horrors befell. That's all there's to tell,
    As far's I recollect.

That's *all*, I said. Not *quite* all.
    The company bestowed
A neat sum fur his sarvice,
ix.  An' free pass o'er the road.
Yes, he's a real hero—
    The title well can claim;
An' long may he live! May all life can give
    Be his—joy, fortune, fame!"

Still it rained! *How* it rained! A wild, eddying blast
    Blew open the door and put out ev'ry light.
As he groped tow'rd the door, to again make it fast,
11.  The store-keeper cried, "What a night! What a night!"
"What a night!" we both echoed, the peddler and I.
    As striking a match, I the nearest lamp lit.
On the floor there was scarcely a spot wholly dry,
    That rain-laden wind-swirl had so deluged it.

On top of a counter we seated ourselves,
    And all for a time exchanged tales new and old,
On various topics. Ghosts, goblins and elves
12.  Played prominent parts in some narratives told;

**47**

Sundry hair-breadth escapes, both by sea and by land,
   Misadventures whose scenes lay at home and abroad,
We recounted, till, leaning m y head on my hand,
   I was lost in the far-away dim Land of Nod.

     \*      \*      \*      \*      \*      \*      \*

I felt myself nudged.  "Come, my partne r, let's go;
   The rain has slacked up, and will presently cease."
'Twas the peddler who spoke.   Said the post-master, "No!

13.    I've a crow first to pick with him!  But—let's have peace!
I'll forgive," he with mock magnanimity said,
   "Your dozing through one of my most thrilling tales.
Was it time to be napping, when pirates with red
   And murderous hands were unfurling their sails?"

"Beg pardon!" said I, "I was weary indeed—
   Could have slumbered through anything -whirlwind—fire—
      flood!"
"Stay! Stay!—have a smoke!"   But, declining the weed,

14.    I prepared to go out in the night—and the mud.
As the peddler was staying half-way 'twixt the store
   And the point I was bound for, together we went.
When my brief but laborious journey was o'er,
   I was worn and bedraggled, and night was far spent.

That I am a dreamer, you *must* needs opine.
   But *that* night—or, speaking precisely, that *morn*—
I out-did all previous feats in that line,

15.    And all other dreamers that ever were born.
After countless adventures, I boarded a train
   Through sublime vasts of space with velocity whirled,-
Borne by wheels formed of rainbows!  'Twere thoroughly vain
   To conjecture our course.—It seemed far from the world.

Soon  down—down—down—down—ever down—ever down—
   Seemed the train straight to  plunge  from  some  horrible
      height,
Through regions abysmal and dismal, whose frown

16.    Nigrescent seemed blacker than Stygian night.
Then ensued a great shock—a most terrible jar—
   A collision—at least, so it seemed in my nap—
And I thought myself pinned 'neath an over-turned car,
   With my dexter foot fast in—a ponderous trap!

"SOME SMART-ALEC SPORTSMEN WHO ROAMED UP AN' DOWN
THE COUNTRY, A-BLAZIN' AT THINGS WILD AN' TAME."

See page 57.

I woke with a dull, throbbing ache in my head,
   While a cold sweat was oozing from every pore.
Obliquely I lay on a much-rumpled bed,
17.   And my head, hanging over, was touching the floor.
Phœbus, soaring on high, in an unclouded sky,
   Was nearing the zenith. I hastily donned
My habiliments, leaving my room with a sigh.
   Of such night-excursions I ne'er have been fond.

---

# Chapter 5.

---

A
TWINGE OF
HOMESICKNESS.—BROWN
AND HIS LETTER.—BROWN AND PRAIRIE-
FIRES UNDER DISCUSSION.—FOSS AND HIS NARRATIVE, "THE
RIDE TO PALE-FACE LAKE."—A LIT-
TLE PLEASANTRY.—THE
OVERLOOKED
LETTER.

---

Sick—home-sick—and gloomy—distressed to the core—
   I lingered that evening quite long at the gate,
Ere moodily saunt'ring away tow'rd the store;
1.   And when I arrived, 'twas, of course, somewhat late.
Nostalgia 's a painful and baneful disease;
   Its attacks are productive of torture indeed;
It harasses sorely—wears out by degrees—
   Ev'ry heart that it causes to suffer and bleed.

No letter! No tidings from home, dearest home!
   With the wildest conjectures my mind straight was rife.
I inly exclaimed: O, what led me to roam
2.   To this out-of-way place, far from child and from wife!
The most awful fancies my fears conjured up;
   They were ill—perhaps dead—or—I could not tell what!
Of bitterness quaffing, I clung to the cup;
   Lost in thought, long I stood as if chained to the spot.

# Tales Told in a Country Store.

From revery starting, I turned to the crowd.
  A man strange to me, but who seemed to the rest
No stranger, was reading a letter aloud,
3.    From friend or acquaintance somewhere in the West.
'Twas a pitiful story of ruin by fire;
  For the writer had recently lost all he had
In a great conflagration that swept, in its ire,
  Many homes from earth's breast, making many hearts sad.

As soon as the reading was brought to a close,
  " Too bad!" a full chorus of voices exclaimed:
And sep'rate expressions of sympathy rose
4.    From various persons, in varied terms framed.
"What an outrage!" the man with the letter then cried,
  "Fur passel o' movers their camp-fire to leave
Unextinguished, to spread o'er the land far an' wide,
  The poor, strugglin' settlers o' all to bereave!

Ther's a law 'g'in sech doin's I reck'n, but how
  To *apply* it 's the problem.  Sech folks jog right on,
An' the difficult thing,"said he, knitting his brow,
5.    "Is to find 'em, an' ketch 'em, when wunst they hev gone.
So engrossed are all hands in attempts to evade
  The danger that's rife, that they fail to keep track
O' the villains that caused it.  The search is delayed,
  An', ten to one, ne'er are the culprits brought back.

I lived in that kentry myself, fur a time,
  An' know very well how sech things happen there.
Sech heedlessness ort to be treated as crime:
6.    Fur sech as indulge it the State ort to care."
Then a man with a very sarcastical smile
  Said: "I s'pose *you* ne'er trained with the emigrant class.
But always have traveled in palace-car style,
  An' cooked all your victuals with lightnin'—or gas."

At this rose a laugh; and the first speaker turned
  The rich carmine of sunset, from forehead to chin,
Somewhat to my wonder.  I soon after learned
7.    'Twas the old case of sinner rebuking for sin.

Rising rather abruptly, he said: "I mus' go;
I ort to gone sooner—forgot myself quite."
And with steps that by no me ans were languid or slow,
He passed to the door, and out into the night.

"My! wasn't he pleased with a pretext to start!"
Said the nearest bystander, half under his breath;
To me then:—"He didn't seem pained to depart,
8.     An' his face didn't wear quite the pallor o' death!
When that chap an' his fam'ly returned from the West
In ol' prairie schooner with loose, wobbly tires.
At a place where they stopped for their noon-meal 'an rest,
They left what made one o' the fearfullest fires.

It ravaged whole townships in fury an' wrath,
An' couresd like a racer both up-hill an' down,
Devourin' all that it found in its path.
9.     It swallowed up many a village an' town.
There were lives lost—full many o' loved ones bereft,
An' all because Brown—that's his name—wouldn't pour.
As his wife wished, the water they chanced to have left
On the embers that smouldered when dinner was o'er.

There were threats o' arrest, an' o' lynchin' much talk.
'Tis said that a party some two hundred strong
Swooped adown, as upon the small bird swoops the hawk,
10.     One evenin', 'bout dusk, as he hastened along.
An' but for his wife's timely pleadin's an' cries,
An' sobbin' an' shrieks o' his little girl child,
He'd died as despised, hunted animal dies,
Out there in the sage-brush in that lonely wild.

What was it some bard 'bout consistency said?
That a treasure it is—no, a jewel, must be.
In some poet's volume—yes, Burns's—I've read
11.     About seein' ourselves same as other folks see.
He might 'a' kep' quiet on *fires*, from mere shame.
'Stead o' that, to the theme he the comp'ny enticed.
He's allers a-huntin' up some one to blame,
Like the Jews that complained o' the woman to Christ."

All this was aside from the talk of the crowd,
    Which, however, went on in a similar strain,
And ended, at length, with a laugh long and loud,
12.    From uniting in which one could hardly abstain.
The humorous phase of the case was so plain!
    "Well, poor Brown's to be pitied far more, after all,
Than many a man with a mightier brain,"
    Said the man with the falsetto tones and queer drawl.

Another laugh rose.  After that came a lull.
    The group's conversation, so lively before,
Dropped.  Ev'rything seemed all at once to grow dull.
13.    I looked at my time-piece, then looked at the door.
Should I linger, or go?  I could scarcely decide.
    I fidgeted, yawned; still a dead silence reigned,
Ev'ry mouth seeming sealed, ev'ry tongue seeming tied.
    Each rigidly sat in his seat as if chained.

Then a Yankee named Foss, who, 'twas rumored, had been
    In every State, and all lands 'neath the sun,
Leaning back in his chair, stroking beard long and thin,
14    Said, "Well, that reminds me!"  All eyes—ev'ry one—
Were at once to the speaker expectantly raised;
    For whenever *he* said, "That reminds me," each man
Knew a tale was forthcoming.  Straight forward he gazed,
    As if sheer *through* the opposite wall—and began:—

    "Did I ever—no, I never—
1.    Or at least, don't *b'lieve* I ever
Told about our great adventure with that mighty prairie-fire—
    Our adventure— mine an' Mary's—
    (That's my wife) out on the prairies.
Well, we hed there an exper'ence such as no one 'u'd desire.

    Though the stage-route ran close by us,
11.    We hed not a neighbor nigh us—
No, the very nearest dwellin's seemed the tiniest o' specks.
    Far away to northward lyin';
    An' in spite of all our tryin'
To refrain from gittin' home-sick, we could not to save our necks.

How we longed to see the mountains,
III.    An' to quaff the sparklin' fountains
That abound in ol' New England—yearned for social
        gath'rin's there—
    Pined to hear the church-bell ringin',
    An' the sarmon an' the singin',
Voices, too, o' feller mortals goin' up to Heav'n in prayer!

    But we hed no time for mopin';
IV.    So we kep' on toilin', hopin—
Prayed for better days—o' settlers comin', day and night we
        dreamed.
    But they came so slowly, slowly,
    It appeared to be unholy
To abide in such a desert as the whole broad region seemed.

    We had been there—well—four Summers,
V.    When, from back East, some new-comers
Came an' settled six miles eastward. We were highly pleased
        thereat.
    In our lonesome situation,
    'Twas a wholesome consolation
To hev livin' human bein's dwellin' close to us as that.

    Well, the years with speed unflaggin'
VI.    Rolled—though time to us seemed laggin'—
Till the seventh;—ah, that Summer was uncommon' hot an' dry!
    Seemed the earth like one vast cinder,
    An' the grass resembled tinder.
An' the sun was simply scorchin', shinin' from a brassy sky.

    'Twas the thirteenth o' September—
VII.    Ah, that day I shall remember
Long as I hev breath an bein'—till I pass from earth away!
    Such a queer haze seemed to deaden
    All the sky—its hue was leaden,
An' the wind rose on a sudden, 'bout the middle o' the day.

From the north the wind came sweepin';
VIII.    I smelt smoke upon it.  Leapin'
From my place at dinner-table I sprang quickly out the door.
There, as sure as shootin'—preachin'—
Was a wall o' fire a-reachin'
Far as mortal sight c'u'd travel—comin' onward with a roar!

I exclaimed, 'God save us, Mary!
IX.    Fire's a-ragin' on the prairie—
Comes this way with force resis'less!  Quick!—Make haste,
for we must take
All that we can safely carry,
An' be off—we must not tarry!—
'Tis a race—all odds against us—twelve good miles to
Pale-Face Lake!'

Out I rushed for team an' wagon;
X.    An' when that abhorred fire-dragon—
How it licked the blackened heavens!—How it bellowed!—
How it roared!—
Was within two miles—less distance,
Like enough,—with wife's assistance,
Things we held most dear an' precious were brought out an'
flung aboard.

This took—well, a minute, maybe;
XI.    Mary then snatched up the baby,
An' we scrambled in the wagon, an' I made the horses go!
Knowin' well that we'd be corses
If too slow, I lashed them horses—
O, I tell ye they were frightened, for I'd never driv' 'em so!

Well, we cast one glance behind us,
XII.    Though the smoke was 'nough to blind us,
An' we saw the flames roll madly over all that we had left—
Saw the house go like a shavin'—
Saw the monster r'arin', ravin',
Rushin' after us.  The welkin its fierce tongues like lightnin'
cleft!

Mile by mile, with speed unbroken,

XIII.    On we dashed—no word was spoken—

An' the horses seemed a-goin' at their very level best—

Ev'ry nerve the brutes seemed strainin,'

Yet I saw the flames were gainin'—

Drawin' nearer—fact grew clearer—an' my heart sank in my breast.


Though I'd used the whip with rigor,

XIV.    I then plied it with new vigor,

Till the beasts waxed furious—frantic—foam from off 'em flecked my face.

Hosts o' animals retreatin'

From the fire, alongside fleetin',

Seemed endeav'rin' to outstrip us in the mad an' headlong race.


On we flew, an' nigher, nigher

XV.    In our rear approached the fire;

Fairly deaf'nin' was its thunder! Ah, its glist'rin'. blist'rin' breath!

It appeared to long to grasp us—

Seemed a-reachin' out to clasp us—

An' I tell ye for a minute we seemed close enough to death!


But the next, as I was peerin'

XVI.    Through the smoke, I felt like cheerin'!

For I saw the goal o' safety—saw the lake shine jest ahead!

Soon we into it were dashin',

Soon the waves were o'er us splashin':

An' the singein' flames, impingin' on the shore, hissed an' fell dead.


'Twas a close shave, no disputin'!

XVII.    Our nerves needed some recruitin'.

Mary, who had borne up bravely, clear broke down an' sobbed at last,

As we sat there safe, rejoicin,'

Thanks to Heaven freely voicin',

With a fervency which never could in mortals be surpassed!

**55**

Baby Gladys, though sore shaken,
XVIII.    Strange to say, did not awaken;
There she lay, sweet slumb'rin' cherub! quiet on her mother's
  arm.
Eagerly I seized—received her
To my bosom—thus relieved her
Worn-out mother, glad our darlin' had been spared all fright
  an' harm.

That was years ago.   That region
XIX.    Now of happy homes has legion——
It has plenty o' good settlers—prosp'rous, active, wide-awake.
Oft while musin' in the gloamin',
Back there goes my fancy roamin'.                    .
Oft in dreams I take it—make it—that wild ride to Pale-Face
  Lake!"

I straightway determined that I would avoid
  The after-discussion and aftermath, too,
Of tales—not because I was bored or annoyed,
15.    But *sleepy*.  I started.  "Here, here!  That won't do!"
Said the store-keeper rising, "We can't allow that;"
  (An attitude striking in pugilist style)
Adding:    " 'Sides,  we're a-goin' to pass round the hat;—
  Now aren't we?"   (With wink at the crowd, and sly smile.)

"Then you might just as well have allowed me to go,"
  I with nonchalance said—"if *that* be your intent;
Very little 'twill lessen the bills that you owe,
16.    If I deign to remain—for I've not a red cent.
But I'll pass round the head-gear, and thus square *my* part."
  "O, waive the affair!  Let's cry quits!  Never mind!
'Twas for Foss here I meant the collection to start;
  *My* bills are all settled—I'm no-ways behind!"

"What's that but a dun for my grocery bill?"
  Said Foss with mock dryness.  "Have patience, dear sir,
And all obligations I'll shortly fulfill.

**56**

17.    I always *have* paid you—in this you'll concur.
I never tell stories for pelf, be it known,
    But our merchant here often tells *stories* for gain."
The latter rejoined in a good-humored tone:—
    "Then the stories I've told *you* have all been in vain."

This badinage quickly, abruptly was dropped.
    A voice clear and strong, from the midst of the throng,
Propounded a query that suddenly stopped
18.    The current of banter that rippled along:—
"Who started it?" "Started what?" ev'ry one cried,
    For the moment forgetting the story, en masse.
"The fire of course. Was the knave caught and tried?—
    Was he one of that poor, despised emigrant class?"

This came from the man who extinguished poor Brown.
    Foss turned:—"Eh?—Who started that ocean o' flame?
Some Smart-Alec sportsmen, who roamed up an' down
19.    The country, a-blazin' at things wild an' tame.
Somethin' small they'd scared up, frightened out o' its wits,
    Was a lurker for refuge in grass monstrous tall.
Six or sev'n o' 'em fired—shot the critter to bits—
    An' the mischief was done beyond any recall.

'Twas ruther dear huntin'. That shootin'-bee cost
    The party their outfit. In *no* time, a wreath
O' fierce flames encircled their camp. All was lost:
20.    They only escaped by the skin o' their teeth.
A pitiful story from each feller rolled,
    When they 'rived at the Fort, twenty-five miles away:
But narratives sadder, far sadder, were told
    By the hundreds o' settlers made homeless that day.

Well, you fellers now may say all that you know
    About fires big an' little—I'm done with my tale.
Like Brown, I've discovered time's fleetin'—must go.
21.    Mister Postmaster, kindly hand over my mail.
You see," said he, smiling, "I ought to be wise."
    With a flourish of mock pride displaying to view
A roll of newspapers of every size.
    With, "Good-night, an' good luck to you all," he withdrew.

The postmaster uttered a grunt of surprise.

"Why, here, Rev'rend Sir!" he exclaimed then to me,

"A letter for you!—I can scarce b'lieve my eyes!

22. Well, well!" he said slowly, "if *that*—don't—beat—*me!*

I must have o'erlooked it in some way," he said.

"Next time I'll be careful, sir, you may be sure."

I eagerly seized it—'twas hastily read.

The loved ones at home from all harm were secure.


That night, strange to say, I had sweet, dreamless sleep.

No unthinking nimrod or emigrant came

To cause me to shiver, or shudder, or weep.

23. By setting the country around me aflame.

I rose much refreshed, with a halcyon frame

Of mind, which continued the live-long day through.

Save when some wild day-dream my fancy would claim,

And fire-demons mockingly danced in my view.

------

# Chapter 6.

TWO

VISITING FRONTIERSMEN.
—ANENT THE KLONDIKE.—RETURN-
ING FORTUNE-SEEKERS.—A NEAT LITTLE
ROMANCE.—GOLD-HUNTING DISCUSSED.—A
RARE AND SUGGESTIVE COIN, STAMPED "1849."
—DROWNS' STORY, "HOW WE HUNTED FOR GOLD,"
REMINISCENTIAL OF THAT PERIOD.—ENTREE OF A
BILL-POSTER.—A STRIKING AND ORIGINAL NOTICE.—
M'CORD'S LOSS, THE PURLOINER, AND PUNITIVE MEA-
SURES UNDER CONSIDERATION.—JUDGE LYNCH HAS
AN ADVOCATE, WHO MAKES A MOTION.—CALKIN'S
STORY, "HOW JUSTICE WAS DONE."—SOME CON-
CLUSIONS.—THE FAMOUS JUDGE'S ADVOCATE
OVER-RULED.—IN THE ROLE OF ERRAND
BOY FOR MY LAND-
LADY.

------

That evening, two brawny frontiersmen were there,

In conventional garb, somewhat awkward and shy:

Related—just how I was not made aware—

1. To their host, an old farmer, whose home was hard by.

"... A STEAMER'S ARRIVAL AT SEATTLE'S PORT,
WITH MINERS RETURNING WITH FAB'LOUS AMOUNTS."

See page 59.

# Tales Told in a Country Store.

They had seen the rough side of the roughest of life,
    Had abode 'mid the cultureless, unpolished, rude—
Dwelt where peril and strife were uncommonly rife;
    But sagacious they seemed—quite observant and shrewd.

They listened in silence, with many a smile,
    To the tales and the pleasantries passed in the crowd;
And after a while, catching spirit and style
2.    Of the company, joined in its laughs long and loud.
Each stranger was cordially, urgently pressed
    Some episode, howsoe'er brief, to rehearse,
Of life in the far-away wilds of the West;
    But each seemed reluctant—to talking averse.

Anon a man read one of many accounts
    Of a steamer's arrival at Seattle's port,
With miners returning with fab'lous amounts,
3.    From the banks of the Yukon, where Fortune holds court.
One man, so 'twas said, a good million brought out,
    Another one six hundred thousand or so;
And others brought sums at which no one would pout—
    All flushed with success—with enthusiasm's glow.

The eyes of the voyagers swept over the group
    At the landing with glances quick, anxious and keen,
Each striving to single out, 'mid the vast troop
4.    Of beholders there massed, those familiar in mien.
There were hats, scarfs and handkerchiefs flourished—hands
        waved—
    There were glad shouts of greeting, the list'ner to thrill,
As the huge ocean-monster, which grandly had braved
    Ev'ry peril swung round, gave a throb, and lay still.

There were men of all ranks, all professions—all kinds—
    The good and the evil, the best and the worst,
From all parts of the land—men of various minds—
5.    Illiterate men—men in lore grandly versed.
Men get down on a level, when seeking for that
    Which to all is so precious.   Partitions of caste
Are o'ercome—broken through—barriers thrown down—
        laid flat—
    For a season at least—till the quest is o'er-past.

# Tales Told in a Country Store.

There were fruit-venders, bar-tenders, grocers and eke
 Undertakers, watch-makers and bakers—a few—
There were teachers and preachers and others who speak—
6. Thugs, highwaymen, and draymen diverse in their hue.
There were sailors and tailors and jailers—'tis true—
 Some sawyers, some lawyers—a score if not more—
There were factors, contractors and actors perdu—
 Inn-keepers, street-sweepers, prize-fighters galore.

There were those over whom the whole earth makes ado—
 Who in various ways won phenomenal fame—
Some whom all fain would seek—some whom most would taboo.
7. There were women of virtue and women of shame.
Takes all kinds of people to make up the world;
 So runs the old adage,—and if it be so—
If truth in that time-honored maxim's impearled,
 The world was there well represented, I trow.

As usual, each one desired to be first
 To reach terra-firma, while those on the shore
With eagerness seemed almost ready to burst,
8. The hinder ones wishing that they were before.
What manifest difference then among men!
 Like a north-wind some blustered—some sunny looks wore—
Some pushed without stint—some apologized when
 They but jostled some one—'tis an old story o'er.

'Twas a scene of rejoicing—at least in the main—
 For the most who returned quite successful had been.
There were some disappointed ones, though, it was plain—
9. Some whose loved ones had failed the bright treasure to win.
Some who landed had sought hidden riches in vain;
 To their friends such returned—some were friendless—
   undone.
But what ship e'er came in bringing gladness and gain
 Unto all who awaited its coming?—Not one.

A common day-lab'rer had competence gained
 In the North's Eldorado. His children and wife
All, breathlessly waiting, their anxious eyes strained
10. To behold him, the joy and support of their life.

With emotion o'ercome, his good angel was dumb.
  Joy's tear, bright and clear, down each faded cheek  rolled.
Thirty-two thousand dollars, I think, was the sum
  Which he had amassed in that country of gold.

A frail-looking clerk, who'd been giv'n up for dead
  By his poor, widowed mother, as if from the tomb
Came back—came ashore with a staunch, manly tread—
11.   Sought his sorrowing parent and scattered her gloom.
With fifty-five thousand, which he had secured,
  He could say to the gaunt wolf: "Avaunt!—Cease to haunt
Our door!"   The privations they long had endured
  Were all o'er.   They no more shall be sore pressed by want.

A struggling inventor, who scarcely could keep
  Soul and body together, while planning to give
The world something useful—revolving schemes deep.
12.   To evolve something grand—may now really live.
By some magic transition—no mortal knows how—
  He turned up at the gold-fields—was crowned with  success,
And, possessing means super-abundant, he now
  May his projects essay— his experiments press.

An artist by no means uncommonly flush
  Took the proceeds entire of the wares he had sold,
Turned back upon studio, palette and brush,
13.   And betook himself off with the mass after gold.
He had won quite a plum—a magnificent sum—
  Let us hope 'twill not claim all his mind, all his heart—
That his soul will not utterly sordid  become—
  Will not idolize Mammon and dis-enthrone Art.

A poet who long in a garret had dwelt,
  Seeming fated—predestined to there end his days,
Left shrine of the Muse, and at Fortune's shrine knelt—
14.   He may now sing in comfort and plenty his lays.
'Neath his own vine and fig-tree, with naught to molest
  Or affright him, he now inspiration may seek;
Chilly Boreas now cannot ruin his rest—
  Hunger make him as slim as a museum freak.

A clergyman, too, who'd been living on air—
   At least on a pittance that scarcely would keep
A government mule—took his chance—got a share.
15. The danger now is—he may worship his heap.
Change so radical sore may unbalance his mind.
   May Heav'n grant him grace his good luck now to stand'
May he "get up and dust," and another flock find,
   With souls less diminutive—more open hand!

A blacksmith, a mason, a carpenter now
   Will handle respectively sledge, trowel, plane
No more. Each a college could amply endow—
16. An orphan asylum establish, maintain.
At ease each may live the remainder of life,
   And bequeath a good portion to quarrelsome heirs
(Unless he possess an extravagant wife,
   Or within him some spendthrift proclivity bears).

A newsboy who'd read all the tales he could find
   In the papers he sold of the gold-fields' new-found.
With fortune-fed smile, disembarked, scarce inclined
17. To again cry the dailies he once hawked around.
An adventurous, indigent urchin, he turned
   To that spot so renowned—the new Wonder of earth.
In the foremost of journals—one not to be spurned—
   He could now own an int'rest—whatever its worth.

E'en a boot-black, gone mad with the mania for pelf,
   Had contrived to make far Dawson City his goal.
He will shine no more boots—he will shine now, himself.
18. For each lick of his pick made the big nuggets roll.
By hook or by crook—how?—Does any one know?—
   From the slums of New York to the slums of a camp
In wild land of snow he had managed to go.
   Could it be in the role of a dead-beat or tramp?

There were sev'ral such cases (you've known some, perchance)
   The newspaper chronicled, too, let me say,
A remarkable, readable little romance:—
19. Two lovers there were o'er the hills far away;
He was only the son of a laboring man,

And could claim no inheritance. She, lovely girl,
Was a millionaire's daughter. The course of love ran
Smooth enough, till a crisis put things in a whirl.

One day the youth asked for his fair lady's hand.
The Crœsus-proud sire said:—"Consent I will give
When you can a suitable fortune command;—

20.   Till then I refuse it—as long as I live."
This indeed was a blow to the fond couple's hopes;
For how could the stripling expect e'er to win
The required amount? As a trav'ler who gropes
In darkness was he—but a light soon broke in.

The discov'ry of gold in the Klondike came soon;
His spirits rose high—he would now do and dare!
Yes, his way now seemed clear—prospects bright as high noon—

21.   Presto! his heart sank, and he groaned in despair!
Far off was the region that held the bright dust;
And minus was he of the metal to pay
For passage and outfit. It seemed that he must
His project relinquish at once and for aye.

But a friend of his father, who knew the case well—
The strait—the dilemma in which he was placed—
Felt his bosom with pity and sympathy swell.

22.   Compassionately the youth's cause he embraced.
He put in his hand the desired amount,
Saying:—"Take this, and wend to Alaska your way.
Whenever your fortune is made, you may count
Out a few paltry shekels, this loan to repay."

Well, he went—made his fortune—returned by that ship.
Fell poverty's barrier being removed,
He was bound to let no opportunity slip

23.   For claiming his prize—the first chance he improved.
At once to Chicago a message he sent:—

"May F———:—
On next Thursday at Denver I'll be;
There meet me. Remember our plan ere I went—
Your promise—your father's. *All's well.*
Yours,
L. E."

"I wonder," said one, "what his fortune might be."
  The reader replied: "The account does not tell;
No doubt something huge. Bet the minister's fee
24.  Will be a big plum.—I'd jes' like mighty well
To be in his shoes—whosoe'er ties the knot!"
  "I don't know about that, though," another man said.
"I 'low 'tisn't always the clergyman's lot
  To be feed in proportion to purse of those wed."

"Ask the parson here—he can decide *that* dispute,"
  Another said, smiling,—referring to me.
It is needless to say, I no longer kept mute,
25.  But gave the results of experience free.
I freely confess, too, I did not confirm
  The first speaker's opinion, and did not deny
The second one's statement. (If you've served a term
  At the business, dear reader, you'll scarce wonder why.)

"Minin's surely jes' sport!" said the man who had read,
  As he folded his paper, and stowed it away
In a pocket capacious. A pause—then he said:
26.  "I've about half a notion to try it some day."
"Minin' sport!—Think it's easy?—Why, bless yer sweet soul!"
  Said a man at his side, "there's a price paid fur greed;
If ye knew half the hardships—but half—not the whole—
  Of the flockers to Klondike, 'twould make yer heart bleed!

Sport indeed! Is it sport to risk all you possess—
  To leave friends, home, relations—leave all things behind
That surround you, your life's path to gladden and bless?
27.  If you try it, no joke in the process you'll find.
I don't say 'twill not *pay*; it may *not* or it *may*;
  *That* matter depends on your pluck an' your luck—
On the latter the most. In that wild far away
  You'll find you've no circus or theater struck!"

"Well, I'd jes' like to try it—jes' gimme the chance!
  O' the puddin', the proof is the eatin', ye know.
Nothin' venture, naught have—Fortune waits our advance"—
28.  Said the man with the paper—"ye know it is so.

# Tales Told in a Country Store.

Who'd 'a' known this New World that we hold is so grand,
    If Columbus had ne'er staked his all an' struck out—
Left his home an' his country—that ungrateful land—
    Spite o' those who his theories gloried to flout?

Where'd our Land o' the Free, our sublime Nation, be,
    If our staunch Pilgrim Sires hadn't fared forth to brave,
With the hope an' the purpose o' thus bein' free
29.    From oppression, all adverse things—foes, wind an' wave?
What would any one know o' the gold-fields themselves,
    If those who discovered 'em hadn't ben bold—
Scorned alike things chimerical—spooks, goblins, elves—
    An' flesh-an'-blood devils, an' hardship an' cold?

No success without *some* hazard—this I hold true—
    To the young and the old I submit it as fact.
Hail and God-speed to him who, with great things in view,
30.    Has the grit an' the courage to strike out an' *act!*
Countless thousands o' men are sech timorous things!
    I admire the man who breaks loose—faces Fate—
From her stubborn grasp wrings the divinest she brings.
    Who would have Fortune woo him a long while must wait!"

"Yes, but minin's a lott'ry—ye *may* draw a prize,
    But more *likely* a blank—it's accordin' to chance—
The craved treasure may mock the most wise while the eyes
31.    O' some dolt a bonanza may find at first glance.
For one who comes home rich an' proud as ye please,
    How many, d'ye s'pose, come back poorer 'n they went—
Less able to revel in luxury 'n' ease—
    With less trust in Providence—more discontent?

The press is one-sided—it gives all the bright,
    But shuts out all the dark—gives the picture no shade.
You'd think minin' one simple round o' delight,
32.    By the representations so frequently made.
The newspapers give us extravagant tales
    About the successful; but what's ever said
About the poor feller that struggles an' fails—
    Returns sick at heart, or lies down with the dead?

**65**

Livin's dear in sech places. One's got to find gold
  By the bushel, to earn e'en the coarsest o' fare,
Or fall back on the savin's he laid by of old—
**33**    Hard-won fruits o' his labors before goin' there.
With the staff o' life one hundred dollars a sack,
  An' bacon nigh on to a dollar a pound,
One mus' pile up the stuff in a purty good stack—
  Else go where purvisions are easier found.

An' think o' the hardships—the dangers to face—
  The perils uncounted by land an' by sea,
En-route to that far-away, out-o'-way place!
**34.**    In jeopardy constant a feller mus' be.
The ocean—the rivers—the bleak mountain pass!—
  One mus' put these behind him—mus' needs penetrate
A vast howlin' wilderness wherein, alas!
  Savage brutes an' wuss humans the unwary wait.

An' then there's the slavin'. From mornin' till night,
  Successful or not, 'tis delve, delve in the soil,
To find the bright particles—work with yer might—
**35.**    No sinecure job—'tis a life o' hard toil.
No convict in pen or chain-gang anywhere,
  Doomed at arduous labor to expiate crime,
Was ever condemned more severe tasks to bear
  Than the searcher for riches endures in that clime.

An' then there's the climate. The waste where the Czar
  Of the Russias sends those who endanger his state,
Or any-wise lawless an' menacin' are,
**36.**    Scarce possesses a rigor more bitterly great.
True, a brief while in Summer the weather's as fine
  As in Araby belst; but when Winter's blasts roam,
Like to demons malign, an' there's nothin' benign,
  One mus' sure feel like sighin' fur home, sweet, sweet home.

Society too!—odds an' ends o' the earth—
  The vilest abandoned—the lowest depraved!
O' all that's ennoblin', upliftin' there's dearth—
**37.**    A man mus' be stanch, if his morals are saved.

There's drinkin' an' gamblin' an' all sorts o' sin.
  What a place fur good people—espeshly the young!
I wouldn't, fur twice what's supposed to be in
  The whole region, sojourn there sech comp'ny among!"

Debate became gen'ral.  Remarks pro and con
  Were advanced on the subject.  Myself I excused,
Remaining a list'ner—a mere looker-on.
38.  To express my own views I politely refused.
There were arguments made that conclusively proved
  The famed Klondike a fraud, a delusion, a snare
(To the framers); and others to show it behooved
  Ev'ry man not insane or a fool to be there.

I waited the out-come—the end was not yet.
  The man who had read showed a feverish state
Of mind—in a pet—quite a fret—half upset—
39.  Complained that his views were esteemed of no weight.
There is no telling where his mad rant would have run,
  Had it not been indeed unexpectedly nipped
By a happ'ning which wholly absorbed ev'ry one,
  And for the time being discussion's thread clipped.

The store-keeper meanwhile went bustling about;
  Trade was brisk, and his patrons all seemed to be flush.
A stream of humanity flowed in and out,
40.  Both arriving and going away in a rush.
At length the stream ceased; then he leisurely drew
  His handkerchief over his sweat-moistened brow.
And, puffing, with cheeks of a roseate hue,
  Exclaimed: "Well, *that's* equal to chas'n' a plow!"

Very brief was his rest, yet his face wore no frown,
  When, as if that sweet respite expressly to stint,
Came a customer, who in repayment, threw down
41.  Piece of gold by its glint, seeming fresh from the mint.
'Twas caught by the payee with motion adept;
  He scanned it, and cried: "Why I thought that was new!
Its date's '49!—Why—why, where have you kept"—
  But the payer had vanished from hearing and view.

As a trophy, he held it aloft in the light,
  Where all could admire its glitter and shine.
"Don't it call back the far Past to some one to-night?
42.  How's this for a souvenir of ol' '49?
Mister Drown (that was one of the Westerners' names),
  Come, relate us a tale—a reel story of old,
When a mania was rampant for stakin' out claims,
  An' the whole country over went crazy for gold."


"I reckin I kin, pard; I'll do as you say.
  I know what *that* means.   Although young in them times,
I went with the multitudes, pickin' my way,
43.  A-seein' successes, an' failures an'—crimes.
I'll give you a chapter o' life in them days;
  As vivid an' fresh in my mem'ry it seems
As anything yesterday brought to my gaze—
  As anything pictur'd last night in my dreams:—


"Away with yer stories o' Klondike!
1.       The furore an' bustle they raise
Can't equal—no, not by a gun-shot—
       The stir o' them '49 days!


Lawzee! what a tumult an' scramble!
11.       Folks 'd sell the las' thing that they had:
They'd work *any* way, 'most, ter get thar—
       Went rushin' pell-mell—good an' bad!


Why, people jes' up 'n' stampeded!
111.       The wildest herd ever ye saw
Ne'er went so decidedly crazy!
       Fur aught else men keered not a straw!


My, my! them war days o' excitement!
1V.       A feller could skursely sleep nights:
An' when he *did* sleep, in his dreamin',
       His fancy took wonderful flights!

# Tales Told in a Country Store.

V.

Some with piles o' the bright dust returnin',
    Give the fever ter them that had stayed;
What they'd got seemed so huge 'n' so temptin',
    The mos' timorous waxed undismayed.

VI.

O' course, some got wondrously wealthy,
    Become millionaires in a week,—
Jes' rolled up the gold—'peared ter sight it
    Wherever they happened ter seek.

VII.

But whar one struck it rich in the diggin's,
    'Bout nine made a wreck o' their all.
Some come back sick, broke down an' discouraged,
    An' some with amounts paltry 'n' small.

VIII.

Some raptured at first when they got thar,
    With the prospec', wrote home ter the folk
Sech marvellous things—an' the *nex'* thing,
    They 'rived at home half-dead an'—broke.

IX.

Some never war furder heard tell of—
    None ever knowed *what* chanced ter them:
An' many war waylaid an' murdered,—
    An' no courts the thugs ter condemn!

X.

Ye can't tell—it's mighty uncertain,
    This minin'—it's like games o' chance;
'F you're lucky, you're in fur a fortune;
    'F ye don't hit it, why—all's askance.

XI.

That'll be jist the way in the Klondike;
    Some'll wax rich as nabobs 'n' kings,
An' some'll git poorer 'n' Job's turkey,
    An' all other lean, hungry things.

XII.

Some prob'ly 'll succumb ter the weather;
    Some others no doubt 'll be starved;
In accidents many will perish,
    An' some will by Injuns be carved.

No one's an idee o' the hardships,
XIII.
    The struggle, the toil an' the strife,
Away from scenes dear an' familiar,
    Afar off from children an' wife.

No man kin half fancy how heart-sick
XIV.
    A mortal kin be till he roam—
Put four or five thousand miles distance
    Betwixt him an' home—sweet, sweet home.

No one's an idee o' the roughness
XV.
    That dwells in sech rude minin' camps.
Whar's little convenience or comfort,
    An' men skursely live better 'n' tramps.

One skurse kin prize civilization,
XVI.
    Till he goes where it's hard ter be found.
Nor priv'leges 'corded him daily,
    Till he gets where sech things don't abound.

Can't tell *how* 'would seem till ye try it,
XVII.
    To live where there's *nothin'* refined,
Naught goin' cept drinkin' an' fightin',
    An' cards—an' all things o' that kind.

Life's wild enough out on the prairies;
XVIII.
    Cattle-punchers' existence is rough,
But 'tisn't like life in the diggin's,
    Whar, like driftwood, floats all kinds o' stuff.

Thar air quarrels—disputes without number—
XIX.
    Fur men in sech places air hogs,
An' no law—nothin' much ter restrain 'em—
    Jes' shoot down each other like dogs.

Ev'ry man fur himself in sech places:—
XX.
    Mus' jes' load yerself *clear* down with arms-
Go purpared any time fur a scrimmage.
    Minin' life has alarms, well as charms.

XXI.
Thar's a dare-devil fierceness an' boldness,
    Unrepressed, undisguised in men's mien—
'Bandoned recklessness sech as is only
    Amid minin' localities seen.

XXII.
If yer claim's rich, thar's some one ter want it—
    Try ter get it by hook or by crook—
If it's poor, why, its wuss than a burden,
    Better stay in yer own quiet nook.

XXIII.
Wall, ol' Ben an' I—Ben's my pardner—
    War young an' gay, gritty an' strong,
Cared nothin' fur hardships an' peril—
    War ready fur what come along.

XXIV.
The craze struck us fairly an' squarely,
    An' nothin' would do but ter dig.
We went ravin' wild at the prospec'—
    Our hopes war amazin'ly big!

XXV.
Day an' night we both dreamed o' the yaller
    Bright stuff;—ah, the dreams o' them days!
We war sure ter be rich—influential—
    An' see all the world an' its ways.

XXVI.
I had planned me a mansion palatial,
    In New York—leastways *some* mighty town;
I'd have sarvants to do all my biddin',
    An' enjoy all a rich man's renown.

XXVII.
I'd arrange a snug place fur the ol' folks,
    Whar they'd never be troubled or vexed,
Whar in comfort this life they might finish,
    An' in ca'mness purpare fur the next.

XXVIII.
I'd set up my brothers in business—
    Or, if one or more didn't like trade—
Loved callin's pertainin' to science
    Art or letters—their way should be made.

XXIX.

I'd give Nell, my sweet little sister,
        'Thorough musical trainin'; an' Nan
Should follow her dream—be an artist;—
        ' O, but mine war a wonderful plan!

XXX.

I jist ached fur a glimpse o' that kentry,
        Jist yearned ter go soarin' above
On a swaller's wings, same as ol' David—
        Oh! guess, sir, you're right—'*twas* a dove!

XXXI.

I jist ached ter seize one o' the chances
        I fancied so common out thar;
Fur I 'magined that fortunes out yander
        War lyin' around ev'rywhar.

XXXII.

I jist ached ter git holt o' a pickaxe,
        An' roll the great nuggets right out,—
Heap 'em up good an' high.—That we'd *find* 'em,
        We hadn't a shade o' a doubt.

XXXIII.

So we rigged up an outfit an' started,
        'Long the famous ol' Overland Trail—
J'ined a party o' jolly prospectors,
        Who with, 'Westward ho!' answered our hail.

XXXIV.

What a long string o' full "prairie schooners,"
        Their canvas, reflectin' the sun,
Gleamed as white as the sails on the ocean,
        I reck'n,—a hundred an' one.

XXXV.

Land sakes! but the journey seemed endless,
        As we snailed along day after day!
Our young hearts war burnin' an' res'less,
        An' we chafed at the slightest delay.

XXXVI.

Clear disgusted with movin' so slowly,
        We drove off—went tearin' ahead;
But the boys brought us back—kep' us with 'em.
        We'd lose our skelps that way, they said.

# Tales Told in a Country Store.

XXXVII.
Pack o' red-skins war hov'rin' around us,
A-doggin' our tracks day an' night,
So the scout said that had the conductin'
O' our caravan—guess he war right.

XXXVIII.
All our safety depended on keepin'
Together, he tol' Ben an' me.
Long's we done so, they wouldn't attack us,
Fur we war too many, said he.

XXXIX.
That night, two adventurous fellers,
Discontented the same as we'd been,
Broke camp, dodged the guards an' skedaddled;—
Two fresh corpses war later brought in.

XXXX.
'Twar a warnin' we chose ter remember:
An' we stuck purty close ter the rest,
Till we got ter the p'int we war bound fur.
'Slow an' sure' we concluded war best.

XXXXI.
Wall, all journeys end. We arrived thar.
We staked a claim jist ter our mind,
An' pitched in an' worked late an' early,
The fortune we'd dreamed of ter find.

XXXXII.
How we toiled! Soon our hands war all blisters—
Our limbs sore in every j'int!—
Precious little rewarded our labors:
Each day would our hopes disapp'int.

XXXXIII.
Whar, whar war the wonderful nuggets
We had seen in our wonderful dreams?
We longed ter behold 'em an' clasp 'em,
Fur in visions we still saw their gleams.

XXXXIV.
Whar air hidden the riches we've come fur?
We sighed;—Echo answered back, 'Whar?'
Nary nugget. Some dust. Though despondent.
We didn't quite wholly despa'r.

We allowed that down deep in thar some-whar
XXXXV.    We'd light on the treasure at last,
An' as diggin' made plaguey slow headway,
    At length we decided ter blast.

So my pardner he took the ol' burro,
XXXXVI.    An' made tracks ter the settlemint nigh,
Fur ter skeer up some sort o' explosive,
    An' purvisions an' sech things ter buy.

We hadn't had meat fur a coon's age;
XXXXVII.    So after Ben started, I took
My rifle, an' crep' up the mountain,
    Fur game o' some natur' ter look.

Wall, Injuns war plentiful round us—
XXXXVIII.    A blame sight more plenty than gold—
An' many a man had his ha'r raised,
    By bein' too temptin'ly bold.

So with eyes peeled, I pushed my way onward,
XXXXIX.    But nary a game-critter got;
Things appeared ter be wonderful wary—
    I didn't get even a shot.

Now Ben he got back a heap quicker
L.    Than I had expected.   Upon
His 'rival, he unpacked an' stacked things
    An' looked fur me—findin' I'd gone.

Not long did he s'arch till he j'ined me;
LI.    We met on the slope high above,
An' *jist* as we met, I glanced downward,
    An' saw a queer sight, sure as—love!

As sure's you're born! dancin' an' prancin',
LII.    With wildest gyrations 'n' springs,
A comp'ny o' painted red devils
    Was round them purvisions an' things!

Out o' sight we stepped—crept—an' then watched 'em.

LIII.
    Purty soon on the ground they all sat,
An' they eat, an' they eat, an' *kep'* eatin';
    An' the powder-keg—one rolled out that.

They reck'ned, sure pop, that was whiskey!

LIV.
    Wall, the buck raised his tommyhawk high,
An' brought it straight down on the head, an'—
    An'—purceedin's war lost ter my eye!

Seemed the mountains ter roll an' ter tumble

LV.
    Like ships in a storm on the sea;
An' a roar like the sound o' a cyclone
    Cl'ar deafened my pardner an' me!

Skies above waxed as gloomy as midnight;

LVI.
    An' the way things went waltzin' through space
Was no joke.—When the smoke-cloud had lifted,
    Straight we gazed down ter spy out the place.

Nary Injun in sight. They'd all vanished—

LVII.
    Gone whar we'd no doubt they belonged—
An' the bowels o' earth war laid open
    Fur rods round the spot whar they'd thronged.

Wall, we went down an' squinted unstinted

LVIII.
    Fur the wealth we'd so long hoped ter shar';
But we found not a sign o' the treasure;
    So we swore off on minin' right thar.

We got out an' skipped out—Ben an' I did—

LIX.
    Both resolved ter turn over the soil
In the ol'-fashioned way—if we turned it—
    So's ter git some reward fur our toil.

We got us a ranch, an' we stocked it.

LX.
    Our herds now are big as ye please;
An' now in ol' age we'll be able
    Ter live with some comfort an' ease.

Don't ever go greedily huntin'
LXI.            In far-away regions fur gold,
But plow, sow an' reap, an' you'll find it—
        As much as yer pockets'll hold.

Gold huntin's a tough, ticklish business.
LXII.          Hold ter what is reliable—sure;
Don't snap like the dog in the fable
        At a shadder—resist sech a lure.

Don't rush ter far-distant Alaska,
LXIII.          Fur treasures the Klondike may yield;
Save hardship an' trouble an' hazard,
        By delvin' at home in yer field."

The man who had read no rebuttal essayed—
    Becalmed, eyeing vacancy, naught had to say.
"How oft of men's fortunes sad ship-wrecks are made.
**44.**    By tryin' to pile up vast wealth in a day!
Far better to seek in the ol'-fashioned way—
    Slow gains an' sure profits by hard, honest toil!"
This came from the postmaster, who in his gay
    Life's Spring was a prosperous knight of the soil.

Just then a man, ent'ring, proceeded to ask
    Permission for posting a notice.   A roll
Of paper producing, he went at the task
**45.**    Of tacking it up on the wall.   It read:—

---

# ST◯LE !!!

out OF.ROb.mc.cord's.BArN.ON.the.*12Th.*—*in.the.*NiGhT—
sorrel MARE,COMiNG *6*—*weight* 100O.

## ReWar*Dl*

FOR.ReCOVeRY,.$25.00,.AT,SiGHt.
.                for DeTecTion of Thief—-tWICe *that* SuM.

--- ---- --- ----

R.Mc.COrD.

---

'Twas, beyond doubt, the work of an amateur hand,
  From a private press issued.   Albeit unique,
He who ran sure might read—at least *part* that  he scanned—
**46.**   Peradventure the *whole*—if his eyes were not weak.
But though finical Art-lovers haply might smile
  On beholding it—scorning to look at it twice—
It possessed what some papers pretentious in  style
  Sorely lack—to-wit, merit of being concise.

The previous subject was instantly dropped.
  All flocked to the bill-poster, hedging him round.
To answer inquiries, a moment he stopped;
**47.**   For each had a query forthwith to propound.
"Hev ye got any clue?"—"Who d' ye 'low that it was?"
  These and similar questions brought gen'ral reply:—
"Wall, the way the wind's blowin', we  'low we've good cause
  To believe we  may soon have the chap in our eye."

At once the most lively discussion arose,
  Regarding the theft, who the culprit might be,
And what he should suffer.   Some  said prison-woes
**48.**   Were wholly too mild for such persons as he.—
"A taste o' the noose would be 'bout the right thing,"
  Said a man with huge beard flowing down on  his breast.
"Let Jedge Lynch perside—from a tree let him swing!
  That's the way they dispense with sech fellers out West."

"Tut, tut, friend! I 'low you're too harsh an' severe,"
  The postmaster said, "Jedgment ought to have sway.
It's different, somehow, out  on the frontier—
**49.**   They manage all things in a different way.
In absence o' courts, judges, juries an' all
  Machin'ry by which the law's business is run,
Offenders to check, Order's foes to appall,
  An' justice to render—what else could be done?

But here where we've law, let the law take its course;
  It's surely becomin' to give it a chance;
Though sometimes it fails—seems to lack proper force—
**50.**   All rules have exceptions, we know in  advance.

Recall all the cases ye ever have known,
  An' see if the law didn't gen'ly succeed.
For what are our off'cers?—For sal'ry alone?
  They're 'lected to serve us in sech times o' need."

"Look-a-here, Mister Calkins!"  (The man thus addressed
  Was the other frontiersman.)  "Your life has been passed.
For the most part, afar in the wild, wooly West;
51.  Amid scenes strange an' thrillin' your lot has been cast.
Can't you give us a page out o' Memory's book?—
  Some episode 'long on this line new or old?"
"Wall, I reckin, postmaster!"  A far-away look
  Stole into his eyes, and this story he told:—

        "Tom Smith was a way-down-east Yankee,
          An' p'r'aps all the better fur that,
        Though when he kem in, our opinion
1.          Wuz diff'rent—yer jest bet a hat!
        But his deal it wuz honest an' upright—
          We couldn't help seein', yer know,—
        An' he minded his business an' paid all his bills,
          An' 'lowed ter give all a fair show.

        The ranch that he bought wuz a small one,
          But he paid fur it all right squar' down;
        An' when he moved in with his fam'ly,
11.          He wuz happy's a king with his crown!
        His wife wuz a nice little critter,
          Ez purty ez purty c'u'd be,
        All healthy an' rosy an' brimful o' hope,
          An' frank 'n' courageous ez he!

        But somehow we didn't quite like 'em:
          Though why 'twould be hard ter explain.
        'Cept most o' us hailed from Missouri,
III.          An' they from the pine-woods o' Maine.
        We held 'em aloof, ter begin with,
          I reckon, by manner an' tone,
        An' so they paid little attention ter us,
          An' we—we jest left 'em alone.

New Mexico seemed a bit lonesome,
  An' wild, too, ter them, I don't doubt,
But whether or not they war home-sick,
  Not one o' us ever found out.
Tom tended his hosses an' cattle,
  An' his flocks an' herds grew an' increased.
He flourished—he prospered the best o' us all!
  He wuz shrewd, wuz that chap from the East!

IV.

Thieves—hoss-thieves in them days war plenty;
  An' many's the long night I've sat,
A-watchin' my nags with cocked rifle,
  Fur fear they 'u'd go—think o' that!
So we raised a 'Committee o' Safety';
  An' I had the honor ter be
Designated ez leader—an office that seemed
  Fur once ruther irksome ter me.

V.

Wall, hosses kep' goin' an' goin';
  Simpson Collinson lost a fine pa'r,
John Toby soon missed a prime roadster,
  An' the next wuz from Franklin Ada'r.
Whenever we coralled a rascal,
  He wuz sure fur ter git a free swing,
Beneath a stout limb o' some huge wayside tree.
  On the eend o' a mighty tough string.

VI.

Still, hosses kep' goin' an' goin';
  An' no one c'u'd skeer up a clew
Ter sev'ral that went in short metre,
  An' rumors they flew an' they grew—
Rumors rank with the breath o' suspicion;
  An' one o' 'em hinted that Smith
Wuz enlargin' his hoss-flock a leetle too fast.—
  I reckoned 'twuz on'y a myth.

VII.

But Smith kem along one fine mornin',
  Past where I wuz breakin' some ground,
On animal noble ez ever
  Wuz seen in the hull kentry round.

VIII.

I skursely c'u'd credit my senses,
 But wuz ready ter vouch then an' thar
The steed that Tom Smith sat so proudly astride
 Wuz the one that belonged ter Ada'r!

I said nary word, but kep' thinkin';
 An' ez soon ez he'd gone on his way,
I sent ter the boys a short notice,
 An' we all went ter Smith's that same day.
IX.
We immejitly trooped ter his hoss-lot,
 An' I ther sez ter Franklin' Ada'r:—
·Kin yer sw'ar that's yer property, now, honor bright?'
 An' he sez:—'I dew solemnly sw'ar.'

'Wall, my friends,' sez I then, 'it's all settled.'
 Smith, wide-eyed an' gaspin' fur breath.
Sez:—'Ye don't mean—ye don't mean I *stole* 'im?'
X.
 His face turnin' ghastly ez death.
Sincerely I pitied the feller,
 But, since jestice hed got ter be done,
I sez:—'Tom, there's some one obleeged fur ter swing,
 An' I'm sorry ter say you're the one!'

His wife hed looked out an' espied us,
 An' wonderin' what c'u'd be meant,
Stepped out fur ter look the crowd over,
XI.
 An' fathom the comp'ny's intent.
I informed her forthwith—broke it gently
 Ez I c'u'd—what we jedged best ter do—
But she breshed me away with a hand cold as ice,
 An' her strength wuz the full strength o' two!

'Assassins! Thugs! Fiends!' she cried wildly.
 'He's honest an' clear as the day!
He's innocent—O, sir, believe me!
XII.
 He'll prove it—he'll *prove* it, I say!'
I half wished he'd skipped 'fore we nabbed him—
 War anywhere else 'neath the sun—
But jestice wuz uppermost still in my mind.
 An' jestice hed got ter be done.

The woman we whisked ter the cabin;
    Smith himself, strugglin', breathless an' pale,
We dragged ter a spreadin' ol' willer,
XIII.    When we heard hoof-beats down 'long the trail.
'Hurry up now!' sez I, 'Lads, be lively!
    We air not doin' this fur a show!'
But the rawhide wuz turribly twisted an' kinked,
    An' the boys seemed amazin'ly slow.

Wall, gentlemen, 'fore we c'u'd swing 'im,
    Kem gallopin' up Sammy Bla'r,
A-leadin' a critter behind him;
XIV.    An', turnin' ter Franklin Ada'r,
He sung out:—'I've brought ye yer hoss, Frank,
    Clear over ter our place he strayed!'
Ada'r, waxin' white ez a stray churchyard ghost,
    Sez:—'Boys, a mistake hez ben made!

*This* hoss is *my* hoss, 'stead o' that one
    In Smith's lot! (They'd make a fine pa'r!)
My brand!— I fergot fur ter look fur 't
XV.    On t' other one—thar it is—thar!'
Now that wuz good news—yer kin bet on 't!
    Wall, Smith wuz that far overcome
He jes' c'u'dn't speak, nor git out nary sound,
    But stood like one nat'rally dumb!

We apolergized freely an' fully,
    An' at last Tom declared he'd fergive;
Then we carried him in on our shoulders
XVI.    Ter his fam'ly—an' long ez I live,
I shall never ferget his wife's gladness,
    Nor her words full o' feelin' an' pith!
An' the order I give as we started away
    Wuz: 'Three cheers fur the Yankee, Tom Smith!'

All had breathlessly listened. A bystander said:
  "Well, the moral, I take it, 's, be sure of your man."
"Be dead sure you are right, before going ahead,
52.    Is the moral *I* draw—an' it's allers best plan,"

Said the postmaster. "Better miss some who transgress,
    Than to punish the guiltless.—Fair play, ev'ry time!
Men should have their deserts—nothin' more—nothin' less:
    But the penalty allers should match with the crime."

The talk was resumed.  Theft and thief were discussed
    In every phase and from all points of view.
Some argued for violence; some in disgust
53.    Condemned such procedure—and these were not few.
The orderly element, gathering strength
    By straight-forward logic, ascendency gained;
And Reason and Judgment prevailing at length,
    Humanity's cause was most nobly sustained.

More quietly now conversation went on.
    I looked at my watch—it was quite half-past ten.
I rose from my chair, and, suppressing a yawn,
54.    Prepared to go back to the farm-house again.
In errand-boy style, tucking under my arm
    Some parcels my landlady sent for by me,
Some sugar, some coffee, some tea and some barm,
    A short cut I took—by-path threading a lea.

---

## *Chapter 7.*

A
MODERN SAUL.
—HIS STORY OF PURDY.—
PURDY'S DISSATISFACTION WITH THE
COUNTRY.—HIS INFATUATION FOR TOWN-LIFE AND
PREDILECTION FOR MERCHANDISE.—HIS NEW-FOUND ACQUAINT-
ANCE.—THEIR DAMON AND PYTHIAS FRIENDSHIP.—
DISILLUSIONMENT.—THE POSTMASTER TELLS GREY'S
EXPERIENCE WITH A KEEN MAN NAMED KEEN.—OF
ANOTHER UNPRINCIPLED GENIUS.—JONES' SONG APROPOS
OF THE EVENING'S TOPIC,"THE PAPER-MADE TOWN."
—A DISMAL RETURN-TRIP.—AS USUAL, A DREAM.

---

As again I drew near to the little brown store,
    I heard a voice speaking in deep, rolling tones,
Which I recognized fully, ere reaching the door,
1.    As that of a man known as "Big Saully" Jones.

"THAT FELLER TOLD TALES O' A WONDERFUL TOWN."

*See page 85.*

# Tales Told in a Country Store.

Though related somewhat—or reputed to be—
    To the man who so wrecked his corporeal frame
By ærial travelling, no one could see     .
    A resemblance between them, except in the name.

And big, too, he was, as his nick-name implied.
    Seven feet and six inches (or thereabout) tall,
And finely proportioned.  He took no small pride
2.    In his ample dimensions—this latter-day Saul.
On the counter he sat.  I need scarcely explain
    The reason—'twas obvious.  No common chair
Could his figure sustain; 'twould succumb to the strain;
    For he was no "light-weight" as all would declare.

"Well, Purdy's got back on his 'eighty', I see,"
    He was saying.  "I reckon he's done with town life.
He 'pears like a bird that's ben lately set free.
3.    Wonder how it is now with his children an' wife.
Poor Purdy! he's lost by that deal, I suspect,
    More'n any one knows—more than he'd care to tell
Yet braces up firmly, an' goes 'round erect,
    An' smiles as ef all things had allers gone well."

To the postmaster all his remarks were addressed;
    There was no one else there.  As I entered, he paused.
With the bit I had heard, I was strangely impressed.
4.    Who was Purdy?  By what was his misfortune caused?
Curiosity wrought on me strongly.  Though not
    A meddlesome man,—though I struggled to mask
My inquisitive impulse, I knew on the spot
    My visage inquired what my tongue would not ask.

He turned to me, seeming to read at a glance
    All my thoughts, and at once volunteered a reply:—
"Ye wonder who's Purdy— an' what the mischance
5.    I referred to?  Sit down—here!—on *this* chair close by."
I expressed my assent, and soon seated myself.
    He, reaching a candy-jar temptingly near,
Though no elf, helped himself without pelf, on the shelf
    Replacing it gingerly.  "Well, you shall hear."

Yes! Purdy is one o' us farmers.   His place
   Is three mile away, down the main-travelled road;
If e'er ye set eyes on it, naught can efface
6.   The scene from yer mind.   Its a harnsome abode.
A whale o' a barn, sheds an' gran'ries to match,
   Big two-story house, painted cream, trimmed with brown,
Lawn, shade-trees, fine orchards, immense berry-patch,—
   But somehow he hankered fur movin' to town.

True, Purdy worked hard, but no harder'n the rest
   O' his neighbors all 'round him; an' oft he would say
That farm-life was drudgery—'lowed 'twasn't best
7.   To spend all o' one's days in that kind o' a way.
His women-folks, too, seemed his notions to share—
   Both his wife and his darter;—wherever they went,
They had a bored air, an' fur naught seemed to care.
   'Twas a household o' murm'rin' an' sore discontent.

Well, the frettin' went on, though the work didn't cease.
   All was worry an' discord the blessed day through;
There was no satisfaction, no joy, an' no peace:
8.   Life was nothin' but hum-drum—at least in *their* view.
People hereabouts *never* turn deaf ears to woe;
   They sympathize *always* with *sensible* grief,
But abominate whinin:— an' some told 'em so.
   This, you may be sure, didn't bring much relief.

Now, Purdy had laid by a neat little sum—
   'Gained', he said, 'by hard knocks'—fur an inclement day,
An' often he'd say that what-*ever* might come,
9.   He would *never* part comp'ny with *that any*-way.
Well, he had a big sale—sold his herds, hosses, grain,
   An' to that precious hoard added one thousand more;
Then declared he'd no longer a farmer remain,
   But remove to some flourishin' town an' keep store.

Just then a slick chap—an' he *was* slick—as oil!
   Came 'long, an' discov'rin' the state o' affairs,
Went straight off to Purdy, an' made him his spoil.
10.   Poor man!   He was taken in quite unawares.

The fool an' his money soon part—so we read
  In the Book, don't we?—*Don't* we?—Well, Purdy's no fool,
But *that* time he missed it—he did so indeed;
  Though his friends all advised, 'Wait a bit an' keep cool.'

That feller told tales o' a wonderful town—
  A new, thrivin' place.   In a *marvellous* way,
He had it mapped out—streets an av'nues marked down,
11.  An' big an' high-flown appellations had they.
  Much he talked o' brick blocks, wholesale houses, an' all
  Sech great things as great cities have—fine churches. too.
All was grand—nothin' small.   Round this huge mundane ball
  'Twould be famed.   O'er its prospec's he made much ado.

He give Purdy papers all brimful o' praise
  O' that place—an' they couldn't be flatt'rin' enough!
An' Purdy, perusin' 'em, squandered whole days—
12.  Swallered every puff—the nonsensical stuff!
  Well, 'The Cassaway Star,' an' 'The Dasher,' I b'lieve,
  Were the names o' them boom-sheets—it don't matter now—
When a month old, they died, leavin' no one to grieve,
  'Cept the printer—who kicked up a turrible row.

'Twas strange what a *cinch* that man Sharp soon acquired
  (An' he *was* sharp, sure 'nough, as his name signified)
On Purdy, who ne'er o' his company tired,
13.  But desired him always right close by his side.
  'Twas Mister Sharp this, an' 'twas Mister Sharp that,
  Wherever he went, both week in, an' week out;
Fur when *Sharp* was with him—why nothin' was *flat*;
  An' when he was absent—why, Purdy would pout.

When he'd got it down fine—blowed the place up sky-high—
  Then the chap got to business;—remarked that he had
Some fine property there, which a good man could buy;
14.  Though to sell it would make him feel solemn an' sad.
  But, since he was embarrassed,—must get out o' debt—
  Though the very thought made him soul-sick an' heart-sore,
An shed tears o' regret (here he made his eyes wet),
  He'd dispose now—"dirt-cheap"—o' his big, well-filled
    store.

He named o'er a good sum—'bout three quarters the pile
   That Purdy'd laid by—the hard earnin's o' years.
Purdy said he'd consider his offer awhile;
15.  He allers says that when he has any fears.
Sharp was sorry to state that he just *couldn't* wait.
   He'd accommodate Purdy with joy, if he *could;*
But his bills *must* be met—'twas a sacrifice great;
   An' if *he* didn't take it, somebody else *would.*

This fetched him—fetched Purdy—his heart he'd so set
   On a movin' to town, an' a-keepin' a store.
Sharp 'sured him that once, only once he'd regret
16.  Not improvin' his chance—that would be ever-more.
So the matter was settled—the bargain was made,
   The contract drawn up, an' the signature giv'n;—
When the money in good legal tender was paid,
   Sharp seemed to reflect—said his poor heart was riv'n.

Sharp informed all the neighbors he met round about
   What a great bargain Purdy had made off o' him;
Which was flatt'rin' to Purdy—removed ev'ry doubt
17.  He'd before entertained—made his vision more dim.
He remained for a week or so after the trade
   (As his guest, Purdy said), seemin' smitten with Pearl.
Purdy's daughter.  The polish an' tac' he displayed
   (He was single, he *said*), might 'a' charmed *any* girl.

Well, Purdy was anxious to move right away.
   Sharp declared there was plenty o' room o'er the store
(It bein' two-story); an' there they could stay
18.  Till a house could be built—this he said o'er an' o'er.
Purdy made his arrangements fur rentin' the farm,
   Little thinkin' he'd soon find himself in a snap—
Little dreamin' o' reapin' the least bit o' harm
   From the sowin' o' that pesky confidence chap.

'Twas strange what a change came about all at once
   In the whole Purdy fam'ly.  They flaunted around,
An' seemed to think ev'ryone *must* be a dunce
19.  Who could stay here contentedly tillin' the ground.

Mistress Purdy an' Pearl both put on city airs,
    An' took up city ways—far's they happened to know——
An' appeared so elated about their affairs,
    That the neighbors all wished they would hurry an' go.

Well, they started—to cut quite a long story brief;——
    Fur their household effec's Purdy chartered a car,
An' they left (while the neighbors drew sighs o' relief),
20.    Bound fur Cassaway—home o' the *Cassaway Star.*
Sharp had 'lowed to go with 'em, to see 'em safe there—
    So he said—but came round 'bout 's the train was to start.
An' averred he'd a message from—dunno just where—
    That his mother was dyin'—mus' go—broke his heart!

So they parted—he goin' the opposite way,
    A chucklin' an' laughin', no doubt, in his sleeve.
At the way he had hood-winked 'em—they with hearts gay,
21.    Believin' the tales they'd ben led to receive.
P'int he claimed to be called to, I now recollect,
    Was some place in Ohio—can't think o' the name.
That the train that conveyed sech a Judas warn't wrecked
    Is a myst'ry—says Purdy—moreover a shame.

They arrived there at last.   They had pictur'd the place
    In their minds as a *very* elab'rate affair.
The conductor came nigh gittin' slapped in the face,
22.    When he told 'em their-stoppin' place reely was there.
They hardly could b'lieve or receive the man's word;
    Vowed he surely was under the inflooence o' wine,
Or suthin' more stout.   But the train-man averred
    There was only one Cassaway known on the line.

What a *come*-down!   If ever a man was amazed,
    It was Purdy.   If ever a person was sold,
It was Purdy.   The place he'd so longed fur an' praised—
23.    Had it dwindled to this?   He felt premature' old.
No street-cars, brick blocks, churches—nothin' at all
    But an alkali waste by a dismal ravine!
A few stragglin' shanties, forlorn, leaky, small—
    That was all o' the "city" there was to be seen!

O' the depot-man, Purdy inquired fur the store.
　'Twas a wood-shed affair—ruther smaller 'n the rest.
At beholdin' his purchase, poor Purdy felt sore;
24.　　His heart like a chunk o' lead sunk in his breast.
　'Thar's his place,' said the man, 'but he's gone—'twixt two days-
　　Vamoosed—shook his friends—give his landlord the slip—
Throwed his wash-lady o'er—sacked what dust he could raise—
　. An' skipped out, I 'low, on an *ex*-tended trip.

Met him, eh?—Bought him out?—Can't get in. 'Tachment
　　served.
　His creditors hev ter be satisfied first.'
Purdy felt, at this news, quite unmanned an' unnerved,
25.　　Then braced up an' swelled as if ready to burst.
He telegraphed straight:—'Here!　Come back here, you black.
　Dirty scoundrel!　You've swindled me!'　No use to carp.
In forty-five minutes, a message came back:—
　'My compliments.　Go to the Devil!'—signed, *Sharp.*

Well, Purdy came purty *nigh* goin'—straight through.
　He fumed an' he fretted, he stormed an' he swore—
Used all o' the cuss-words that ever he knew,
26.　　An' wished that he had at tongue's end a few more.
But profanity-spasms—eruptions o' ire—
　Wouldn't bring back his money, nor open the door.
O' explosions like that he began soon to tire,
　An' indulged in ca'm thought when his ravin' was o'er.

He concluded 'twas no use to cry o'er spilt milk,
　Nor get down at the mouth, inconsolably sad,
Nor to keep cussin' Sharp an' the rest o' his ilk.
27.　　So he'd just make the best o' a deal that was bad.
He settled Sharp's bills—'bout a hundred or so—
　Squared 'em up one an' all, an' re-opened the store.
The goods—they'd all seen their best days long ago—
　Were appraised fifty dollars- -wuth not a dime more.

He *wanted* to 'rect a big store—big as that
　Which he thought—fondly thought- -poor, duped man!-
　　he had bought;
But, havin' ben bit, he took warnin' thereat,
28.　　An' resolved that he'd look 'fore he'd leap—as he ought.

So he fixed up the shanty as well as he could—
    An' the goods—hired the best o' the shanties near by,
An' ensconced there his fam'ly.  'Twas strange how they stood
    Sech a low, humble nest, after soarin' so high.

Well, the place was as dull as a place could be.  Trade,
    To use Purdy's words, was 'eternally slim.'
Lapse o' days didn't help it.  The longer they stayed,
**29.**    The poorer they got—an' the outlook more dim.
But the worst was to come.  While a-twangin' a harp
    One day—killin' time with a song he'd composed—
He was 'prised o' the fac' that a mortgage which Sharp
    Had giv'n on the lot had ben promptly foreclosed.

The last straw, they say, breaks the poor camel's back:
    An' this was the last straw that broke the backbone
O' poor Purdy's pluck.  Like a man on the rack,
**30.**    He writhed in his mis'ry—did scarce aught but groan.
He vowed 'twas no use to try Cassaway more;
    'Twas tried an' found wantin'—in all save renown.
The dream o' his life with its beauty was o'er;
    The star o' his hope in the dust had gone down.

They ordered a car, packed their things an' returned.
    Purdy bought off his renter an' so—here they are,
More sad an' more wise;—some things sure they have learned.
**31.**    An' not least o' 'em's not to trust strangers too far.
If you want to cut Purdy clear into the core—
    If you want to do worse than to knock him right down—
Just request his advice about how to keep store,
    An' inquire his opinion o' livin' in town."

All was quiet as sleep, till the big man had ceased
    His remarks.  Then the store-keeper hastened to say:—
"I have known sev'ral cases in which men were fleeced
**32.**    By unscrupulous strangers in 'bout the same way.
They come an' with blandest an' grandest o' tones
    The praise o' some make-believe city they sing.
Now, there was Tom Gray—you remember him, Jones,—
    Moved back to Mass'chusetts a year 'go las' Spring.

**89**

A sharper besieged him—'twas some years ago—
　　Tellin' tales o' a new town with big-soundin' name—
Can't quite recollect it—with words all aglow,
33.　　Makin' pictures as lovely as language could frame.
'Twas a wonderful, wonderful, wonderful town,
　　In a wonderful, wonderful, wonderful place,
An' 'twould soon have a wondrous an' thund'rous renown.
　　Its inhabitants 'clipsed all the rest o' the race.

All its streets an' its av'nues with taste were laid out;
　　All its houses were built in the very best style.
There was nothin' at all the most cultured would flout.
34.　　'Twas an up-to-date town, said this smooth man o' guile.
He bragged o' its churches, an' *speshly* its schools;
　　Each public improvement indeed was a gem.
The town had no sinners, no drones an' no fools—
　　In all things 'twas next to the New J'rusalem.

He had property there which 'twould pay him, no doubt,
　　To retain for a rise; this he wished could be done,
But he guessed, after all, that he'd have to sell out,
35.　　Though advised not to do so by every one.
It had doubled in worth since the day it was bought,
　　An' would double ag'in, in a year or less time.
Couldn't do as he *wished*, but mus' do as he *ought*;
　　He must square off his debts—if it took ev'ry dime.

He'd several blocks he'd sell 'way down fur cash.
　　Gray said 'he would think of it'—man couldn't wait.
Like Sharp, all his bargains he drove with a dash.
36.　　His name it was Keen—an' he *was* keen, sure's fate!
'What a pity 'twould be'—an' his words fell like dew—
　　'For you to neglect such investment to make!
What a pity indeed fur a shrewd man like you
　　The chance o' a life-time to spurn an' forsake!'

So he argued an' flattered most ably by turns.
　　Gray, ruther suspicious, remained cool as ice.
An' the man, somewhat taken aback by his spurns,
37.　　Descended at last to 'bout half o' his price.

**90**

Gray finally melted. From wise scruples freed,
  He ventured to count out his silver an' gold,
Receivin' a paper marked 'Warranty Deed.'
  He has the thing yet—but the 'warrant' won't hold.

Gray started at once for the prize he had bought;
  But he jest *couldn't* find it—that *no* one could do.
No person knew aught o' the mammoth town sought.
38.  In his search, he got lost in the woods time or two.
  'Twas a fake—hoax—canard—'twas a swindle complete.
  There was no sech place known—never *had* ben at all.
So he beat a retreat in a heat, as 'twas meet,
  Feelin' chopfall'n an' crestfall'n—unspeakably small.

Well, Tom didn't swear—didn't rave like a Turk,
  Nor load up a shot-gun—that wasn't like Gray.
He set himself quietly, stoutly to work
39.  To locate the swindler, who'd made tracks away.
A man o' few words, great to calc'late 'n' plan,
  An' as resolute 's ever the breath o' life drew,
Was Tom Gray— ye know that *that* sort o' a man
  Gen'lly follers a thing till he sees it clear through.

Tom advertised freely—sent bills far an' wide—
  All over the world, 'most, describin' the scamp.
But *he* could read faces; an *Gray's* never lied.
40.  Keen knew from the first he mus' quickly decamp.
'Twas learned that in far-off Australia he ranged.
  Tom put a detective at once on his track;
But name an' location so often he changed,
  That, baffled, the sleuth-hound o' jestice come back.

Disappointed was Gray. He said 'Try, try again'
  Was his motto. But figurin', countin' the cost,
He decided 'twas best just to drop matters then,
41.  An' consider both money an' man same as lost.
An' he did. From that time he'd have nothin' to do
  With folks that came round—agents, peddlers—all such
Though like pure doves they'd coo, or like warm lovers woo.
  He said 'twouldn't do to b'lieve strangers too much."

He paused, then resumed:—"Thirty-eight year ago,
  When this region was new—sparsely settled an' wild—
When red-men roamed over these hills we well know,
**42.**   An' the prairies in sweet virgin loveliness smiled—
When the land here had scarce any value at all—
  Could be had fur a song—a smart chap from the East—
I remember him well—keen-eyed, slender an' tall—
  Came around an' secured 'bout three sections at least.

He parceled a third out in town-lots. The town
  He named fur himself. When he'd got it staked out,
An' all on a chart with precision marked down,
**43.**   An' fancy price set on each parcel, no doubt,
He departed, returnin' the way whence he came.
  In a tour o' New England, fur buyers he fished.
He was foundin' a colony—that was his claim:
  He would furnish good homes—town or country as wished.

He had town-lots an' farms. What he wanted was *men*—
  Men with fam'lies—or 'thout—made no *great* diff'rence
      which;
But they all mus' be *good* men. Again an' again.
**44.**   He declared that he'd make ev'ry colonist rich.
Great things 'bout the country he told—o' its charms—
  Its nat'ral resources—its crops an' its herds—
Enlarged on its fertile an' broad rollin' farms—
  O, he was a painter, I tell ye,—with words!

He told thrillin' things 'bout his newly-made town,
  It had fact'ries an' foundries an' fine mammoth stores:
An' steam-boats, he said, daily plied up an' down
**45.**   On the river 'twas built by (a mere creek) by scores.
There was plenty o' food an' employment fur all—
  O' all that conduces to comfort no dearth—
An' he hinted that gold—not in quantities small,
  But *hunks*—could be found by jes' probin' the earth.

Well, he sold ev'ry 'farm', an' he sold ev'ry 'lot',
  Fur what seemed back there but a moderate sum.
But exorbitant prices he really got
**46.**   Fur all he disposed of—the news struck us dumb.

The colonists started. At length they arrived.
    They formed quite a party—'bout three hundred strong.
Strange how they survived, but they somehow contrived
    To weather that winter so stubborn an' long.

If ever poor mortals were taken aback,
    It was them hopeful colonists. Scarce could they b'lieve
The man they'd so trusted a villain so black;
47.    'Twas a hard, bitter fac' they were 'bliged to receive.
Disappointed? Enraged? Words are faint to portray
    Their condition o' mind! But at length they cammed
        down--
O' the wild land made farms—they are nice farms to-day—
    Made a town on the town-site—a fair country town.

The rascal that sharked 'em? They took it so cool—
    Didn't hotly pursue him with firearms or law—
He thought they'd o'erlook it. He acted the fool
48.    At least *once* in his life—big as ever ye saw.
A year or two after, he came to the place--
    Dunno why—p'r'aps to see how 'twas gettin' along—
Was recognized—fled—all the settlers gave chase!—
    He jes' missed stretchin' rawhide—or somethin' quite strong."

Jones, who had been writing and listening both—
    Or trying that feat—picking up the brown sheet—
On which he had scrawled, said if we were not loath
49.    To give our attention some verse he'd repeat.
Or p'r'aps he would sing it;—he thought of a tune
    He believed would just suit. In a low and soft tone,
He hummed a few bars—paused a crude line to prune —
    Then these stanzas he sang to an air quite well known: —

            "When a shrewd chap tires of making
            Honestly his way— then taking
            His farewell of good—forsaking
                All that's virtuous, no doubt,--
1.            Not rememb'ring life's a vapor --
            Then he burns a midnight taper--
            And constructs a town on paper,
                And proceeds to sell it out.

Then of all prevarication
Ever known in state or nation—
Ever heard in all creation—

11.     All the *lying*, sooth to speak,—
All the tales of sinful bias
Since the death of Ananias,
To afflict the truly pious
    Comes forth something huge, unique.

Then of marvellous surprises
The superlative arises,
When, unblinded by disguises,

111.     Sees the victim what he's lost—
Lost for ever and for ever
In a fruitless, mad endeavor,
Having striven to be clever
    To his everlasting cost."

I wondered somewhat, though I did not express
   My wonderment, why in the world on that eve
No others came in—could not fancy or guess—
50.   But found out the reason, on taking my leave.
'Twas raining, though softly.  The drops fell so soft
   That not one of us, being absorbed with our talk,
Had heard them.  How dark!  Not a ray from aloft!
   I again had a muddy and desolate walk.

In my visions that night, I beheld a strange sight—
   A genuine, *literal* paper-made town!
All the houses were paper—some black and some white,
51.   Some crimson, some purple, some gray and some brown.
*Ev'rything* was of paper, straight, twisted or curled;
   And I was possessor, methought, of the whole.
To be owner I fancied I'd given the world,
   And lost (I imagined) both body and soul.

"I'VE BEN AXED FUR A SPEECH, SO I'LL JES' GO AHEAD."

*See page 97.*

# Chapter 8.

My good hostess commissioned me duly once more
   To procure for the household some needed supplies.
As I started away on my trip to the store,
1.    She approached me, admonishing me on this wise:—
   "Now *don't* get loaf sugar—the common'll do—
     And *don't* get Blank's coffee—the brand we have had
Is good enough—plenty—don't *you* think so, *too*?
     *Don't* get *fancy* tea—kind we're usin' 's not bad."

Well, if this isn't frankness without cloak or mask!
   I reflected, sore tempted to call for a string
To affix to my finger; but ere I could ask
2.    For that old-fashioned, time-honored, magical thing,
She resumed thus:—"Be *sure*, now, and *don't* you forget
     Any articles named—p'r'aps I'd best speak 'em o'er."
Drawing forth a small note-book (while list'ning) I set
     Down a list headed "*Don't*," with a strong underscore.

Of my hostess, kind woman, most motherly soul!
   I would nothing whatever detractingly say.
My remembrance of her, as the years onward roll,
3.    Shall grow more and more precious each vanishing day.

**95**

So here's to her mem'ry, and here's to her health,
   In a full crystal goblet which need none appall,
(I take nothing stronger—not even by stealth.)
   She was honest and plain and straightforward—that's all.

But gen'rally speaking, one looks for the best
   When he pays for a first-class *menu*. Without doubt,
My mind's ruminations my visage expressed;
4.   For she eyed me quite keenly, then boldly spoke out:—
"You think I am sparin' concernin' expense;
   But you know the ol' maxim 'bout dollars an dimes?
To make the ends meet—it's no flimsy pretense—
   I hev got tew be savin'—it's mighty hard times."

"It's mighty hard times!" O'er and over again
   Rang these words through my brain—in my ears they would
      dwell.
"It's mighty hard times!" Ah, sad children of men!
5.   Earth has groaned 'neath hard times ever since Adam fell.
Hard times! 'Tis a cry that's familiar to all,
   Wherever man struggles, around the whole world—
To youthful, to aged, to great and to small;
   And *will* be till Time's fleeting pinions are furled.

Hard times! How that wail has gone out from the lips
   Of the hard-toiling masses—wan wrestlers for bread—
Whose hopes, 'neath the stress, were well-nigh in eclipse—
6.   Thousands scantily clothed and more scantily fed!
Hard times! Let us trust their worst pressure is past;—
   That abroad in the world and throughout our loved land
Ere long will Prosperity's full glow be cast—
   That her clearest refulgence is now close at hand.

Meditating on this wise, I came to the end
   Of my walk. As I leisurely entered the store,
I beheld a man nick-named "The Workingman's Friend"—
7.   So yclept from his use of that term o'er and o'er,
Designating himself. On huge box in the rear
   Of the store-room he stood—waved his long arms aloft,
And demanded attention. All smiled and gave ear;
   Straight were newspapers dropped, pipes laid by and hats
      doffed.

Perhaps 'twill be well, ere I pass on, to trace
  An outline your fancy may fill as it glows:—
A short and thick figure—a round, puffy face—
8.   Wide mouth—pale blue eyes—very pale—stubby nose.
And now as to raiment, a few things to note:—
  A "hickory" shirt that had long borne the brunt
Of battle with wear—worsted "claw-hammer" coat,
  Much worsted at elbows—frayed badly in front;—

A pair of tight trousers, worn thin at the knees,
  Hung by one lone suspender—a buttonless vest.
These few rapid strokes of the pen you may seize
9.   As suggestions—I leave to your fancy the rest.
Though his manner of speaking was surely unique,
  His discourse was not void of rhetorical flowers;
And although he could quote neither Latin nor Greek,
  He had faith in his own oratorical powers.

"I've ben axed fur a speech, so I'll jes' go ahead;
  Fur to speak is as easy to me as to eat."
(I can scarce now recall ev'rything that he said,
10.   So you need not accept this report as complete.)
"The topics I *gin'rally* handle the best
  Appertain to fi-*nances*. My subjec' tonight
Is 'long o' that line. Friends, I'm not here to jest;
  I'm in *live* or *dead* airnest—whichever term's right.

We air nowadays havin' some mighty hard times;
  An' it's hard on us all! (All was hushed in a trice.)
What's the matter?—What's gone with our dollars an' dimes?
11.   They are sca'ce! (He repeated this truism thrice.)
It's *hard* times!" His voice like a clarion rang.
  Now, that's what's the matter with Hannah, thought I.
(Excuse my *apparent* descent into slang;
  But Hannah's the name my good hostess went by.)

"Why on airth is this thus? What's the reason? *I* say
  We're *im*-posed upon by *on*-principled men.
We mus' fight fur the rights they air takin' away—
12.   Contend fur 'em boldly with tongue an' with pen!

We'll use the *sword*, too,—that we will—that we will,
    If they keep on oppressin' us same's they air now!"
His accents grew more and more piercingly shrill.
    With a flaming bandana he scrubbed his wet brow.

"What use dew we hev fur the stuck-ups—the rich—
    Bloated loaners o' money an' owners o' land?"
His voice here attained an astonishing pitch,
13.    An' his gestures were striking—all made with closed hand.
  "There's the gover'ment officers—conscienceless class—
    The way they get fortunes is wust o' all crimes.
By a fash'nable thievin' their wealth they amass —
    It's *them* as is makin' these mighty hard times!

An' then there's the bankers—a scoundrelly pack—
    When gain's to be sighted, they're all eagle-eyed.
A smooth set o' sharpers!  Their hearts air as black
14.    As midnight itself—O, they're villains deep-dyed!
To men o' that soul-less an' merciless stamp,
    The jingle o' money's the sweetest o' chimes.
Down, down with each crafty an' honey-tongued scamp!
    It's *them* as is causin' these mighty hard times!

An' then there's the lawyers—a rascally lot—
    They rival in mischief the ol' Nick himself.
They talk an' they talk, an' they plot an' they plot
15.    An' set folks a-quarrelin',—merely fer pelf.
They laugh in their sleeve, when they get men at odds;
    All *they* want's tew get holt o' dollars an' dimes—
To rake in the money by han'fuls an' wads—
    It's *them* as is causin' these mighty hard times!

An' then there's the doctors—a pitiless set—
    Makin' poor people sick jest to run up a bill.
They care naught fur suff'rin' so money they get:
16.    So they dose 'em an' dose 'em with powder an' pill.
They get 'em down low, an' they *keep* 'em down low,
    Humanity stiflin' fur dollars an' dimes.
What keer they if men to eternity go?
    It's *them* as is makin' these mighty hard times!

An' then there's the *preachers!*" "Now, Rev'rend, look out!"—
  Said a man at my side—"he's a-goin' at you."
"They're after the shekels;—there isn't a doubt."
17.   The orator thundered—"at least in *my* view—
That they air a burden o' needless expense!
  The Book gives them d'rections fur all lands an' climes—
Furbids 'em to hev purse or scrip—that's good sense!—
  Its *them* as is makin' these mighty hard times!"

"There's many responsible—'cordin to him,"
  Said the man at my elbow, with grotesque grimace,
"There's multitudes makin' our prospec's look dim;
18.   To get rid o' 'em, one'd have to kill half the race.
Well, I warrant he'd sanction a-takin' 'em off,
  An' 'low sech deeds oughtn't be reckoned as crimes.
(Here the speaker was forced to repeatedly cough)
  Jest now he's *sure* havin' some mighty hard times!"

"An' then there's——!" The speaker stopped short, and
      turned pale;
  Like one sorely smitten with ague he shook,—
Appeared all at once unaccountably frail.
19.   'Twas strange what a change came o'er manner and look.
His knees knocked; his articulation was gone;
  His breath he drew in with a quick painful gasp;
He seemingly could not get down nor go on!
  He reached for support—there was nothing to grasp!

Before one could guess what the trouble might be,
  A feminine voice sharply rang through the store.
Half sad and half angry its tones seemed to me.
20.   All eyes were instinctively turned to the door.
A woman in plainly-made calico gown,
  With a dull-colored shawl loosely flung o'er her head,
Had entered.  Her once handsome face wore a frown.
  Pointing straight at the speechless speech-maker, she said:-

"Jeremiah! I told ye to bring me some wood.
  Now the fire's gone out, an' you're hangin' round here.
Makin' anarchist speeches an' doin' no good.
21.   Sech purceedin's 'll make no hard times disappear!

*Good* times *never*'ll come while you're loit'rin' around,
    A-ravin' away like a heathenish Turk.
Prosperity 'll *never* in *that* way be found.
    The bes' cure *I* know for hard *times* is hard *work*.

Jeremiah! That big pile o' beans mus' be thrashed,
    An' this very evenin' the job can be done—
Hang yer lantern up high, so's it sure won't get smashed—
22.    There's lots o' things waitin'—a thousan' an' one.
*Less* work with yer *tongue* an' *more* work with yer *hands*
    Would suit *your* condition, an' bring in more dimes.
Leave spoutin' to them as the art understands.
    It's lazy louts *gen'lly* complain o' hard times.

Jeremiah! *Stop* makin' a fool o' yerself!
    You *know* you're a doin' it right straight along!
Quit yer *nonsense*, an' *work!*—Ye can't live like an elf,
23.    On dew-drops an' sech things,—don't *need* to—you're strong.
Jeremiah! Ye *never* hed *extra* good sense;
    But *where* has the *small* wit ye *had* gone to roam?
Do give up speechifyin'—make no more *pretense*—
    Climb down from yer perch—git yer hat an' come home!"

Our hero, who wilted at first like a flower
    That feels the full force of a late autumn frost,
Now slowly recovered his usual power
24.    Of motion and language so suddenly lost.
Bracing up, he appeared somewhat more like a man—
    At least less like a corpse—more like some one alive.
What to do or to say he seemed trying to plan,
    As his wool-gath'ring senses began to arrive.

At last, with a sigh like the sigh of the Moor
    When he left fair Grenada forever behind,
As one would relinquish the Great Kohinoor,
25.    Or a similar treasure, his post he resigned.
Like a sad deposed monarch deprived of his throne,
    His sword and his sceptre, his purple and crown,
From whose bosom forlorn hope's last vestige has flown,
    "The Workingman's Friend" stepped reluctantly down.

"Yes, Mandy, I'm comin'.—Excuse me, my friends,"—
  Here his spouse interposed:—"Why, o' *course* you're ex-
      cused.
*They*'ve no use fur yer speech—makes no odds *how* it ends.
26.   Strange they'd *hear*—mus' be *'customed* to bein' abused."
To this winding-up thrust at his speech-making powers,
  The poor, fallen orator naught had to say;
But dejected as anything living that cowers,
  Took leave, his extinguisher leading the way.

"*She*'s a terror, *I* wager!" said one in the crowd,
  As the door with a rattle behind the pair closed.
" She jes' *hez* to be,—sure's you're a-livin', McDowd."
27.   Thus the store-keeper on her behalf interposed.
"*He*'s the shiftlessest, triflin'est sort o' a cur
  I've ever set eyes on in all my born days.
Though sech lectur's are no special credit to *her*,
  They do good to *him*—make him 'shamed o' his ways.

By seein' right after him— spurrin' him up—
  An' takin' him down when he gets up too high,
She gets *somethin'* out o' him—worst is the *cup;*
28.   He *will* take a sup— allers *has*—on the sly.
Once a month, too, he'll lurk round that swill-shop at Kirk,
  An' no one can tell when his jubilee 'll end.
It's good-bye then to home-scenes, to Mandy an'—work.
  But still he's a 'labor-man'—'Workin'-man's Friend.'

He's eternally havin' all kinds o' ill luck,
  An' blamin' the times—*allers* says they are bad.
Now, whatever the times, if a man's got no pluck,
29.   There's somethin' forever a-makin' him sad.
The bes' times *I* ever exper'enced or knew,
  Folks had somethin' to do to get dollars an' dimes.
If people don't hustle, o' course coins are few.
  It's *himself* that is makin' *his* mighty hard times.

"Times are hard 'nough for *her* ev'ry day o' her life.
  She takes washin'—makes clo'es—does a'most anything.
I remember her 'fore she become Jerry's wife;—
30.   She was lovely an' happy's a bird on the wing.

What a change! What a change! But it's not a bit strange,
  She's had such a struggle a-scratchin' fur dimes.
I hev wondered sometimes that it didn't derange
  Her mind—but she never finds fault with the times.

She frets quite a little fur fear that some child
  O' the lot—they have seven—a nice-lookin' flock—
May take after him, an' be—well—kind o' wild,
31.  Slack an' easy, moreover,—a chip o' the block.
Well, *she* has *her* faults. If they'd take after her,
  They wouldn't be angels—to say that's but fair.
But she's to be pitied—she is *so.* Yes, *sir!*
  Her face is beginnin' to show lines o' care."

"Two speeches—or three, if we reckon *your'n* in—
  We've heard. Mr. Postmaster;—now I'll make mine,
Though sca'ce knowin' just how or where to begin,"
32.  Said Foss, who was present, with visage benign.
"The problem we've heard so *elab'rately* solved
  I've revolved an' revolved in the depths o' my brain;
An' finally, gentlemen, I have resolved
  My deductions to give you—my views to explain."

All were willing and ready to hear his remarks;
  For he always had something worth hearing to say,
Interspersed with keen sayings, which sparkled like sparks.
33.  Not infrequently brilliant and burning as they.
And now as he spoke on the theme of the hour,
  All with close, deferential attention gave ear,
Convinced of his rare conversational power.
  Full expecting they something of int'rest should hear.

"Now a word at beginnin' regardin' the cause
  O' the hard times:—it's diff'cult to locate the same:
Some declare its a judgment—some say it's the laws—
34.  Some avow—'s we've just heard—certain folks are to blame.
Who or what *is* responsible?—Where may we seek
  Fur their origin?—Ev'ry man has his own view.
Speculation aside, whether trite or unique,
  In respect to their *source,*—that they're *here*'s one thing
      true.

Such depressions *will* come in commercial affairs,
　　An' *will* affect all, high an' low, great an' small;
　　Like convulsions o' Nature, they come unawares;—
35.　　No power o' man their approach can forestall.
　　Like a hateful, ungrateful an' fateful disease,
　　　They come oft by degrees—ere you know, here they are,
　　An' insidious, invidious, perfidious, seize
　　　On the country, our pleasures an' prospec's to mar.

The highway o' life runs both up-hill an' down,
　　Like the highway out there;—now we're flush, now we're not;
　　High prices, then low—Fortune's smile, then her frown,—
36.　　Now the sweet—now the bitter—that's ev'ryone's lot.
　　Since this is inevitable, what is best?—
　　　To go heedlessly on like the unthinkin' steed
　　That rushes to battle, till, sorely oppressed,
　　　We encounter the pangs o' misfortune an' need?

'In time o' peace, make preparations for war.'
　　So runs the ol' maxim—it's good advice, too;
　　An' though Christian lands strife an' bloodshed abhor,
37.　　That's what, if their gover'ment's wise, they will do.
　　From this model, a proverb I'll make, new an' pat:—
　　　'In season o' plenty, prepare for grim want.' —
　　If the people would all for a pattern take *that*,
　　　But mighty few spirits hard times'd ever daunt.

The *main* problem's *not* to prevent the hard times,
　　Nor to drive 'em away when they're once fully on,
　　But this—it's the same in all countries an' climes—
38.　　*How to meet an' endure 'em until they are gone.*
　　What folly—indeed, there can *be* nothing worse,
　　　From a standpoint financial, although it's oft done,—
　　To encounter hard times with a poor empty purse!
　　　That means mis'ry unbounded for—well, *any* one.

In good times, when money comes easy, men spend
　　Vastly more than they ought—they're not willin' to *crawl—*
　　Mus' *fly*—mus' soar *high*—an' when hard times descend,
39.　　They must run then on credit—or not run at all.

That is jest the way  hundreds fall 'way, 'way behind—
  Countless thousands break up—hampered then all their lives.
To the fore-handed man fickle Fortune is kind,
  For he's kind to himself— an' that's why he survives.

'Way down in ol' Egypt, when Joseph was head,
  Under Pharaoh the king, there was plenty sev'n years:
An' durin' that season, prosperity spread
40    O'er the kingdom—unknown were Want's piteous tears.
But Joseph, with wisdom obtained from on high,
  Knew Scarcity'd follow in Plenty's bright track,
An' stored up provisions to have by an' by;
  An' so they were safe when the hard times came back.

Great trouble is, men, as a general rule,
  Are not savin' enough, an' don't oft make the most
O' all that they get.   They can chuckle or pule
41.    O'er the bright or dark present, but blind as a post
Are they to the future.—An' then again, some,
  Forever an' ever a-lookin' ahead,
Live 'cordin' to what they're *expectin'* will come,
  An' draw on the future until they are dead.

Shun extremes.   When you flourish, don't eat all you make,
  Nor wear it all out— lay a good portion by;
For prosperity soon may your pathway forsake,
42.    An then you'll need somethin' the wolf to defy.
Be no miser, no spendthrift; but when times are good,
  Make sure o' your share o' the dollars an' dimes—
Nothin' more, nothin' less; for, in all likelihood,
  You'll need 'em ere long—there'll be *other* hard times.

But good times are comin'—they're now on the way:
  Hard times can't last always—they never have yet—
They're goin'.   'Good-bye, an' good riddance,' we say,
43.    Without any sorrow or twinge o' regret.
Prosperity's comin'—look out for her car,
  All temptin'ly laden with dollars an' dimes!
Hark!—Hear it a-rollin' an' rumblin' afar?
  Wave hands in farewell to departin' Hard Times!

Business men talk o' confidence bein' restored,
 An' ev'rything soon'll be boomin', say they.
Lab'rin' men expect soon to make more than their board—
44. P'r'aps 'nough for their keepin' some distant dull day.
The way's growin' clear, an' a brighter day's near:
 "Twill bring us less worry an' care—fewer crimes.
With mirth an' good cheer, we'll behold it appear!
 God speed the times comin'—the prosperous times!"

With fervor poetic, the speaker expressed
 His trust in approaching Prosperity's sway.
He spoke with great zest. All who heard acquiesced;
45. No demurrer arose—no objector said nay.
His statements all seemed with his hearers to weigh;
 For they knew he had travelled and greedily read,
Though careless of language—near uncouth as they.
 Warmest words of approval were frequently said.

"Now, where's our musician? Here, Lemwel, step out!
 You're wanted!" The store-keeper gayly exclaimed.
"Come give us a song!—You've a new one, no doubt;
46. My boy, don't be backward, nor loth, nor ashamed.
I saw ye a writin' a minute ago;
 I reckon, inspired by our friend Foss's talk,
With soul all aglow an' the rhyme-tide in flow,
 You've made somethin' splendid. Come, now, toe the chalk!"

Toe the *mark* was his meaning. Well, "Lemwel, *my boy*,"
 As he dubbed him, was surely, as none would deny,
An unusual character. Half bold, half coy,—
47. Half ungainly, half polished—half open, half sly—
Half urbane and half rustic in manners and dress;
 In writing precise, but in speaking uncouth:
Middle-aged, and yet seeming youth still to possess.
 He was of extremes a strange mixture, in sooth.

In his physical make-up were wondrous extremes.
 His arms were quite lengthy—his nether limbs short;
While his eyes bore the azure with which Heaven teems,
48. His hair was tar-black, and his countenance swart.

A dual voice—rather *two* voices seemed his;
    While his tones were in common speech guttural, gruff,
Whene'er his soul revelled in song's harmonics.
    They were soft past description—no woman's less rough.

His gait was slow, shuffling; his hands were as quick
    In their motions as swallows' wings.  As from the dim
Corner where he had sat he advanced, through his thick,
**49.**    Paderewski-like locks he kept running his slim
Hand with marvellous swiftness.  This genius unique
    Had published some songs in sheet-form—half a  score—
Which betokened celebrity.  Meek—O, so meek
    He seemed—but with Lucifer's pride took the floor.

"Wait a bit!" cried the postmaster, stepping within
    The railing dividing post-office from store.
From a nail there he took down a large violin,
**50.**    And blew the dust from it.  With eyes brimming o'er
With something suspiciously like unto tears,
    He twanged the strings lightly, then taking the bow,
Played softly a tune none had heard for some years—
    An air that was popular long, long ago.

"Here!  Take my ol' fiddle—I guess it'll go;
    It's lately ben fixed—with new catgut supplied.
How *I* used to saw it in days gone!  My—oh!
**51.**    Can't do it, though, now—been so long sence I tried.
Now tune her up brisk!  What's the name o' yer song?—
    'Prosperity's Comin'?'  That's proper an' good!
Lift boldly yer voice—make yer words clear an' strong,
    So's each one can hear—make yerself understood!'"

"The music's mine, too, friends," the singer explained,
    His bow deftly poising, as if to begin.
Unrestrained, he refrained;—as if chained he remained,
**52.**    While expectancy reigned.  From his lapel a pin
He drew forth—fixed his scrawl—his MS.—to the wall,
    Pausing yet somewhat further its contents to scan,
And make sure 'twould not fall.  A relief came to all,
    When he swept waiting strings, and his lay thus  began:---

# Tales Told in a Country Store.

"Hard times have reigned throughout the land,
　　And caused sore want and grieving;
But brighter days are near at hand—
　　The darksome days are leaving.
In words of welcome, lift your voice!
　　Her chariot-wheels are humming;
She comes our spirits to rejoice—
　　Prosperity is coming!

The army of the unemployed
　　Will have a chance to labor,
And plenty soon will be enjoyed
　　By each man and his neighbor.
The wheels of Progress, so long checked,
　　Will soon be rolling, humming;
With all her grand insignia decked,
　　Prosperity is coming!

There's growing life in business now;
　　The prospect's daily brightened.
The cloud is lifting from man's brow—
　　His burden being lightened.
Soon, as in glad days long ago,
　　The fact'ries will be humming;
Hope forward points with eyes aglow—
　　Prosperity is coming!

There's growing life in commerce, too;
　　She'll soon pour in her treasures
In wonderful profusion.   Who
　　Can not sing happy measures?
The foreign nations send their gold,
　　Which makes the wheels go humming;
Our mines unfold their wealth untold –
　　Prosperity is coming!

The struggling workman shall receive
　　For toiling worthier wages;
For those who aught in Art achieve
　　The outlook now presages

More ample guerdon.   Men will soon
   Be gains, not losses, summing.
With many an undreamed-of boon
   Prosperity is coming!

Thank Him who sends both gloom and light—
   The bright day and the other.
'Tis wisdom guides His hand of might.
    All bitter carping smother.
Take heart!   Awake to newer life,
   And to your task go humming
Some song with grateful praises rife!—
   Prosperity is coming!

Without dull days, how could we prize
   The coming days of splendor?
If ne'er a cloud came o'er the skies,
    What were the sunshine tender?
Then let us recognize the Hand
   That sets the wheels a-humming
In ways we scarce can understand.
   Prosperity is coming!"

Vig'rous clapping of hands and like rapping of feet
   (Some boots that were heard must be classed No. 10)
Showed the crowd's approbation was full and complete.
**53.**   Encored was the singer again and again.
With the rest I approved and applauded the song.
   (In conventional style) for 'twas "proper and good,"
As the postmaster said.   'Twas enjoyed by the throng,
   For 'twas simple—its theme something all understood.

Now a spasm of modesty seeming to cross
   The musician's high soul—he would fain be excused.
How with grace to retire, he appeared at a loss
**54.**   To decide—so to sing more he simply refused.
The postmaster came to the rescue; he seemed
   To wield over "Lemwel" a more potent sway
Than any one else; on him blandly he beamed,
   And before his persuasions the minstrel gave way.

"Ye don't need to sing over the song we've just heard,
   Nor grind us out anything specially new;
Give us that on the ladies.   I feel bad—reel sad—
55.    For a feller as smart an' good-lookin' as you
To be down on the fair sex;—I'm 'stonished thereat.
   I'm sure you'd make some purty girl a nice mate.
I'm quite puzzled—but there!   I forgot!   All o' that
   Yer song'll explain.—Hurry up, fer it's late!"

The singer once more to his audience turned:—
   "Friends, I've tried to decline—tried my post to resign—
But you will not listen.   This song may be spurned,
56.    By you all—for 'tis quite on a different line.
You may like it or lump it—may ha-ha or groan;
   It carries my sentiments—maybe they're wrong—
But if bored or annoyed, the fault's wholly your own.
   The lyric's entitled—

# THE BACHELOR'S SONG.

O, of all the queer objects that I've chanced to view,
      The queerest I ever did see
Was a woman!—And here let me tell it to you—
      The women are nothing to me.—
1.    She wasn't an angel—though free from remorse—
      For she hadn't the harp nor the wings—
But wore her hair long—like the mane of a horse—
      And displayed at least three shining rings.

She would charmingly smile upon that one or this—
      Unless 'twere more easy to scoff—
And her cheeks, red as roses, looked never amiss—
      Except when the paint got rubbed off.
11.    And talk—she could chatter when minutes seemed long,
      And laugh with a silver te-hee,—
But here I'll remind you again in my song
      The women are nothing to me.

Her cloak and her hat were most stylish—perchance
  E'en such as no princess would scorn;—
Religious?—Oh, yes!—Half the way to a dance—
III.  And when she got home the next morn.
That *all* are like her I'll not venture to say,
  But *seem very much so to be;*
So here I'll repeat it again in my lay—
  The women are nothing to me.

Just look at their fashions!—They're fickle as straws!
  (All works of the Devil, no doubt.)
Ah, little *I* care for their gauze and gew-gaws
IV.  Or what they may simper about!
They may say this is only a bachelor's whim,
  And laugh in derisory glee,
But unmoved I can say with a countenance grim.
  The women are nothing to me.

Though they call us old bachelors crusty in mind—
  Sneer and fleer at each odd-sounding phrase—
Where on earth a more heartless concern can you find
V.  Than a woman—of fash'nable ways?
And I'd just like to ask any married man nigh
  What virtue in them he can see,
For if one can inform me, why,—I'll tell you why
  The women are nothing to me."

    Comment surely is needless.  I'm not much inclined
      To essay it.  A laugh arose, lengthy and loud,
    Which was far from applause; for the mass of mankind
57.   Are averse to such sentiments—so was the crowd.
    At what's laughable men laugh, however.  "The boat
      Only big 'nough fur one is too small by jes' half
    What it orter be," said a dry wag, as, *sans rote,*
      Broke the throng.  Quoth the singer: "Such talk is mere
        chaff."

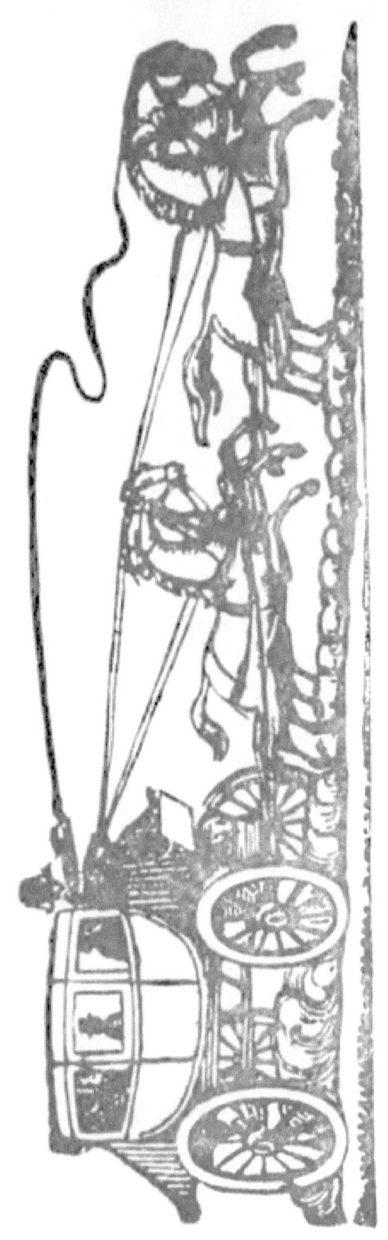

"AS WE RUMBLED THROUGH THAT REGION,
FANCY CONJURED UP FOES LEGION."

*See page 132.*

# Chapter 9.

---

---

The time of my sojourn had speedily drawn
  To a close; and so, packing my trunk and valise,
I made due arrangements at once to be gone,
1.    Somewhat sad, and yet glad at my brief stay's surcease;
For though I had love for that sweet rural place,
  For its beauty, its quiet, its novelty's charms,
I found myself yearning to gaze on the face
  Of each loved one—to clasp those at home in my arms.


"*Must* you go, Rev'rend Sir?"—said mine hostess—"go *now?*
  Can't you stay a *while* longer—a week *any*-way?
*Do* drop us a card when you're there, tellin' how
2.    You got through with your journey. You've made a *short* stay.
Now, if *ever* you come to this part of the sphere,
  *Do* call round an' see us—*do* make this your home!
I'm in *hopes* you've enjoyed yourself while you've been here.
  Remember us kindly, wher*ever* you roam."

**111**

Mine host called his youngest son John from the field,
    And gave him instructions my driver to be.
Much joy this would yield.  He with pride unconcealed
**3.**    Made ready.  A natural Jehu was he.
"Twas his favorite pastime a good whip to wield
    Back of spirited horses—a well-matched, fleet span.
Much adroitness and tact and true skill he revealed
    In his coachmanship—far more than many a man.

The stage would be due twenty minutes past four
    At the store; so at four my young coachman drove round
With team and spring-wagon appeared at the door.
**4.**    Bag and baggage aboard, myself ready I found.
Then a shaking of hands, and exchange of farewells,
    And I mounted the seat, and awayward was whirled,
Like a leaf on the wind, over hills and through dells,
    While the dust far behind us in clouds streamed and curled.

This was not the first time I had ridden with John;
    He had taken me several times for a ride,
Here and there through the hills; and as now we sped on
**5.**    He seemed rather uneasy, and frequently sighed.
A mile and a quarter at that rapid rate
    Is soon passed.  As we went up a hill somewhat steep—
The last on our journey—he slackened the gait
    Of the horses—and truly I thought he would weep.

"This ride is our last one together—perhaps"—
    He said, with averted and far-gazing eyes.
"You're out in the world, and are used to young chaps;
**6.**    You've thought, studied, travelled, observed and grown wise
Through experience.  Now, as we're going to part—
    I've wanted to say this before, but failed twice—
(I guessed when the times might have been) from your heart
    I want you to give me some parting advice."

Some parting advice to a soul in life's morn!
    Opportunity golden!  (I said to myself)
It should not be treated with lightness or scorn.
**7.**    I replied:—"My dear boy, this remember:  That pelf

Should not be your object. Ne'er let that control
  All your thoughts, wishes, deeds—live for something sublime;
Be noble, magnanimous—*wealthy in soul;*—
  Live for riches enduring beyond earth and time.

Live not for mere pleasure. Enjoyments all cloy
  That are won in defiance of Duty and Right.
Live for principles noble, uplifting, and joy
8.    Will be granted in fullness, your course to requite.
Live not for renown. Though the bruit of your name
  Encircle the globe, if your life be not pure,
'Twill serve to perpetuate merely your shame.
  Build character—that will forever endure.

Live not for yourself.—The life centred in self
  Is of no use at all in this great world of ours.
You might as well be but a gauzy-winged elf,
9.    To disport amid Fairy-land's fabulous bowers,
As to live for your own, and for no other's sake.
  Seek to make those around you both happy and good;
And the joy that within you such strivings will wake
  Will make blessed existence.—Be this understood.

Live neither for self, nor for others alone;
  Live for Him who has made you, and given you breath.
By whom all your thoughts and your feelings are known.
10.   Who is Lord over life—also Master of Death.
Let nothing about you be grov'ling or base:
  Let your eyes sweep the heights by the Shining Ones trod;
Let the blest Word of God be your guide in life's race:
  Live for truth, virtue, purity, holiness—God.

I have given the highest advice I can give.
  But hearing and doing are different things;
It is one thing to know, and another to live
11.   According to knowledge. From purpose good springs.
The life that is right will not simply evolve
  Itself out of chaos—must have a *high aim;*
The soul that mounts up must first firmly *resolve,*
  Then *strive*—or go downward in sin and in shame.

This may sound like a very old story to you,
  My dear boy,—you may say that *all* preachers talk so:
But you know 'tis sincere, and you know it is true.

12.  'Tis the best admonition I have to bestow.
  Bear in mind that this life with its tasks is soon o'er—
    Transient quite in God's sight as this afternoon ride—
  Live it well." At this juncture we drew near the store.
    "Thank you much—very much!" the lad softly replied.

Seed sown by the wayside! (So inly quoth I)
  Heaven grant where it fell may prove good, fertile ground—
A hundred-fold harvest bring forth by and by,

13.  To the glory of God and His cause to redound!
  I alighted. My baggage disposed of, I gave
    A hearty "Good-by" and warm hand-grasp to John:—
  Musing watched him drive homeward. He turned round to
        wave
    His hand at the brow of the hill—and was gone.

Beneath the store-awning a group of men sat,
  Among them were Foss, peddler Thompson, McDowd.
I wondered what furnished the theme of their chat,

14.  But found out at once, on approaching the crowd.
  "The 'Workingman's Friend' lost his dwellin' las' night:—
    Got ablaze about midnight—burned clear to the ground."
  Said Foss. "All who came worked with all o' their might,
    But we jes' couldn't save it—to go it was bound.

Saved nothin'—lost ev'rything—'bout—jes' got out
  An ol' rockin'-chair, which her gran'-mother gave
To her for a keep-sake. To-day, I don't doubt,

15.  She's sheddin' some tears, though so gritty an' brave.
  She had a small sum—recent earnin's—laid by,
    An' she told where 'twas kep'—the identical spot—
  We tried to get at it, but couldn't get nigh:
    Had to give up the effort—the flames were too hot.

Caught afire from the chimney—at least we suppose
  That's the case—for 'twas sadly in want of repair:
Bein' patched late las' fall, the material froze,

16.  An' has been droppin' out all along here an' there.

Did they know its condition?   O, yes, well enough;
   But his wife couldn't fix it, an' he jes' delayed—
Put it off same's he always does jobs he thinks rough—
   Could 'a' done it well's not—is a mason by trade.''

I remarked that 'twas likely the house was insured.
   McDowd said:   "The policy lately expired;
Agent asked a renewal, but only secured

17.   A 'Some day' from Jerry.   As soon's he'd retired,
He heard Jerry say, in his slow, easy way,
   To his wife:—'We have never burned out heretofore.'
She said:—'Well, we may—better 'range it to-day;
   Can't tell what'll come—may not have a chance more.'

He'll be spoutin' again about 'hard times.' "   "You're right!"
   Thompson said, quickly raising his eyes from the ground.
"He'll be ravin' distracted—be ready to bite

18.   All professional men that may happen around.
Don't care much for him, but I pity his wife;—
   Makes more up-hill scratchin' for her an' her brood.
An' he—O, well, somehow such men get through life—
   They gen'lly get clothed, an' have plenty o' food.''

I looked at my watch—'twas a quarter of five—
   Remarking to Foss that the stage was quite late.
" 'Tis, sure's you're alive!   Ought to promptly arrive

19.   On time, for his nags are good trav'lers—fust-rate.
No wash-outs, no burn-outs, this time o' the year—
   Naught hind'rin' his progress, far's any one knows.
It's strange; but no doubt pretty soon he'll appear,
   An' then he'll explain the delay, I suppose.''

At this moment, the postmaster came to the door,
   With a puzzled expression upon his mild face:—
"Billy's tardy; he seldom has ben so before.

20.   Wonder what 'tis has chanced!   Somethin's sure taken place.
What could it 'a' ben?   Can't imagine or think!"
   Said he, with a sweeping glance far up the road.
"Held up, like enough," said McDowd, with a wink,
   "Like Tim—jes' a-waitin' an' holdin' his load.''

The postmaster simply replied, "Reckon not!"
   And vanished within.  McDowd turned then to me:--
"Jes' jokin'," he said.  "The stage-driver we've got
21.    Is brave an' as faithful as mortal can be.
But ol' Maybell's son Tim – driver jest afore him—
   Was clear different— queerest case ever one saw—
Allers lookin' fur robbers:—'twas only a whim,
   But his wild notions kep' him furever in awe.

My, but *wasn't* he skeery!  Like all coward men,
   He loaded himself with revolvers an' knives—
Was a reg'lar live ars'nal.  Again an' again,
22.    He came purty *nigh* takin' other men's lives
By mistake--thought o' course they were layin' for his,
   When they never had dreamed o' sech measures as that.
Their designs bein' far as the northern pole is
   From the line– far's Pike's Peak from ol' Mt. Ararat.

Ol' Sammy McCoy went out huntin' one day;—
   I think—yes, 'twas rabbits he wanted to fetch;
An' one played him sharp.  He had twice blazed away—
23.    Both times failed to down him.  The cute little wretch
Led him quite a long chase, then tacked into a clump
   O' thick briars that stood 'bout a rod from the road.
Partly hid by some saplin's, Sam perched on a stump,
   Mopped his brow, stopped to take a short rest an' reload.

Jest then Tim came drivin' along with the stage;
   An' catchin' a glimpse o' a man with a gun,
An' thinkin' he'd war with a bandit to wage,
24.    'Lowed the man that shot first was the fortunate one.
So he pulled up his team, an' like lightnin' whipped out
   A self-cockin' six-shooter--the king o' the pile
Pumped until 'twas clean empty, then turnin' about,
   'Stead o' comin' down here, drove like mad back to Kyle

The passengers thought there was *somethin'* to pay;
   He a-nigh overset 'em in turnin' around.
They thought first the horses were runnin' away,
25.    Till they heard Tim a-urgin' 'em over the ground.

An' I tell ye them steeds didn't loiter nor creep;
  Tim soon dropped his whip, an' fur dear life hung on.
While the people inside were all tossed in a heap,
  An' thought fur awhile they were certainly *gone*.

He was speechless with fright till he'd gone a good mile,
  Then uplifted his voice in a panther-like yell.
Well, in no time—at least, in a *very* brief while—
26.   Back he swep' into Kyle like a cyclone—pell-mell!
He uttered a war-whoop that brought the whole town
  A-surgin' around him, excited's could be!
'Highwaymen!' he shrieked.   'Git yer guns an' go down!—
  I shot five or six!'—he was *rattled*, ye see.

The passengers *they* couldn't tell—didn't know—
  More 'n what they'd *experienced*—'cept what *he'd* said.
They reckoned there *must* 'a' ben *some* sort o' foe,
27.   To skeer him like that—make him *clear* lose his head.
One an' all advised searchin' the place where he thought
  They'd met the fell enemy—so a good squad
Started out, well-equipped an' well-mounted.   They sought
  The spot in great haste—saw a sight ruther odd.

There stood poor ol' Sam, gazin' blankly around,
  Now here an' now there, with a dazed sort o' mien,—
Now up at the sky, an' now down at the ground.
28.   He seemed at a loss—couldn't make out the scene.
There were two clean-cut holes through the crown o' his hat,
  An' two through his coat; there was one through his hand—
Wound he'd somehow got stanched—he had sense 'nough fur
    *that*,
  Though jest how things chanced he could not understand.

Well, the stage was late *that* night; fur Tim wouldn't start—
  Naught could budge him an inch till the party came back,
Tellin' what they had seen.   Then he *longed* to depart,
29.   Fur o' jokes an' o' banter there wasn't a lack.
Here we waited an' waited.   I stayed an' stayed on
  Till at last he hove in—fur my wonder ran high—
But not much would he say—seemed in haste to be gone.
  Soon the news got around, though,—ye know sech things fly.

We chafed him an' guyed him unmerciful' then,
   An' whenever he chanced to be five minutes late,
We'd say: 'Well, I spose you've ben held up again!'
30.   'Twould a ripple o' merriment allers create.
My sakes, how he'd squirm!—Like a poor, impaled worm
   On a fish-hook! 'Twas cruel, yet somehow 'twas fun;
We kep' it up, too, till he finished the term
   O' his contract—he must 'a' ben glad when 'twas done.'

That taught him a lesson, but wasn't a cure.
   Though he let up on shootin', he still lost his wits
Now an' then—nursed his whim, an' was frequently sure
31.   He was laid fur—was twice skeered—once clear into fits.
That he fought hard ag'in his fool notions an' fears,
   I haven't the slightest o' reasons to doubt;
But as these were born in him, an' swayed his young years,
   To oust 'em was like castin' sev'n devils out.

Middlin' early, one evenin', I started to go
   To a pastur' I have, lyin' east 'bout a mile
From the home place, an' 'lowin' I might see a crow,
32.   Or a hawk, or some game, or spy *somethin'* wuth while,
I jes' shouldered my gun. Well, I'd passed through that strip
   O' woods, an' was crossin' the big iron bridge,
When I saw Tim a-comin', a-makin' his trip,—
   He'd got almos' down to the foot o' the ridge.

The low sun a-strikin' him full in the face,
   He didn't have quite the best use o' his sight,
An' so didn't know me. In that lonesome place,
33.   He jumped to conclusions—an' drew the lines tight.
He set the brake hard—hauled his hosses right up.
   Soon a head was poked out—some one glanced all about:—
A voice I heard say:—'D'ye expect us to sup
   In this out-o'-way spot?—Want us all to get out?'

No reply reached my ear. Why on earth had he stopped?
   I at first had no s'picion he *could* be afraid,
Thought that somethin' had broke, or that somethin' he'd
      dropped;
34.   But no movement he made—jes' delayed—simply stayed.

**118**

# Tales Told in a Country Store.

Bein' quite a bit weary—or lazy, perchance,—
  I leaned back 'g'in the rail, with my gun in my hand,
An' observed him, expectin' that soon he'd advance;
  But he didn't. His course I could not understand.

The longer I looked the more puzzled I was;
  An' after I'd loitered ten minutes or so,
I said to myself that there mus' be a cause
**35.**   Fur Tim's cur'us actions that *I* didn't know.
Suthin' surely had happened—he needed some aid—
  An' there I was standin' an' gawkin' the while!
So I started that way. To my s'prise, Tim essayed
  To turn round an' flee in a panic-struck style.

It dawned on me then what he'd taken me for—
  A lurkin' highwayman—a desperate knave—
An' he'd chosen flight in the place o' grim war.
**36.**   The thought made me smile, though the prospect was grave.
I'd 'a' stood in the road there an' laughed till I cried—
  Mebbe died—if I hadn't feared some one'd get hurt;
For that reason I looked on the serious side,
  Takin' measures disaster at once to avert.

Straight I shouted:—'Come on! I'm a peaceable man!
  I don't want yer money—I don't want yer life,
Nor the lives o' them with ye! I've no evil plan;
**37.**   The weapon I carry 's fur huntin'—not strife.'
Well, that reassured him—my voice he well knew—
  But if he didn't look like a sheep as he passed!
He claimed 'twas a put-up-job all the way through.—
  I was innocent's *could* be, from first to the last.

Well, the *wust* skeer he got was a month later on,
  On his out-goin' trip, mile 'n' a half west o' here,
At the ol' Walford place—Walford's sold out an' gone,
**38.**   But the place bears his name—will fur many a year.
The farm's by the highway cut 'zactly in twain.
  A long row o' cherry-trees runs on each side,
So close that their boughs a'most meet o'er the lane.
  There's ben but scant room fur a roadway supplied.

Well, ol' Nathan Cunnin'ham—man who presides
  There nowadays—has for that v'ri'ty o' fruit
Particular pref'rence.  Whene'er aught betides
39.    The cherry-crop, *he* cannot keep still or mute.
The cherries were rip'nin'; they bore a high price
  That year, fur the birds were uncommonly bad.
As soon 's red an' nice, they were gone in a trice.
  Some farmers lost purty nigh all that they had.

He fretted an' fumed—an', I'm sorry to say,
  Profaned quite a bit.  Though he handled his gun
With tellin' effect, they would not stay away—
40.    Jes' settled right back, soon 's the shootin' was done.
He rigged up a skeer-crow—the ol'-fashioned kind—
  Pole an' ol' clo'es an' hat—but they wouldn't heed that;
Not blind, skurse behind human-kind, they divined
  (He opined) what in mind he'd designed—scorned thereat.

He was madder'n' a hatter, an' goin' to town,
  He visited all o' the clothin'-stores there,
An' returnin' at eve, in great triumph set down
41.    Twelve large tailors' dummies, well-clad—debonair.
He the very nex' day took the skeer-crow away,
  An' put up the dummies ('Twas after Tim passed
On his trip back this way); quite imposin' were they.
  The birds in flocks vast held aloof, quite aghast.

Well, Tim drove along somewhat later that night
  Than usual—twilight was cov'rin' the land—
An' glancin' up there in the dim, fadin' light,
42.    An' seein' men's forms in the dark tree-tops stand,
Concluded some outlaw's notorious band
  Was 'bout to pounce on him.  He whipped up his team,
But somehow the lines both slipped out o' his hand;
 . He fell an' rolled under the seat with a scream.

Quick as lightnin' they dashed down that long stretch o' road,
  (Tim was havin' a fit, an' jes' didn't know beans)
Till they met Kirby Mounts comin' home with a load
43.    From the coal-mine—'twas over jest yon side o' Dean's.

Kirb tried hard to side-track his big load o' coal;
  'Twas useless:—he hadn't half time to prepare;—
Tim's team struck his wagon, an' jes' made it roll.
  A-scatt'rin the 'black diamonds' everywhere.

Kirby picked himself up 'bout a good rod away,
  Much bruised, badly shaken, but able to go,
An' began to investigate.  Tim's hosses lay
44.  Disabled by broken legs, writhin' in woe.
The coach, strange to say, was not damaged, except
  At the tongue, which was broken.  Its inmates, unhurt,
Though sadly demoralized, leapt, stepped or crept
  From its doors, an' demanded, 'What's up?' in tones curt.

Kirb's wagon was kindlin'-wood—fine, too, at that—
  Battered, shattered an' scattered—beyond all repair—
In shivers an' slivers.  A moment thereat
45.  He directed his gaze with a blank, absent air.
'Well, the fuel's all ready—now who's got a match?'
  He said with a humor unspeakably grim.
Then a thought seemed to strike him, while nursin' a scratch:
  'Why, say!  Where's yer driver?  What's happened to *him*?'

Sure enough, where was Tim?  They looked all up an' down
  The highway, fur what seemed to all longest while,
Findin' naught but his hat, with a badly-mashed crown,
46.  Though searchin' the back-track fur p'r'aps a good mile.
At last one detected a moan or a groan,
  Which seemed to his ear to proceed from the coach,
First skursely perceptible, swellin' in tone,
  An' growin' more audible on his approach.

There was Tim, jest recov'rin', though turribly dazed;
  What had happened he didn't remember or know.
When upraised, round he gazed, all amazed.  'Bout half crazed
47.  He appeared by his stare in the lantern-light's glow.
Well, when they had found him 'twas quite late indeed;
  An' the passengers bein' both hungry an' tired,
Were anxious at once on their way to proceed.
  But the question was, *how* to proceed as desired.

Well, as Tim an' his hosses were helpless, an' since
   Kirb had nothin' to hitch to, they laid siege to him
To convey 'em to Ware.  First he didn't evince
**48.**   A big int'rest in doin' so.  Sore in each limb,
An' sort o' bewildered at thought o' his loss,
   At first he said, "No"; but they wouldn't hear.  So
Without further parley—'thout words short or cross—
   The coach-tongue he patched, an' got ready to go.

Tim's broken-legg'd nags, by some well-d'rected shots
   Were removed far beyond life's distresses an' cares:
An' at the next farm-house—ol' Bill Holverstott's—
**49.**   He was lef' fur safe keepin'—laid up fur repairs.
Informin' his own family o' the affair
   (They live jest out here), so's they'd know where he'd gone,
Kirb went with the stage, as requested, to Ware,
   Arrivin' there jest at the first peep o' dawn.

When he'd made the round-trip, an' got back there again.
   Tim was ready fur business; worn off was his fright.
An' his ep'lepsy ditto.  Kirb said there an' then
**50.**   That he'd better resign.  Tim replied p'r'aps he might.
But he didn't: he drove till his contract expired,
   Though the butt o' all jokes.  People wondered thereat.
To bear *half* what *he* bore, wouldn't many be hired.—
   But his passenger-traffic was slim after that.

What right has a timorous critter like Tim
   Fur any responsible post—any trust?
*I*'d want to go hide where the light's low an' dim-
**51.**   Git out o' the range o' the public's disgust.
'Does he live round here yet?'  Yes, a mile off—about—
   An' is allers a-tryin' fur office to run:
But in ev'ry campaign, his ol' record's brought out,
   An' his race is a short an' a humorous one.

But Billy's all right.  Though a man o' few words,
   An' plain, unpretentious—no discount on him!
'Twould take suthin' more than what skeered ol' Nate's birds
**52.**   To shake him or make him a whit out o' trim.

He's up to his business—he hasn't a fear—
  Hark!—Didn't I hear the faint rumble o' wheels?
He'll shortly be here—in a bit he'll appear—
  An' make it all clear—not a jot he conceals."

The lamps were all lighted, the awning drawn up,
  And all went within.   I now preyed on my lunch,
And thought, had I known, I had had time to sup!
53.   The rest bought some cheese and some crackers to munch.
Both Calkins and Drown, the frontiersmen, were there;
  Like me, they were waiting the stage to depart
For home—to their loved ones afar to repair;
  And also, like me, they were anxious to start.

All eyes sought the clock, which was ticking away
  In the post-office corner—'twas now after nine.
Our hunger appeased, we had little to say;
54.   With his thoughts each was busy—or I was with mine.
One after another, we went to the door,
  And blankly stared out on the gloom of the night.
This act was repeated by all o'er and o'er—
  No coach came in range of our hearing or sight.

"This waitin' 's tough business!" said Calkins at length—
  "More tedious than herdin' or turnin' the soil —
Not tryin', o' course, to one's physical strength,
55.   But hard on the mind—more depressin' than toil.
It makes a man fidgety, narvous an' sour,
  To remain as we've ben. on the very tip-toe
O' thrillin' expectancy hour after hour—
  It's the quintessence—climax—the acme o' woe.

Some poet has sung o' the pangs o' suspense;
  I reck'n we're feelin' 'em right here an' now,
As real an' potent, as sharp an' intense
56.   As anyone—keenly enough, anyhow.
Uncertainty's killin'.   Whene'er a man's sure
  O' what is before him, he makes up his mind
To meet it—the wust to o'ercome or endure;
  But one in suspense is jes' goin' it blind.

I remember a time when the stage-coach war late—
  'Twar in ol' Californy, in days long ago;
An' the ones as war ling'rin' its comin' to wait
**57.**    Must 'a' 'lowed Father Time war remarkably slow."
"Come. give us the narrative!"  Somebody cried.
  "If the stage isn't comin'," he answered, "I will."
He strode to the door—stood a moment outside—
  Harked—re-entered—proceeded his word to fulfill:—

    "Journeyin' from San Francisco
    Down ter mountain-walled Camp Brisco,
    Nigh ter shanty-town called Liscoe,
**I.**        Once I had experience queer—
    Somewhat serious—ruther shockin'—
    Grave beyond all jestin', mockin'—
    In the thrifty fall o' '50—
        Ever memorable year.

    Oft I'd shifted my location—
    Sought a better situation—
    Still fur gold made excavation,
**II.**        Though fur me it didn't pay:
    All my ventures war unlucky—
    Ev'ry one; but I war plucky:
    Though repinin', I kep' minin'
        Without whinin', day by day.

    Still I delved away at Brisco.
    I'd ben up ter San Francisco—
    Thar war no great shakes at Liscoe—
**III.**        Naught that sure returns would give—
    But the outcome war not flatterin':
    Places ter my taste seemed scatterin';
    Fortune stern, hopes batterin'—shatterin'
        Tol' me I mus' dig ter live.

    All the land war full o' danger
    Fur the pilgrim an' the stranger:
    Gold had hardened hearts unpardoned—
**IV.**        Souls o' gholes in form o' men:

# Tales Told in a Country Store.

Cut-throats worked along the highway,
Lurked an' smirked by trail an' by-way,
Gatherin' gold up—bloodiest hold-up
    'Currin' ev'ry now an' then.

Men with burnin' dust returnin',
With their breasts fur loved ones yearnin',—
Home-turned faces—war in places
    Unfrequented, dreary, lone,
Straight relieved o' their subsistence,
An' bereaved o' their existence,
An' their fate in full ter waitin'
    Friends an' kindred ne'er war known.

The huge coach with men war laden,
'Cept two women—one a maiden,
Seemin' pure as sprite from Aidenn—
VI.    Much they cheered that tedious trip.
Men observed as strict decorum
As a staid an' stately forum;
With the fair ones' influence o'er 'em,
    No coarse word crossed any lip.

Might war right in that wild period.
Or esteemed so by a myriad—
By the darin' an' unsparin',
VII.    Bearin', wearin' loads o' arms:
Pity seemed a total stranger
Ter each Godless, Christless ranger,
Who, eschewin' virtuous doin',
    Found in ruin untold charms.

Soon a man learned ter be wary,
In his words discreet an' chary,
In a shack or on a prairie—
VIII    Keep close mouth, ye understand,—
An' his vision clear as crystal—
Ter be handy with his pistol—
Make improvement in his movement,
    Lookin' out on ev'ry hand.

'Tis a fine thing in sech places
Ter be able ter read faces,
Make chance actions well's transactions.

IX.
      Useful knowledge, too, impart.
I could soon form calculations—
Accurate prognostications—
From mere sweepin' observations—
      Found it a most helpful art.

On that trip, though, I war puzzled,
An' my jedgin'-power seemed muzzled,
That's no stigma.  An enigma

X.
      Saw I then in human guise—
Failed that countenance so stoic
Ter decipher, though heroic
In endeavor aye an' ever;—
      'Twould a-baffled *any* eyes.

One day. at a way-side station,
Singularly styled Darnation—
Smooth yer faces; thar war places

XI.
      Rougher, tougher named than that—
Came aboard a leetle feller,
With a grip-sack small an' yeller,
B'iled shirt snowy—necktie showy—
      Glossy, glowy stove-pipe hat.

I engaged in specerlation
'Bout his prob'ble occupation;
Fur by me he chose location,

XII.
      With his grip-sack 'twixt his feet.
He seemed well-informed an' clever,
Ruther reticent however.
When he *did* speak, it war never
      Save in tones soft, meller, sweet.

He is surely not a miner,
Or else *I* am no diviner,
War my first thought as opiner,

XIII.
      As I took a gen'ral look;

He is far too fond o' riggin'
Fur a man that's used ter diggin'.
P'r'aps from tailors he's ben priggin'—
    Fitted out by hook or crook.

He is certainly no hunter,
Nor a follower o' Gunter—
Nor a ranchman—skurse a stanch man
    Sure no soldier, neither scout;
Surely he is not a trapper—
He is much too spruce an' dapper.
All at sea in the time bein',
    I war left in dark an' doubt.

XIV.

He's no husbandman—too handy
At the art o' playin' dandy;
Hands so dainty, arms so fainty
    Ne'er swung hoe nor guided plow—
Never wrought in field or garden—
Never knew 'nough toil ter harden
Narve an fibre—p'r'aps a giber,
    Scornin' sech things anyhow.

XV.

He's no peddler—place fur peddlers
Is whar redskins air not meddlers,—
Ter marauders an' defrauders
    O' all orders less exposed;
'Sides the stock that one might carry
In that hand-bag 'd shame a fairy—
'Less that 'ceptacle so airy
    Jew'lers gimcracks gay enclosed.

XVI.

He's no plains-man—that I'll warrant—
Out-door life's ter him abhorrent;
He loves neither turf nor torrent,
    Steed o' speed nor scaly spoil;
His physique is altogether
Free from press an' stress o' weather;
Sun's not browned him—wind played round him—
    He's too free from tan an' soil.

XVII.

XVIII.

Mebbe he's a mine-inspector,
Or a revenue collector,—
P'r'aps a peekin' nov'list seekin'
        Some new scene ter suit his plot—
P'r'aps a poet, seekin' sweeter
Things ter grace his rhyme an' metre—
Huntin' glory fur his story
        In some rare, sequestered spot.

XIX.

Mebbe he's some rich investor—
Or assayer—p'r'aps—gold-tester—
Tired theol'gist—hired geol'gist,
        Lookin' fur some curi's stone—
P'r'aps some shrewd detective, seekin'
Some one who's revenge ben wreakin'
On some human —man or woman—
        Or a-takin' more 'n his own.

XX.

Mebbe a purfeshnal gambler,
One from camp to camp a rambler—
Comin', goin', few a-knowin'
        When or how he comes an' goes:
Hard as flint, yet sweet as honey
In his ways—o' time an' money
Men bereavin'—hosts deceivin'—
        Makin', leavin' countless foes.

XXI.

Mebbe some embezzler, wanderin'.
Other people's funds a-squanderin',
Deeply ponderin', inly maunderin'
        O'er the perils o' his course—
Some default cashier or treasurer,
O' his chances a ca'm measurer,
Still a-schemin', deemin', dreamin'
        O' evadin' the law's force.

XXII.

P'r'aps a trav'lin'-man—a drummer—
Sech war skurse then—p'r'aps a mummer—
A theatrical new-comer—
        Stray play-actor passin' through—

# Tales Told in a Country Store.

P'r'aps in that small grip o' yeller
In his 'make-up' fur Otheller,
King Lear hoary—Richard gory—
    Or fair Venice's base Jew.

P'r'aps some treacherous, lecherous bein'
From the hand o' Vengeance fleein'—
Blamed annoyer—home-destroyer—
XXIII.        Human wolf in sheep's attire—
Thar air sech the round world over—
Mebbe he is but a rover,
Measurin' gravel jes' ter travel;—
    'Tis some hearts' supreme desire.

Mebbe he's some Eastern banker—
Wall, thar!   Like a ship 'thout anchor,
Tossed my mind with wonder ranker
XXIV.        On conjecture's boundless sea:
Vague an' variable opinions
Crowded fast through Thought's dominions:
Still no nearer—no jot clearer
    War the actual fac's ter me.

Still concernin' him I wondered,
As o'er knoll an' dale we thundered—
Rolled through canyon—our companion
XXV.        An' his closely-watched valise—
Wondered 'bout his destination,
His vocation, age an' station,—
Yearned an' burned fur information,
    An' my wonder would not cease.

How I longed an' ached ter ask him!
Should I with sech queries task him?
Quizzed a chap *once* ter unmask him—
XXVI.        Got a bullet fur my pains—
Purty nigh furever stilled me—
Mighty nigh completely killed me—
On this p'int it sort o' chilled me:—
    'D ruther save my blood an' brains.

**129**

'Ter that grip-sack he seemed married;
Day an' night the thing he carried,—
When we rode an' when we tarried—
XXVII.     When he'd sit an' when he'd stand.
Oft at wayside stations lunchin',
In our haste each other hunchin',
From one hand he'd food be munchin--
     Grip-sack'd be in t'other hand.

Sometimes in the night I'd waken,
When the coach war rudely shaken,
An' I'd see—I warn't mistaken—
XXVIII.     That man, sleepless as an owl.
On his lap that satchel holdin',
Round it fondly his arms foldin',
As you'd fold yours—as you'd hold yours
     Round yer bes' friend--How I'd scowl!

All opined he had a treasure—
Riches almost without measure—
In that bag which 'peared ter pleasure
XXIX.     Heart an' soul—the whole o' him;
'Twar despised by all who scanned its
Saffron shape—seemed bodin' bandits—
Made our outlook dark with doubt look--
     Prospec's grim an' slim an' dim.

Stranger's caution war one-sided—
'Twar not evenly divided;
Though himself on it he prided,
XXX.     He war keerful not a whit
'Bout appearances;—the needy
An' the seedy an' the greedy
On it doted—'pon it gloated—
     As he toted, noted it.

Day by day, he sadly vexed us,
O'er an' o'er more sore perplexed us.
Himself scand'lin', that grip handlin'
XXXI.     In that dandlin' style o' his:

Had he only kep' it hidden,
We might all in peace 'a' ridden,
Though by acrid glances chidden,
 He maintained impassive phiz.

Seemin'ly all peril scornin',
He displayed it night an' mornin',
An' paraded, spite o' warnin',
XXXII. At each stated stoppin'-place—
War the Jonah o' our party.
All with one consent most hearty,
Sayin', 'Blast him!' Could 'a' cast him
 O'er, but forbore with good grace.

Drive' seemed a bit hard-hearted.
'Fools an' money soon air parted,'
Hand on weap'n, back'ard stepp'n',
XXXIII. Sotto-voce-like he said.
Leetle man, with eyes a-snappin',
Vowed that he war not a-nappin'.
'Fools by babblin' known are—gabblin'—
 Wise men keep an eye ahead.'

By the wise a hint is heeded,
Whether justified or needed:—
'Tis sufficient, 'tis conceded.
XXXIV. Jehu's orbs sharp look-out kep'—
Speshly on account o' lack o'
Caution in one coach-seat back o'
Him;—like beagles'—hawks' or eagles'—
 The route o'er before him swep'.

We were passin' through scenes dreary;
E'en the blades o' grass seemed eerie;
An' ter say we skurse war cheery
XXXV. Air a-puttin' matters mild:
Ev'ry man his shooter fingered,
By it close his right hand lingered;
Faces pallid feelin's tallied,
 Women's eyes war bright an' wild.

But the stranger smiled serenely,
An', I fancied, ruther greenly;—
Seemed ter sense—I watched him keenly—

XXXVI.      Naught o' what perturbed the rest.
I concluded as I pondered,
"Twar some lunatic who'd wandered—
By cute peepers dodged his keepers,
    An' war roamin' through the West.

As we rumbled through that region,
Fancy conjured up foes legion—
Now rapacious an' voracious

XXXVII.      Reds—now truthless, ruthless whites;
Nothin' chanced, though, in disorder—
Nothin' that war held ter border
On the tragic. till, like magic,
    One morn, crossin' chain o' heights.

On a steep hill overtowerin'
Nighly all the country,—cowerin'—
Quakin'—shakin', as if achin'

XXXVIII.      With the ager in each limb—
Kem the driver, havin' halted.
Ter the door:—'We'll be assaulted;
Quick be ready, an' be steady!
    Hope yer weepons air in trim!

Havin' let my vision wander
Ter that leetle copse down yonder,
I've detected half-expected

XXXIX.      Comp'ny c'lected thar in wait!'
Yer kin guess, 'thout hesitation.
What in sech a situation
War our notions an' emotions,
    As we stared at—glared at Fate.

Narrow way—arrowy road—no turnin'—
Bank too steep—this fac' discernin',
Driver flustered waxed an' blustered—

XXXX.      Could in no shape 'scape by flight!

All allowed our case war serious.
Suddenly, with tones imperious,
Said the leetle man mysterious:
    'Ladies, gentlemen, alight.'

Skursely knowin' why we paid him
Any heed we all obeyed him.
Unaffrighted, first he lighted—
    Carryin' his grip, o' course.
Ter our great amazement, stridin'
Ter the hill's brow 's if deridin'
All with scornin', he with warnin'
    Hailed that sulkin', skulkin' force.

In stentorian tones o' thunder,
Called he:—'Here, you!—Come from under
Cover!—Here, you imps o' plunder!
    You're discovered!—Do you hear?
Come an' your submission tender!
You'll be *spar'd*, if you surrender.'
Jeers an' fleers an' laughter after
    This demand which seemed so queer.

'Come, give up, you dirty knaves, you!
Come an' yield, or nothin' saves you!
Come an' *beg* while this hand waves you.
    Or this arm will *vengeance* wreak!
Seek, before the storm, fair havens!
Come, you villains! Come, you cravens!
Or be given to the ravens!'
    Words ter paint their rage war weak!

How they howled! We vowed him crazy—
Classed his reason mighty hazy—
Sure he'd made our case more mazy.
    Fur we now could skurse expect
Any quarter. Sech defiance—
Sech uncommon self-reliance—
All hopes, save through martial science.
    Seemin'ly'd completely wrecked.

# Tales Told in a Country Store.

From their lurkin'-place advancin',
They in anger upward glancin',
Ceased abscondin', an', respondin',

XXXXV.　　Told us one an', all ter go
Ter a place devoid o' pleasure.
They their strength with ours would measure.
As fur Mercy's nonsense (curses)—
　　'Twar a thing they didn't know.

Leader said:—'Come down here, Colonel!
Fur by all that is eternal,
Fur example, we'll jes' sample

XXXXVI.　　That air trav'lin'-sack o' yours;
Come right down, ol' Legal-tender,
An' we'll talk about surrender!
Yer a suave one—naive one—brave one!
　　Come—we'll see whose word endures!'

'Villains! Do you court disaster?
Know,' said he, 'I am your master!
At your pleasure—at your leisure—

XXXXVII.　　*Take* my treasure!' then, in ire,
Round an' round his head he whirled it,
Faster—with speed vaster—twirled it,
Then, ter our surprise, he hurled it
　　Downward with momentum dire!

Struck the head-most squar' on shoulder!
'Fore I war a jiffy older,
I war senseless as a boulder

XXXXVIII.　　By the side o' that air road.
When I come to, I war lyin'
On my back. Some one war tryin'
Ter arouse me—had ter souse me
　　In a spring that near clear flowed.

I said, 'Well, air you a bandit?'
I jes' couldn't understand it—
Didn't know the scene, an' scanned it

XXXXIX.　　Fur what seemed the longest while.

**134**

Slowly I my wits recovered,
An' the man who o'er me hovered
Saw discernin' powers returnin'
    With appreciative smile.

'Twar the leetle dapper stranger:—
'You're all right—you're out o' danger.'
'An' them robbers—Devil's jobbers?'
    'O, they're out o' danger, too,—
Out o' danger o' disturbin'
Trav'lers more—they needed curbin'—
Most derisory, spurned advisory
    Words—experience 'll do.'

Quietly I lay, reflectin',
Past an' present scenes connectin,'—
What had transpired recollectin.'
    Soon I formed a venturous plan.
'May a feller make a query?—
Will it not yer patience weary?'
He replied in accents cheery:—
    'Ask;—I'll answer, if I can.'

'So they got yer bag o' treasure?'
'Yes; they got it in full measure.'
He vouchsafed no more.  With pleasure
    Beamed his keen eye—visage thin.
Said I:—'Would ye tell a feller
What war in that sack o' yeller?'
'Yes;' he said in tones so meller—
    'It was—nitro-glycerine.

Now a myst'ry I'll unravel.
Fur a factory I travel,
An' to save a deal o' cavil,
    An' a deal o' trouble, too,
I bore in that hand-bag—ample
For each necessary sample—
(Which I watched that none should trample)
    What has made all this ado.'

'Fore the day closed, I war hearty—
Well as ever.   O' our party,
None met harmin' much alarmin';
LIV.        I war bruised—contused by fall—
All the rest. though shocked an' shaken,
By their wits war not forsaken.
An' the plucky ladies—lucky—
        Had no casualties at all.

Though our leadin' span o' horses
Lifeless war as any corses,
Still the second pa'r, though reckoned
LV.        Blinder 'n' two bats, could be used;
An' the coach, sore rent an' riven,
Yet war sound 'nough ter be driven,
Though it badly, sadly, madly,
        From its look, had ben abused.

More war done by that explosion
Than by ages' slow erosion.
Yawned a dismal chasm abysmal
LVI.        Whar the road war lately seen;
We war 'bleeged ter make a by-way,
Ter avoid the ruined highway,—
Trees an' under-brush ter sunder,—
        Stumps, tumps, clumps o' briars keen.

But all difficulties vanished—
By our energy war banished;
All war longin'—for'ard throngin'—
LVII.        Ter do all within our might
Ter effect our extrication.
All worked with determination:—
Thankful fur deliveration,
        Toiled unroiled with spirits light.

'Twar a task slow an' laborious;
But at length we war victorious.
Perseverin'.   In the clearin'
LVIII.        Process e'en the ladies lent a hand,

Hackin' down the tiny saplin',
With the smaller boulders grapplin'.
All war plastic ter the drastic
    Force o' our united band.

So at last we got in motion.
Couldn't move, though, ter our notion:
Skurse one plug-team—Land o' Goshen!—
    Could that big rig drag along.
Coach, though, war in no condition
Fur much lightnin'-like transition.
Makin' best o' our position,
    Whiled we time with rhyme an' song.

We war jes' twelve hours belated—
Seemed an age! An' them as waited
'Lowed us fated—'magined hated
    Redskins barrin' all approach.
When we 'rived, a band war ready,
Formed o' stout an' staunch an' steady,
With a leader hot an' heady
    At their front, ter hunt the coach.

All war in an upset humor,
Havin' that day caught a rumor,
Which each should a ben presumer
    War o' dim an' doubtful stamp:
Band o' cow-boys, tootin', hootin',
Glarin', tearin', swearin', shootin',
On their r'arin' nags come scootin'
    Ter the drink-hell in the Camp.

One o' these tol' that his brother
Fetched the news from some one 'r other
(Hatched or dreamed it, one or t'other,
    Likely) that the reds war out.
Troopin', whoopin', swoopin', slayin',
In Apollyon-fashion playin'
Havoc—waste the country layin',
    Through which wound around our route.

Some eye'd spied (progressed the story)
Signs o' strife—no transitory
Scrimmage, but a tussle gory—
LXIII.        Up the track an' back a way;
Wolf-picked bones war thar a-gleamin',
Eerie—vastly ghastly seemin'—
Rid but freshly o' their fleshly
        Coverin', whitenin', brightenin' lay.

An' 'twar said—the cow-boy said it—
Fancy fed it—Gossip sped it—
An' so spread it it won credit—
LXIV.        The wild devils, havin' spilled
The crowd's blood, took huge an' small things—
Vehicle—bags—baggage—all things—
Made a bon-fire—no wee, wan fire.—
        O, it war a tale that thrilled!

Lay in hard charred heap together
All us birds o' ev'ry feather—
Scraps o' wraps an' bits o' leather—
LXV.        Rings an' springs an' twisted tires;—
Sudden shower's precipitation
Had snuffed out the conflagration,
Ere complete the ruination
        Ter their worst accurst desires.

Yes, they 'lowed we'd prob'ly perished.
Meager hope most eager cherished
They should spy us—should descry us—
LXVI.        Ever eye us—one o' us;
But had planned, ter stand suspenses
Stings off, s'arch, when—could their senses
Be deceivin'?—or wuth b'lievin'?—
        'Mazed they gazed upon us thus!

Wall, ter folks in their condition,
Sight seemed hoax or appyrition—
We like eerie sprites from dreary
LXVII.        Regions o' the legions dead!

Yer may guess with shouts they hailed us.
Who 'mos' good as skelped bewailed us.
Joyed fair Fortune had not failed us.
 Flowin' glowin' words they said.

When we tol' our hero's story,
Bathed an' swathed war he with glory—
Leetle dapper whipper-snapper,
 Climax-capper o' the hour!
On their shoulders, big men bore him,
Loud avowed none proud afore him.
Thus with us great fuss made o'er him,
 Zealous,—none war jealous, sour.

'Mong the anxious ones at Brisco,
When we 'rived from San Francisco,
War my cousin an' a dozen,
 At the least, from 'way back East;
They war narvous—'lowed the Red Man
Had swooped down—made me a dead man
Sweet our meetin'—meet their greetin',
 From their cheatin' fears released.

'All that ends well's well.'—Some poet
Said that—'s if we didn't know it.
Ride from Frisco down ter Brisco,
 Close ter Liscoe, ended well.
Soon enough, o' all the veriest
Mirth-mad crowds we war the merriest—
No-ways hateful, bateful—grateful
 Nothin' fateful more befell."

When Calkins had ceased, fast diminished the group,
 For fatigued and aweary of waiting were they;
They left one by one, until out of the troop
 That had gathered—so far it had dwindled away—
There remained very few. These by fits nodded, drowsed,
 Yawned, joked, proposed puzzles, diversion to make.
"Has it come?" They would say now and then, half-aroused,
 But we who were going were quite wide-awake.

Now once more to the door the proprietor went,
  And with steadiness list'ning, peered into the dark.
All on hearing were bent—not a sound the air rent—

59.   Not a sound! All around reigned profound stillness—hark!
A low, distant rumble distinctly we heard.
  "It's coming," the postmaster quietly said.
"It's coming!" With joy we re-echoed that word.
  Each grabbed his valise—jammed his hat on his head.


With mail-pouch on shoulder, and lantern in hand,
  And a hearty "Hello!" which a cheery ring bore.
The postmaster sallied forth, taking his stand

60.   On the platform, as dashed the coach up to the door.
"You're late?" He in tones interrogative said.
  "You're right, sir!" was Jehu's laconic reply.
"I'll let the nags puff, 'fore I urge 'em ahead,
  An' tell—fur you're wond'rin'—the *how* an' the *why*."


Three persons had meanwhile alighted, but we—
  The frontiersmen and I—who a moment ago
Were full as impatient as mortals could be,

61.   Were by this more than anxious Bill's story to know.
With satchels in hand, by the postmaster's side,
  With the handful who lingered awaiting their mail,
We stood on the platform, with ears open wide,
  While the driver related a somewhat strange tale:


"You well know the ol' proverb—'The longest way round
  Is the shortest way home'—well, in this case, it *was*,
An' the longest way round was a long way, I found.

62.   Fur it led round by Payson's.—Now as to the *cause*.
I progressed all O. K. to the bridge just this side
  O' Sac's—found the ol' mammoth structure down flat
As the flattest o' pancakes. Jake Simmons had tried
  To cross with steam-thresher—it wouldn't stand that.


The engine went down with a crash (so they say)
  That was heard a good mile—up to Joshua Mean's.
On sharp rocks below the destroyed puffer lay—

63.   An' the sep'rator, too,—very best o' machines—

Total loss!—Well, no fordin'—too deep.  The back-track
 I took—went by Payson's, as stated afore.
Haven't ben o'er that road fur a long, long while back—
 O, mebbe five years—or perhaps trifle more.

Well, the big bridge down there—county bridge 'tis, ye know.
 Is becomin' at last mighty shaky an' old;
It by rights should 'a' ben torn away long ago,
**64.**   An' a new one put in—that's the plan now, I'm told.
I wasn't aware—hadn't ben nigh the thing
 Fur years—o' its state—didn't know but 'twas sound,
So trotted right on it, which caused it to swing
 An' quiver an' shiver an' teeter around.

I'd disposed o' my ol' team—I skursely know why,
 I avow, fur they never were up to tricks bad:
An' we hadn't got 'quainted—my new nags an' I—
**65**   Got some whoppin' big bays fur them black ones I had.
When the bridge begun shakin', they jes' stood up straight,
 Danced an' pranced where it chanced, standin' on their
  hind feet.
Wuss they jumped, wuss it shook; an' I thought sure as fate
 Ev'rything 'd be demolished—a ruin complete.

While they were a jumpin' an' thumpin' about,
 An' I strove to be doin' my dead level best
To bring 'em to time—while I still was in doubt
**66.**   How I would should or could their wild antics arrest,
 Chancin' jes' to glance up—horror seized on my mind!
 I saw a board sign which could scarce be contemned:
Strange I hadn't observed it before!—Was I blind?.—
 It read in big letters:—

# THIS BRIDGE IS CONDEMNED!

The passengers somehow wrenched open a door,
    An' takin' their lives, so to speak, in their hand,
Sprung out. When on good terra-firma once more,
**67.**    They stood wringin' fingers—a horror-smit band.
While a-viewin' my struggles, they spied out the sign
    Which I'd jest descried. "Oh!" in chorus they wailed.
'He'll be killed jes' as *sure!*' Sech a fate was not mine:—
    Thought, though, that it *might* be—my pluck a'mos' failed.

Will ye b'lieve it?—That minute, when luck seemed to frown,
    The hosses cammed suddenly—stood still—inert.
Well, I wondered at that, an' at once clamb'rin' down,
**68.**    Examined the critters;—they wa'n't a bit hurt.
I remounted the seat, an' essayed to drive on,
    Kinder slowly an' gently, so's not to give shocks
To the flimsy ol' structure. Their terror seemed gone,
    But they jes' wouldn't budge more 'n a pair o' big rocks!

How things rocked!—Yes, they'd balked;—all my urgin' they
           mocked—
    Might jest as well speechify unto the wind!
I'm afeard that the language I used ruther shocked
**69.**    Them as heard it—too bad—I'll own up that I sinned.
'Twill a big wonder be, if none enters complaint
    Ag'in me fur 'busin' dumb critters. I trow
Could they 'a' talked back, we'd a made someone faint.
    Well, I wore out my 'black-snake'—they *still* wouldn't go!

There they stood with their legs braced like so many posts—
    Jes' 's if they'd a certain foundation beneath
'Em fur footin'—an' snorted as if seein' ghosts,
**70.**    An' grinned in defiance—at **least**, showed their teeth.
Surely no equine statues were ever more firm!
    Each brute was as rigid—unyieldin' as steel!
When I lashed 'em an' thrashed 'em, they'd jes' kind o' squirm,
    An' try to let on that they didn't half feel.

No go. They refused to be coaxed, driv' or led.
    I never had fooled with sech critters afore.
From cuts I had give 'em, like stuck hogs they bled.
**71.**    I yelled until hoarse—yanked until I was sore.

No use.   So I left 'em in speechless disdain,
  An' went up to Payson's an' borried a span.
My own?—Like as not, where they were they remain—
  I left 'em in keer o' ol' Payson's hired man.

'Bad trade?'  Well, I guess so!  I'm bit, I confess.
  I'd no business tradin'—no jockey am I—
Come not o' that stock.  'Look out *nex'* time?'  O, yes!
72.  Experience teaches us things by an' by.
  It's dearly bought *some* times.  Got tired o' black;
  But what's in a color?—Not much, sure as fate!
Good service is main thing.  'F I had my team back,
  I'd give suthin' purty.—No use—it's too late.

Sech is life!—Well, these nags have recovered their breath;
  They're goers—they're willin' to hustle an' climb;
Brisk but steady.  Am 'fraid, though, I'll drive 'em to death.
73.  A-foolishly tryin' to make up lost time.
All aboard!" he sang out in tones ringing and clear.
  We entered the coach, our good-byes having said
To the few we were leaving.  The clear atmosphere
  Was rent with a whip's crack—away we then sped.

'Twas a ride uneventful—that night-trip to Ware—
  Neither spectres nor brigands disputed our way;
Safe and sound, well and hearty, the morn saw us there,
74.  Having met with no accident, fright or delay.
I departed at once on the "limited" train.
  The frontiersmen had just an hour longer to wait.
They were pleasant companions, those Westerners twain—
  Each had many a noble, agreeable trait.

## I. 'ENVOY.

Home again!—Not from a famed foreign strand,
   But home-coming always is sweet—it is bliss—
Whether returning from far-away land,
1.   Or from a short tour or excursion in this.
   O, well the loved Poet of Home has portrayed
      The feelings that throb in man's innermost heart,
   As all will attest, I doubt not, who have strayed
      From cherished abode, and from loved ones apart.

And truly indeed did another bard say
   That the best of a journey is getting back home.
Whatever may lead us or lure us away,
2.   In the broad, busy world that surrounds us to roam—
   Yea, whether we seek from our cares a release,
      Or relief from some grief we have scarce strength to bear.
   We find sweetest peace when our wanderings cease—
      When we cross our own threshold—embrace dear ones there.

One learns to prize that from which one is debarred
   By time or by distance—or aught—for a space;
What we are dissundered from grows in regard;
3.   'Tis so in respect to a man's dwelling-place.
   'Tis so in respect to the ones whom we leave
      Behind when abroad in the vast world we go;
   How precious they are we can scarcely perceive,
      Till far from their presence—their smile's genial glow.

Though not long was my trip, and not lengthy my stay—
   My allotted vacation in that calm retreat—
Doubly dear—ah, yes, I may veraciously say
4.   Trebly grateful to me—trebly precious and sweet

Did my home-threshold seem, as with hastening feet
    I in eagerness crossed it, upon my return;
Trebly precious the cherished ones waiting to greet
    Me with love's warmest tokens—its tend'rest concern.

No happier home, I am free to declare,
    Was ever known, pictured, or dreamed of than mine
The eve upon which I arrived safely there:
5.   Fair Fortune seemed gracious and Heaven benign.
That night with my loved ones I sang "Home, Sweet Home."
    (For domestic affections and joys inspire song)
And, rapt, felt I never should care more to roam—
    Seek for solitude's haunts or the world's busy throng.

But renewed and endued with fresh vigor and life,
    Rugged energy born of diversion and rest,
I resumed my campaign against sin—endless strife!—
6.   And the great task of caring for souls with new zest.
Though home's next to Heav'n—none who scorned it e'er
         throve—
It is often a blessing to fly the routine
The hum-drum of one's occupation, and rove,
    Free as air, 'neath skies azure—o'er flow'rful meads green.

A fortnight's reprieve from a hard round of toil
    Is worth all the nostrums the whole world contains—
More potent than all pill-dispensers to foil
7.   The ghastly Destroyer—bring health to the veins.
Spend not, like the woman of Scripture, your all
    On drugs and physicians, and rather grow worse;
A respite, though small, wan disease may forestall—
    The ills that afflict you or threat you disperse.

"Throw physic to dogs—I'll have none of it!" cries
    The vexed man in the drama—but not so say I;
Though not lauding "doctors' stuff" sheer to the skies,
8.   I would not to mankind the profession deny.
Though of potions and lotions wild notions have some,
    Yet the "M. D." has surely a place in the ranks
Of the world's benefactors—is worthy his crumb,
    Merits, quite sure am I, fewer curses than thanks.

"Give the Devil his due!" retorts one who has lost
    All faith in remedial agents.  Be sure
Some antipathy groundless your mind has not crossed,
9.    To warp your best judgment—breed prejudice pure.
"Give the Devil his due"—'tis a handy old saw:
    But be sure 'tis a devil you give devils' pay.
There are tyros, pretenders—hands careless or raw
    In all lines—all professions.  Discriminate, pray.

The best of physicians is only, at most,
    An assistant of Nature.  Does health fly or flag?
Cease work—play the shirk—hie away to the coast,
10.    To the woods or the fields—do not loiter or lag.
Are your nerves all unstrung?  Are you spiritless, sour?
    Does your life seem a burthen too great to be borne?
Seek some halcyon bower, and do all in your power
    To forget what has made you so worried and worn.

Lay by book or pen—quit your post at your desk,
    No matter how eager for money or fame;
Change scenes dull, prosaic for scenes picturesque,
11.    Where health waits the seeker— earth's richest prize claim.
Find the best of all tonics in fresh, balmy air;
    Find the best of all nervines in Sol's grateful ray.
Nature heals, soothes and blesses.  Ere one is aware,
    She works wonders.—I this from experience say.

But you murmur:  "I cannot;—my purse is too lean,
    My income too meagre—my bank-account short—
Yes, and wardrobe too scanty;—I'd blush to be seen
12.    At noted or notable Summer resort."
Let me whisper: "Tis not necessary to go
    Where the *swells* congregate—give the false notion o'er.
'Tis mere Fashion that costs—Nature's free as you know.
    Seek such place as I sought when I found that lone store.

There the sunshine is fully as golden and sweet,
    And the grass is as green and the sky is as blue,
As at any retreat of the haughty elite;
13.    For impartial is Nature—her best all may view.

No respecter of persons, to no select few
  In one thing or one spot she defers merest jot—
Makes more brilliant no hue—clearer no drop of dew
  (This is true) than for you—or those humbler in lot.

But enough on this line.—To my wife and my child,
  As time and my tasks would permit me, I told
All these tales; and 'tis needless to say they both smiled,
14.   At least, at some things that these Chapters unfold.
Of the sundry narrations which these pages bear,
  My good-humored help-mate a pref'rence expressed
For the trap episodes, while my wide-awake heir
  Account of the ride to Camp Brisco liked best.

Adieu, gentle reader.   Your pardon I crave,
  If aught in these lines has offended your taste.
I have no excuse, no apology, save
15.   The one the old farmer gave—"Written in haist."
To the too-hasty critic, however, I say:
  If you venture to censure with rancor my pen,
I will write again—hastily—some other day.
  You may wish you had been somewhat less hasty then.

Adieu, *gentle* reader.   If language of mine
  Has but smoothed out one wrinkle, or chased from your
          brow
One frown—banished tears—caused you gloom to resign—
16.   I am amply repaid for my task, even now.
And if e'er I again turn my back upon care,
  And forego pressing tasks to rove thither once more,
I may give you some word of my visit down there—
  Tales that yet may be told in that lone country store.

# WAR

# POEMS

# War Poems.

~MMMM~

## THE FATE OF THE MAINE.

Havana Harbor, Feb. 15th, 1898.

I CAN sing to-day no cheery,
          Gaysome strain;
     Sad as dreary miserere
          My song's vein!
Seventy million voices blent
Raise a Nation's deep lament!
Ah, the mourning they give vent!
O, the requiem up-sent
          For the Maine!

Grandly swept she through thy surges,
          Ocean! Deign
To prolong thy solemn dirge's
          Sad refrain!
Dolesome Winds, fresh sighings waft!
Ah, she was a gallant craft!
Stanch and trim before and aft,
At your wildest mood she laughed—
          Noble Maine!

Night came down with dusky, eerie
          Shadow-train,
And our Country's sons, aweary,
          Doubtless fain

Welcomed sleep—refreshing sleep—
With no thought that at morn's peep
They unwaking rest would keep,
'Neath the woesome waves that sweep
    O'er the Maine!

Peace was regnant o'er the billows'
    Aqueous plain;
Well repose might woo men's pillows,
    'Mid her reign!
4.
Nature's self was all serene:
All unruffled was her mien.
Who would guess horrific scene
Would so shortly supervene
    On the Maine?

In a moment—in a twinkling!
    None could gain
Of disaster omen, inkling—
    Sign obtain—
5.
With an earthquake shock and burst,
An explosion dire, accurst,
On the proud ship wreaked its worst—
Down she went! Alas! submersed,
    Shattered Maine!

Ah, the scores of dead and dying!
    Ah, the pain—
Moans and groans of maimed ones lying
    'Mid the slain!
6.
Ah, that night of death and gloom!
Those cut off in manhood's bloom
Little dreamed of such a doom—
That thou thus wouldst be their tomb,
    Fated Maine!

Throughout all our land is weeping!
    Sorrow's rain
Falls for those untimely sleeping,
7.
    Vilely slain—

For the youthful, strong and brave,
Those whom naught availed to save.
Whom far Southern waters lave—
Those who sank beneath the wave
    With the Maine!

Could they but have fallen battling
    Not in vain,
'Mid war's missiles round them rattling
    War's red stain!—
But to perish unaware,
Like dumb brutes within a snare,—
Those who any foe would dare,—
Such a fate was hard to bear!—
    O, the Maine!

Ah. 'twas treachery infernal—
    Dark its grain!
Let the record be eternal,
    In terms plain,—
Of a nation's breach of trust,
And of blood its cruel lust,
Which inspired that fateful thrust—
Blow that smote our loved august.
    Stately Maine!

Thrills each heart at the recital—
    Throbs each brain!
Such dark wrong demands requital!
    Take heed, Spain!
Ah, wilt thou decline to heed.
Gloating o'er thy most fell deed?
Treachery may have its meed:—
Justice yet thy doom may read,
    O'er the Maine!

Land of crowned and crownless Neroes,
    Gory Spain!
We remember our lost heroes—
    Not in vain!

Stay!—We plead not, but command!
Stay thy barb'rous, murd'rous hand
In the lovely bleeding land
'Neath whose waters, off whose strand
    Lies the Maine!

Cease thy misrule and oppression—
    Blackest reign!—
Cease yon forfeited possession
    To enchain!
Bloodiest nation ever was,
At whose vitals ruin gnaws!
Warning take, and timely pause!
We remember Freedom's cause—
    And the Maine!

12.

# THAT DAY AT MANILA.

### May 1st, 1898.

WE hailed it indeed as a glorious presage—
    That word to our Chief, as at Hong Kong we lay,
    That message—that pithy, laconical message
    Which bade us at once make Spain's squadron our prey.
With gladness and pride we made swift preparation,
    And soon at full speed we were taking our way
To scenes soon to witness our triumph's elation.
    We swept on and on till the dawn of the day—
That Day of proud days in the Bay of Manila—
The day we demolished the Spanish flotilla!

Right boldly the mouth of the Harbor we entered,
    Ere midnight's black shadows were over and gone.
No foe proffered challenge—his guns on us centered—
    We filed on in silence to meet the gray dawn.
Now hark! On our right there resounds a deep booming'
    Sharp eyes at Restingo seem hitherward drawn!
Corregidor lies on our left dumbly glooming.
    Thus spoken, we answer—in kind—and pass on—

2.

Pass on till we enter the Bay of Manila,
Where, waiting its fate, lies the Spanish flotilla.

We know that before us, beneath the dark water,
   Lurk mines such as brought the lost Maine to her grief;
And these in a flash may bring ruin and slaughter,
3.    More deadly by far than the wave-hidden reef.
What says our Commander?  He deigns not to palter,
   Nor even to falter in doubtfulness brief.
Our chances we take, nor our forward course alter.
   "Steam on!" is the signal displayed by our Chief.
And so we steam into the Bay of Manila—
Steam in to demolish the Spanish flotilla.

At dawn we discover the enemy's station—
   In front of grim Cavite lieth the foe.
A shot is their hail, and their morn salutation.
4.    Pursuant to order, straight at them we go.
Now backward and forward our fleet sweeps before them,
   As passes the mower the grasses to mow.
And cool is our aim.  How our heavy shots gore them!
   How reels ev'ry craft from each thunder-bolt blow.
As fast, on the beautiful Bay of Manila,
Our cannon demolish the Spanish flotilla!

Still back and forth sweeping with steady progression,
   We ever draw nearer the foe's shaking line.
Our Commodore's ship heads the stately procession—
5.    Ah, how her bright colors aloft proudly shine!
The enemy's flag-ship presumes to assail her,
   But soon her rash project is fain to resign;
Our gallant Olympia's crew does not fail her!
   Yon hostile craft flies—burning drifts on the brine—
The Reina Christina, queen of the flotilla,
Soon, soon to go down in the Bay of Manila!

Two deadly torpedo-boats now would destroy her,
   Our Commodore's vessel, so stately and staunch;
These only a moment annoy her, employ her,
6.    As seek they their missiles dread at her to launch.

Beneath the thick smoke-cloud of battle they hover,
  As sea-monsters waiting some victim to craunch;
The huge cruiser's guns each slight craft at once cover.
  And quick each recoils as a steed on its haunch!
They cannot escape. be they swift as Camilla!
One sinks—both are wrecked in the Bay of Manila!

Our volleys incessant the heavens have blackened;
  We scarce can discern either foeman or friend;
And now for a space we our fire have slackened,
7.    And over the waters our glances we bend.
Five times we with easy manœuvre have passed them.
  Our shells with precision among them to send.
Ah, into disorder most sore we have cast them!
  The enemy surely is nearing his end!
Ships burning, ships sinking! The Spanish flotilla
Will soon be no more on the Bay of Manila!

Two hours and a half of uproarious battle!
  Now (is it not cool on our brave Leader's part?)
A respite *for breakfast!*—That o'er. our shots rattle,
8.    Directed with vigor—fresh rigor—and art.
Ah, soon is the task we had almost completed
  Achieved, and with transcendent lightness of heart.
We catch the glad word, o'er and o'er fast repeated.
  "The foe has surrendered!" and blithe shouts upstart!
Yon westering sun sees no more the flotilla
It saw yester-eve on the Bay of Manila!

Of all the foe's squadron escaped not a vessel:
  We sent them all reeling down under the wave!
Miraculously we emerged from the wrestle—
9.    We lost not a ship, nor a sailor-boy brave!
And when we had placed ev'ry hostile craft under
  The deep, and full many in watery grave.
Upon the shore-batteries turning our thunder.
  A speedy quietus to each one we gave:—
We silenced the forts as we stilled the flotilla,
And masters were we of the Bay of Manila!

All honor to Dewey, our noble Commander,
   Who ordered with wisdom the battle's array!
Ah, never was triumph completer or grander
10.    Than that which we won 'neath his guidance that day!
All hail to the Hero whose prudence and daring,
   Whose foresight and genius for vict'ry made way,
That shrewd down-east Yankee, of calm, quiet bearing,
   Who brilliantly, coolly directed the fray—
That world-renowned fray in the Bay of Manila,
Wherein we demolished the·Spanish flotilla!

All honor to Dewey! A nation of freemen
   Its thanks promptly, graciously tenders to him,
And through him to all his unwavering seamen!
11.    Its gratefulness words cannot tell—fancy limn!
A sword and a flag for this Hero of Ocean—
   An Admiral's flag—may its stars ne'er grow dim!
We greet it with pleasure and loyal emotion!
   Long, long may it float over vessel so trim,
As floated our Banner unscathed at Manila,
That day we demolished the Spanish flotilla!

All hail to the Flag we call fondly "Old Glory"!
   Three cheers with a will for the Red, White and Blue!
A red-letter day has augmented its story!
12.    All hail, Stripes and Stars, crowned with laurels anew!
The Star-Spangled Banner for ever and ever!
   For aye may it float as in grandeur it flew
That day of our grand and successful endeavor,
   When haughty Spain's squadron we banished from view —
When deeply we buried the Spanish flotilla
Beneath the blue waves of the Bay of Manila!

All praise unto Him who this triumph has given,
   Of whose blessed fruits all Mankind may partake!
Loathed bonds of Oppression our conquest has riven:
13.    The chains of the fettered we glory to break!
The blow we delivered smote Tyranny's minions:
   'Twas dealt for the world—for Humanity's sake.
Soar, Emblem of Freedom, with joy-impelled pinions!
   Proud Eagle! with loudest scream glad Echo wake!

Come make thee an eyry by wave-kissed Manila,
Since sleeps 'neath her Harbor the Spanish flotilla!

Our Father!  Great God of our homes and our Nation,
    From whom, as we own, comes each glorious gift!
May we, in this hour of our Land's jubilation,
14.    Our hearts' to Thy throne with due reverence lift!
May we as a people ne'er slight or ignore thee,
    Conceited and vain in the midst of our thrift!
Our Ship of State guide evermore, we implore Thee,
    That we amid breakers or shoals may not drift!
In Thee may we trust as we did at Manila,
That day we demolished the Spanish flotilla!

# THE SINKING OF THE MERRIMAC.

Feat of Lieut. R. P. Hobson and Seven Seamen at the Entrance of Santiago Harbor.

"A PROJECT I conceive,
        And, Admiral, by your leave,
            Will stop the channel there
        With barrier none will flout,
    So ships shall not steal out;
            My plan is laid with care.

Give me the Merrimac;
    Thrice will her worth come back
2.            In service she shall yield;
    She shall be sunk across
    The harbor's mouth.   Her loss
            Is naught, so that be sealed.

Who will lament her wreck,
    If thus the foe we check—
3.            His squadron so confine?
    Approve, and it is done—
    The hostile fleet is won:—
            'Twill  skim no more the brine."

162

# War Poems.

Granted is his request;
Swells with proud joy his breast:
4.        Now for a crew he asks,
To aid him in adroit
Details of his exploit—
        Most hazardous of tasks!

Gauntlet of with'ring fire,
Aimed by the foe in ire,
5.        The band that goes must run.
Now who will volunteer?
Expect no cowards here;
        Ready is ev'ry one;—

Ready to dare and do—
Ready swift death to woo—
6.        To face with dauntless glance
Ready to ride yon ship
Into Destruction's grip,
        If it our cause advance.

Seven will his purpose serve.
Avers this man of nerve,
7.        And these are given him;
Arranged is all—complete;
They on their mission fleet,
        At early morning dim.

More gallant deed ne'er was!
Into the harbor's jaws
8.        Flies that devoted craft!
How the fierce batteries rave!
Yet she still swims the wave.
        Though raked both fore and aft'

How the shells round them scream!
Boldly they onward steam—
9.        Heed not the iron hail!
Let the wild tempest burst—
Let the foe wreak his worst,
        He shall not see them quail'

Seamen with anxious hearts
Watch as the gloom departs—
10.      Yearn for some sign or trace!
What is their comrades' doom?
Lie they in watery tomb?
      Or share they Fortune's grace?

The world well knows the rest,—
How they endured the test,
11.      And did not blench or quake,
That through its narrow mouth
That harbor of the South
      Spain's ships should not forsake.

True to the hero's dream—
True to his brilliant scheme—
12.      Just at the spot desired,
The ship is swung about—
Her anchorage made stout—
      Prepared explosives fired.

All the world knows the rest—
North and south—east and west—
13.      'Tis breathed on ev'ry shore;
In story and in song
'Twill be remembered long—
      Applauded evermore!

Honor each seaman brave
Who such bold service gave—
14.      Scorned countless cannons' breath—
Counting his life not dear,
Flung to the winds all fear,
      And dashed in face of Death!

Honor to him who planned
Feat so heroic, grand;
15.      Not for mere noisy fame—
Nay, not for men's applause,
But for his Country's cause.
      Homage to Hobson's name!

# LANDING OF HUNTINGTON'S MARINES.

Guantanamo Bay, June 10, 1898.

GLADLY we press this Southern strand.
   Here to await our soldier band;
   Though our foes lurk on ev'ry hand
      Amid these tropic scenes,
   Here on this height we take our stand,
   First of our Country's sons to land.
   First to unroll her Banner grand—
      United States Marines.

Here shall our Starry Standard wave
   Till from the spoiler's grasp we save
   Region as sweet as waters lave,
2.      Amid these tropic scenes;
   Thus we attain to what we crave—
   First on his ground the foe to brave!
   Let the war-tempest round us rave—
      United States Marines.

Let the Castilian make his boast!
   Ready is he to yield the ghost?
   We at all odds will keep our post
3.      Amid these tropic scenes;
   We will defend to uttermost
   From the most fierce assaulting host
   What we have seized of this fair coast—
      United States Marines.

Every whit of tyrant sway
   Banished must be for aye—for aye!
   Here with Old Glory we will stay.
4.      Amid these tropic scenes:
   Soon will the transports come this way—
   Anchor, we trust, within this Bay;
   Patiently wait we that blest day—
      United States Marines.

# CHAMPIONS OF FREEDOM.

The American Army of Invasion, Enroute for Cuba, June 14th, 1898.

**S**AIL we from fair Tampa's Bay,
        Champions of Freedom,
Out upon the deep away,
        Champions of Freedom!
Yes! we have a mission grand,
Given us by our great Land:—
'Tis to wrest from tyrant hand
Bleeding Isle hard by our strand,
        Champions of Freedom!

Voices call us o'er the sea,
        Champions of Freedom,
We at last accord their plea,
2.        Champions of Freedom!
Seek we land whose blood and tears
Have been flowing countless years!
We will end its sighs and fears—
We will break its chains with cheers.
        Champions of Freedom!

That torn land we will not leave.
        Champions of Freedom,
Till our purpose we achieve,
3.        Champions of Freedom!
On that melancholy Isle,
Gladsome day eftsoon shall smile!
Soon unblushing Misrule's guile
Shall no more its shores defile,
        Champions of Freedom!

From this Western Hemisphere.
   Champions of Freedom,
Must Oppression disappear,
   Champions of Freedom!
From this glorious New World—
Edens in its seas impearled—
Despotism must be hurled—
Only free flags be unfurled,
   Champions of Freedom!

We Apostles, too, must be,
   Champions of Freedom,—
Teach men to be truly free,
   Champions of Freedom!
Freedom's doctrine must be spread
Wheresoever we shall tread:
'Tis the Gospel rightly read—
Righteously interpreted,
   Champions of Freedom!

In the Infinite we trust,
   Champions of Freedom,
He is with the true and just,
   Champions of Freedom!
He who said. "Let there be light,"
When all earth lay wrapt in night,
Will assist us with His might—
Aid us make that dark spot bright.
   Champions of Freedom!

Tyranny the gauntlet flings,
   Champions of Freedom,
At her feet who humbles kings,
   Champions of Freedom!
In her name—belov'd of God!—
Name of her we love and laud,
Who can ne'er be overawed,
Fearlessly we go abroad,
   Champions of Freedom!

# THE BATTLE OF CUSCO HILL.

### (A Participant Speaks.)

YOU see, we so oft had borne stealthy attack
    From the treacherous, barbarous, murderous foe,
We felt not a little like paying him back—
    As we pay anything—any debt that we owe.
Day in and day out, we found scarce any rest,
    And in slumber had hardly a lot or a part;—
The Dons strove to oust us their dead level best,
    But notoriously failed to induce us to start!

By day, in wise dread of alert cruisers' shells,
    They were wont to keep warily somewhat aloof;
But when night came down, crept through dingles and dells.
2.      And of bushwhacking talents gave questionless proof.
Their Mausers made round us a girdle of flame,
    And constrained were we sans intermission to fight.
Though Morpheus wooed us, no wink could we claim
    Through the whole of each livelong and torturous night.

Utter savages never were ever more sly,
    Or illusive, delusive, elusive than they.
When we thought them afar, they'd be oft-times hard by,—
3.      When we thought them a-nigh they'd be oft far away.
But soon we were up—as we say—to their tricks,
    And were able to duplicate all of their games—
Knew just how—beg pardon—to get in the licks—
    Knew their tactics as well as we know our own names.

But the thing got monotonous after awhile—
    For endurance has somewhere a limit and bound—
Outraged Nature revolted in usual style,
4.      As the sleepless hours rolled in rotation around.
Why, "weary" 's no term to apply to our state! .
    We were perfectly fagged —indescribably tired!
The President's English (though quite up to date)
    Couldn't give to your mind the idea required!

It couldn't last always.  The troops didn't come.
   (Though plenty more Spaniards undoubtedly did)
And we were too drowsy to feel even glum;
5.    And still was repose absolutely forbid.
Yet bound were we stoutly to maintain our Camp.
   And o'er it Old Glory in grandeur afloat.
Ah, how we did long for our soldier-boys' tramp—
   Their drum's lively roll. and their bugle's blithe note!

But certainly something. we knew, must be done
   To put our swart foemen to shame or to rout:
For, should they continue as they had begun,
6.    Ere long they would have us worn totally out.
So our shrewd Leader drew on his brain for a plan,
   Embarassing harassing forthwith to stop;
'Twas a shining success—so declares ev'ry man—
   At least—as the boys say—we "came out on top."

When next the foe faced us in pretty full force,
   And a fairly good scrimmage (for Spanish) got up.
Supposing us all in the Camp there, of course,
7.    We administered to him a bitterish cup.
While some of us well entertained him in front,
   Part struck out round the bluffs to his left flank and rear.
And—well, he made tracks faster far than his wont.
   Though he'd likely disclaim any symptoms of fear.

We caught him and roasted him 'twixt two good fires,
   And had him in no time persuaded to run
With briskness commensurate with our desires;
8.    And then in a trice began something like fun!
The party dispatched to his rear (our Allies)
   Just then came upon him with jubilant strides ..
A band from our front next swept over the rise,
   And he was well penned—corralled in on three sides!

Good land!  How the patriots peppered away,
   And slashed right and left with their corn-fodder knives!
Like redskins they whooped and sailed into the fray,
9.    For their share of glory, of spoils and of lives!

The only available way of escape
   Was most greedily seized by the horror-struck foe;
His force disappeared without order or shape
   As a snow-drift would melt in the tropic sun's glow!

Up the head of the gulch they all fleeted like deer—
   Up the steep ridge they flew, seeking safety beyond!
It was running the gauntlet—no lark, it is clear,—
10.   And their only desire was at once to abscond.
Before they could vacate that bleak exposed slope,
   The fugitives dropped—were killed off by the score,
As, blazing like hunter at scared antelope,
   At long range each man took his pick. —'Twas soon o'er.

Well, I guess that is all that is worth while to tell—
   Save perhaps that the lesson the foe there received
Seemed to answer its purpose remarkably well.
11.   Of attentions unwelcome we straight were relieved.
And maybe we didn't feel ripe for repose!
   Ah, never did mortals a respite enjoy
More fully than we, when our meddlesome foes
   Resigned their perpetual deadly annoy!

Though dreary was waiting, we still held our own
   Till the army, delayed, to the Island came down,
The enemy letting us mostly alone;—
12.   Little more did we see of his blood-thirsty frown.
The Mausers no longer each hour cracked and gleamed
   From tree, bush, shrub, boulder—from nooks and ravines!
The Star-Spangled Banner inviolate streamed
   Above Camp McCalla's undaunted Marines!

# GUASIMAS.

## SONG OF THE ROUGH RIDERS.

COW-BOYS from far Western prairie,
　　Dandies from Gotham the proud.
Seek we the swart adversary.
　　With the same fervor endowed!
Caution!　Like savages lurking,
　　Wait they to deal a dread blow!
Here is no recreant shirking—
　　Eager are all for the foe!

What though some hail from the border.
　　Some from rich drawing-rooms fair?
Have we no harmony—order?
2.　　Cavilling critic, beware!
Who speaks of discipline lacking—
　　Want of affinity—force?
Such carp, of ignorance smacking.
　　Must have contemptible source!

Elbow to elbow, together
　　March we, or toil we. or fight,—
Hands imbrowned—cheeks tanned like
　　　　leather—
3.　　Hardships we share and invite!
Ready for anything—ready!
　　Caustic fault-finder, be dumb!
You shall not see us unsteady
　　When chance for action shall come!

On through the chaparral tangled
　　Naught can our progress arrest!
On 'neath the Banner star-spangled—
4.　　Fairest and brightest and best!

Ha! from the thicket before us,
  Whistling, a rifle-ball flies!—
Scores hum around us and o'er us—
  Falls down our foremost and dies!

Ah, we are in for it now, boys!—
  Matters it whose life is stopped—
Whether a dude's or a cow-boy's?
5.    'Twas a leal patriot dropped
One of the staunchest and bravest
  Ever your vision may scan,
Though perchance one of the suavest —
  Though a society man!

Scarce catch we glimpse of our foemen--
  Skulking in ambush are they;
Ah, there is every omen
6.    Of a most sharp, bloody fray!
Quick shoot we hither and thither,
  Where a sly enemy seems!
Thought they our courage to wither?
  'Twas the most airy of dreams!

Fast waxes hotter and hotter
  Contest so fiercely begun:—
See yonder officer totter!—
7.    Sad work a Mauser has done!
Murderous volleys they give us
  From their invisible ranks!
Ah, they not all shall out-live us--
  Shots we return are not blanks!

Forward! The foe must be driven!
  Forward! This hill must be ours—
Proof of our prowess be given!
8.    This is a test of our powers.
Forward! Our Flag must be planted
  High on the crest of the height!
Long for this hour have we panted!
  Hail, opportunity bright!

# War Poems.

On! Fearless leaders we follow—
  Braver the world never saw!—
Up! Beat the Castilian hollow!
  Strike him with terror and awe!
Fancy sees all the world gazing;
  We must prove worthy our sires—
Heroes Earth long has been praising!—
  On through this hottest of fires!

Victory crowns our endeavor;
  Flees in confusion the foe!
Foiled we his scheme neat and clever—
  Taught him a lesson, we trow!
After him, cow-boy and dandy!
  Give him a close, hot pursuit!
Now with your weapons be handy—
  Deign him a parting salute!

Plant we in triumph Old Glory
  Where the foe's banner went down!
See! He has left a trail gory,
  Tow'rd Santiago's doomed town!
Freedom! Thy cause is advancing!
  Score we one blow in thy name!
Inland all eyes are now glancing—
  Soon may we yon city claim!

Cow-boys from wild Western prairie,
  Dandies from Gotham the grand,
Wide though our fortunes may vary,
  We are as one—heart and hand!
Hardy Rough Riders, we mingle
  Aye as true comrades and peers,
Plunging through jungle and dingle,
  Boldest of bold volunteers!

# THE BATTLE OF SANTIAGO.

Storming the Heights, July 1st, 1898.

NOWHERE on History's manifold pages
   Find we recital of deeds more sublime—
     Nay, though we search through the volumes of ages,
   Sweeping our eyes down the annals of Time!
Possible only such feats were to heroes—
   Heroes who any achievement would dare!
Never their rivals beyond the broad sea rose—
   Ne'er their superiors breathed anywhere!

Oh, it was wondrous beyond all expression—
   How our troops challenged the besom of Death,
Forging ahead with no dream of recession,
2.     Grimly defying each volley's hot breath!
Ay, 'twas a scene of rare grandeur and beauty—
   Ev'ry one valiantly doing his best,
Mindless of all save a stern sense of duty,
   Till they swarmed over each conquered hill's crest!

High on each slope, by his deep trenches shielded,
   Viewlessly, ceaselessly fired the foe;
Out in the open, assailants' forms yielded
3.     Target-like marks for his rifles below.
Fairly alive seemed the air with balls humming—
   Bullets dispatched with deliberate aim—
Ah, through them all could the Yankees be coming?
   Ay, even so—onward, upward they came!

Who would rush into the swirling tornado?
   Who would dash into Niagara's flow?
Yet without flinching, though sans vain bravado,
4.     Into worse peril seems each man to go!
On up the heights!—Up San Juan—steep El Caney!—
   No one can rest till their crowns shall be won!
Ah, but by warriors both brawny and brainy
   Could such exploits—yea, such marvels be done!

Ah, how the Mausers above them are cracking!
　　How the swift missiles around their ears sing!
Weighed in the balance, not one is found lacking—
5.　　Up go they all with alacrious spring!
Nay—nay, not all!　Here and there men are falling—
　　Some must lose life on occasions like this—
On through the storm—through the torrent appalling!
　　No one is laggard, and no one remiss!

Now up yon steep see our fair Banner sweeping—
　　Steadily, swiftly and surely it goes!
Out of his trenches the baffled foe leaping,
6　　Stays not in hand to hand struggle to close!
Down goes the ensign of red and of yellow!
　　Now in its place see Old Glory appear!
Cheer upon cheer, by the echoes made mellow,
　　Rings from each height through the cleared atmosphere!

Ah, far beyond all description 'twas glorious—
　　Far beyond all tongue or pen can portray!
They but conceive of it who were victorious—
7.　　· Conquerors proud on those summits that day!
In the wide world is there post or position
　　Soldier-Americans dare not confront?
Freedom's born Champions know no submission:
　　In her name seek they the fiercest strife's brunt!

# THE NEWS FROM SANTIAGO.

July 4th, 1898.

O N this day to Freedom sacred—
　　Glorious Independence Day—
What word comes on wings of lightning
　　From the South, far, far away?
Victory crowns once more our Banner,
　　So our last dispatches say;

We have won a brilliant triumph!
   Let our hearts be doubly gay,
On this blessed Day of Freedom—
   Day to be revered for aye!

*Let us raise a mellifluous, grateful pean,*
*For the victory won in the Caribbean!*

2.

From their mine-defended refuge,
   Where beleaguered long they lay,
Issued forth Spain's steel-clad vessels—
   Eager for escape were they;
They would shun the dreaded Yankees—
   Fain would not become their prey:
But our heroes were not napping;
   'Twas a dangerous game to play—
'Twas a hope forlorn and fruitless:—
   Tell the tidings this glad day!

*Let us raise a mellifluous, grateful pean,*
*For the victory won in the Caribbean!*

3.

Sallied forth the fleet Teresa,
   And to westward took her way.
After her the swift Vizcaya—
   How her bow flung off the spray!—
And the Colon and Oquendo,
   All in battle's grim array;
And the Pluton and the Furor
   These to follow made essay:—
Tell the tale of their rash venture
   On this joyous, joyous day!

*Let us raise a mellifluous, grateful pean,*
*For the victory won in the Caribbean!*

4.

Forward sprang our ocean-monsters.
   Calling all their powers in play.
Sending forth a storm of missiles—
   Hurling scarcely one astray—
Brooklyn, Oregon and Texas,
   And the Iowa *au fait,*—

How they raked the fleeing cruisers!—
    Ah, the scene who can portray?
Tell to all the thrilling story
    On this memorable day!

*Let us raise a mellifluous, grateful pæan,*
*For the victory won in the Caribbean!*

With their utmost force and fury,
    Strove our foemen to repay
Shot for shot, as on they skurried,
5.    Thirsting to destroy and slay;
But the fugitives were baffled;
    Naught could their pursuers stay:
Soon the quarry was o'ertaken—
    Quickly forced to turn at bay:—
Tell it on this Day of Gladness—
    Tell the news from far away!

*Let us raise a mellifluous, grateful pæan,*
*For the victory won in the Caribbean!*

One by one, with dark frames riddled,
    Wreathed with flame and smoke-clouds
        gray,
Tow'rd the coast the doomed ships headed—
6.    Soon upon the rocks they lay!
And the vaunted fast destroyers—
    *Hors du combat* soon were they—
Quick they sank beneath the waters,
    Each the plucky Glou'ster's prey!
Tell our seamen's deeds of prowess,
    On this doubly glorious day!

*Let us raise a mellifluous, grateful pæan,*
*For the victory won in the Caribbean!*

From their burning, smoking vessels,
    On whose decks they could not stay,—
Floating—sinking pens of slaughter—
7.    Leaped our swart foes every way!

They were gathered up by hundreds,
　　With their captains—Admiral gray—
Ah, our prisoners are legion!
　　Let rejoicing have due sway,
On this blessed Day of Freedom—
　　Liberty's own storied Day!

*Let us raise a mellifluous, grateful pœan,*
*For the victory won in the Caribbean!*


In such grand, decisive combat,
　　What our casualties, pray? *
*Only one killed and two wounded!*
8.　　With just pride the list display!
Though War's annals from beginning
　　To the present we survey,
Scarce can History show its rival,
　　Turn we wheresoe'er we may—
Save the record of Manila!—
　　Tell it on this glorious day!

*Let us raise a mellifluous, grateful pœan,*
*For the victory won in the Caribbean!*


Thanks to God—the God of Battles—
　　Who upon His holy Day
Gave us victory o'er our foemen—
9.　　Triumph in that mighty fray!
Yield we heart-felt adoration—
　　Soul-felt homage duly pay—
Praise Him for His signal favor,
　　And for its continuance pray,
On this day by Freedom hallowed—
　　Made most glorious for aye!

*Let us raise a mellifluous, grateful pœan,*
*For the victory won in the Caribbean!*

# THE FALL OF SANTIAGO.

An Infantryman LOQUITUR.

WITH staunch lines we compassed the city,
Which sulkily waited its fate;
By turns we were solemn and witty;
The Mausers sang spitefullest ditty.
From pits from which foes without pity
Or mercy sent shots at a pretty
Good rate.

Our cordon we constantly tightened;
By rush after rush we close drew;
Whenever a foe's head was heightened
2. To view, our guns thundered and lightened;
Our prospects and hopes daily brightened;
Our foe waxed more hollow, more frightened—
More blue.

Successively charging, we routed
The Don from his ditches profound;
His meshes of barbed wire we flouted,
3. His forts and his block-houses scouted,
Nor once of the issue we doubted,
Ah, how as he scudded we shouted,
Joy-crowned!

We summoned the foe to surrender;
Though starving, he haggled for time;
His honor must maintain its splendor;
4. On this point exceedingly tender,
Of negative message a sender,
He still played the role of defender
Sublime.

With steady advance, we yet cited
    The foeman again and again
To yield, but our offers he slighted,
5.  Like one either daft or benighted.
With vow to bombard, if requited
Thus still, once for all we invited
    Him then.

When Sampson—strong man of our era—
    Began fresh display of his might,
(That Sabbath-Day trip of Cervera
6.  Ere this had half wrecked the chimera
Made Don in his own eyes appear a
Grand hero who never need fear a
    Huge fight)

He weakened perceptibly, quickly;
    His thread-bare bravado was gone:
His struggles grew feeble and sickly,
7.  When shells began playing round thickly;
Our bayonets looked a bit prickly,
And soon he was talking more sickly—
    The Don.

At length, after wearying truces,
    And numberless tedious delays.
And various baseless excuses,
8.  As countless as bubbles in sluices,
Which only as quibbles had uses—
Devices akin to the Deuce's
    Own ways,—

The city gives in—we have gained it!
    Our flag floats in all of its charms—
Dispels theirs who fain had profaned it!
9.  Our flag!—Have we not well sustained it?
"Old Glory!"—Dishonor ne'er stained it!
Our foeman lays down—he has deigned it
    His arms.

What next?—Whither turn we *manana?*
        (To-morrow, in language of Spain)
San Juan, Porto Rico?—Havana?—
10. To Madrid?—We care not!   Hosanna
To Him who gives triumphs as manna!
Our Leader has only to plan a
        Campaign.

# CUBA LIBRE.

A BEAUTIFUL Isle, lying out in the sea,
        Long thralled, Uncle Sam one day vowed should be free;
        And on this same point quite decided was he.
        Although Uncle Sam is a peaceable man—
Keeps clear of all squabbles whenever he can—
1. Yet, nevertheless he has back-bone—is mettled—
And this is the way he was finally nettled:—
He had on the waters a very fine boat,
Which bore crew as gallant as e'er were afloat;
Said boat 'twixt two days was exploded and gone;—
The cause was a trick of the swarthy-faced Don.

        *CUBA LIBRE!*
Uncle Sam heard the poor, half-starved Patriot crying;—
That the shibboleth pleased him, there's no use denying;
And so, when the Don made this dark demonstration,
He heartily joined in the blithe exclamation—
        *CUBA LIBRE!*

A "notice to quit" he then served on the Don,
And signified mildly his patience was gone,
And told him what might be depended upon:
But Don he was surly, as ev'ry one knows,—
That such is his character history shows—

181

2. And upon this occasion he waxed even surlier—
Said he'd go when he pleased—not an iota earlier—
Uncle Sam's final message refused to receive,
Whereupon Uncle quietly rolled up his sleeve:
And thereupon Don got his fighting-tools out,
And dared Uncle Sam to the chance of a bout.

### CUBA LIBRE!

Uncle Sam raised the cry, and declining to knuckle,
Straight proceeded his sword-belt around him to buckle:
And now in mood not at all adverse to fighting,
Prepared for a tilt without farther inviting.

### CUBA LIBRE!

Sam still said the island should surely be free,
But with him Don utterly failed to agree:
And so on the subject they twain were "at sea."
But good Uncle Sam ne'er was known to back down—
This fact you'll be told by each person in town—
3. And he was not likely upon this occasion
To vary his custom by any persuasion.
When the Don like his favorite beast turned at bay,
Uncle Sam fell to work in his business-like way.
He had said to the Don, "Leave the isle—let it be,"
That he meant what he said all the world could now see.

### CUBA LIBRE!

Uncle Sam and the Patriot chimed it together,
And at once for the Don made some very warm weather:
Made it hot for him truly—increasingly hotter,
Insomuch he repeatedly *got under water!*

### CUBA LIBRE!

The Don was convinced, in no very long while,
That no further use he would have for the isle;
And (hastened no doubt by Sam's vigorous style)
Arrived at the horse-sense conclusion, at length,
'Twould be just as well to save temper and strength.

4.  Uncle Sam, though so cool in his shrewd meditations,
    Is remarkably prompt to discharge obligations.
    Sharp proof of this fact made the Don ope his eyes,
    And gave him a genuine fit of surprise.
    He had called Sam a pig—this proud Son of Castile—
    But howe'er that may be, *he* was first one to *squeal!*

### CUBA LIBRE!

Good-bye to the Don! Let him waive his claims insular,
And take himself home to his region peninsular—
Go back to his bull-fights and other diversions,
In future abstaining from westward excursions.

### CUBA LIBRE!

Be joyful, O, beautiful Nymph of the Sea!
Henceforward be happy and tranquil and free!
For safety you have Uncle Sam's guarantee.
Oppression his blood-thirsty, mad course has run—
The foe cries, "Enough!"—The affair is now done.

5.  And now 'neath your Champion's ample protection,
    To whom you are bound by firm bonds of affection,
    Stand, Daughter of Freedom! Stand forth in your pride,
    And wait the broad sweep of prosperity's tide!
    Your sons will enjoy what so long they have sought—
    For which they have bloodily, bitterly fought.

### CUBA LIBRE!

His watchword the Patriot gayly is crying;
No more is he famished and tortured and dying:
And the Don no more proudly despises the lanky
Individual known as the typical Yankee.

### CUBA LIBRE!

# Odes
# Written for
# Patriotic
# Occasions

# Odes Written for Patriotic Occasions.

## A TOAST--OUR FLAG.

COME, drink to our Flag! Let the draught be of water—
    Sweet Nature's own beverage, clear, pure and free—
    Let all Freedom's children— each son and each daughter—
  Now drink to the weal of the old Flag with me!
From the East, where Mount Washington soars in his glory
  To the West, where the Rockies rise crag upon crag,—
Where Mount Rainier towers aloft, high and hoary,—
  Drink we all to our peerlessly glorious Flag!

    Let us drink to the Banner whose Stripes iridescent
    Graced of old Saratoga's immortalized field!
    May those colors ne'er pale, nor become obsolescent,
2.    Nor their laurels so valiantly won ever yield!
    To the Banner whose Stars shed at Yorktown their splendor,
    Borne by columns disdaining to waver or lag,
    Lift a bright brimming goblet, and leal homage tender
    To that noblest of ensigns—our world-honored Flag!

    Let us drink to the Flag which the Demon of Treason
    Strove to humble forever—to tread in the dust!
    Though the dark clouds of strife hid its folds for a season,
3.    Soon it grandly emerged, for in God was our trust!
    Ay, drink to the Flag that gave Liberty's treasure
    To multitudes doomed slavish fetters to drag—
    To all 'neath its sway equal rights in full measure!
    Drink, drink with a zest to our joy-giving Flag!

# Odes Written for Patriotic Occasions.

Let us drink to the Flag which at distant Manila
  Waved in victory brilliant as earth has e'er known
Which triumphantly flew when a proud foe's flotilla
  In the blue Caribbean was quickly o'erthrown—
To the Flag which by virtue of unsurpassed valor
  Floats o'er fall'n Santiago— o'er Morro's grim crag-
Which oppressors behold but with tremor and pallor
  Freedom's own chosen favorite emblem — our Flag!

Freely drink to the Flag that is symbol and token
  Of all that is noble and holy and pure!
May it float on in grandeur, in triumph unbroken,
  As long as the orbs in yon welkin endure!
Ay, drink to the Banner of ever-blest omen,
  From sea to sea waving o'er vale and o'er crag,
To friends a delight, and a terror to foemen!
  Anew we our fealty pledge thee, O, Flag!

A glass to our Banner! As now, may it ever
  Stand for gallantry, progress, enlightenment, truth—
For honor— for virtue—for earnest endeavor—
  Yea, for all that is sacred to age and to youth!
Ev'ry cause of humanity nobly advancing,
  May it ever go forward, nor falter, nor lag;
May the eyes of the world, ever hitherward glancing,
  On thy folds view no blot—find no stigma, O, Flag!

A drink to our Banner! Let all who revere it
  Give proof of allegiance, deference due;
While patriot fervor imbues ev'ry spirit—
  Now here's to our Flag—to the Red, White and Blue!
Set down the drained glass! As the crystal ware rattles,
  My fancy, aroused, will not loiter or lag;
With mind's eye I witness the myriad battles
  Where thou hast waved proudly in triumph, O, Flag!

Again fill the glasses—brimful—but with water!
  Bring forth no decanter of death-dealing wine,
The stripling to tempt, or the maidenly daughter;
  Inebriants deadly abjure and resign.

With Nature's elixir fill up to o'erflowing
  The once-emptied goblet—let ardor not lag:
With heart fitiy buoyant and soul meetly glowing,
  Drink—heartily drink once again to our Flag!

Ah, yes! Let us now pledge undying devotion
  To the Pride of our Nation—the beautiful—grand!
Unite with me, freemen, with loyal emotion,
9.    Through the length and the breadth of our marvellous Land-
From the East—from the shores where the stormful Atlantic
  Oft urges his surges high up on the crag,
To the West, where unrolls the Pacific gigantic!
  Now quaff we the bumper—ay, here's to our Flag!

# OUR DAY OF DAYS.

### FOR THE FOURTH OF JULY.

WHY is to-day our Day of days?
    Why are those Stripes with the rainbow vying.
Stars like the stars which Heav'n displays
    Ever before us thus floating, flying.
Whithersoever we turn our gaze.
    While glad sounds rise—
      While cannons' roar
Shakes earth and skies
      From shore to shore?
Now whence all the grand
    And wondrous commotion
That thrills our broad Land
    From ocean to ocean?
Whence the gay scenes the eye surveys?—
Why is to-day our Day of days?

Why is to-day our Day of days?
    Why do the people of this great Nation
Gather in 'crowds, with stirring lays—
    Strains that wake gladness and exultation?

**189**

# Odes Written for Patriotic Occasions.

Why do we thus our voices raise?
    Why wend we, why blend we
        Together in throngs,
**2.**      Rejoicing and voicing
        Our jubilant songs?
And eloquence, aye
        Most enchantingly flowing—
Why lauds it this day
        In words goldenly glowing?
Whence all the joy our land displays?
Wherefore is this our Day of days?

Why is to-day our Day of days?
    Ah, IT IS SACRED TO FREEDOM EVER
While a grand Past his glance surveys.
    What is the orator's high endeavor?
*That* to make clear he well essays.
    To-day is the day
        Of our Nation's birth,
    The grandest for aye
**3.**        Of the days of earth—
    Most jocund, most gay
        And most meet for mirth
    A tyrant's chain
        On this day was broken—
    Spurned—rent in twain;—
        Past redemptive token.
    Made void and vain
        The harsh mandate spoken
Therefore our land such joy displays
Therefore is this our Day of days!

Why is to-day our Day of days?
    Ever this day evokes the story
History's page so well portrays –
    That of our Land's birth, progress, glory
Things that have filled earth with amaze
    Of fields of old—
        Each well-won field

Where foes most bold
    Were forced to yield—
Of Ticonderoga
    With pride ever named—
Famed Ticonderoga,
    And triumphs more famed—
Renowned Saratoga
    And Yorktown acclaimed—
Red scenes of yore
    Where our sires victorious·
Yon banner bore
    Which we hold so glorious!
Hence all this day's sublime displays—
Therefore is this our Day of days!

Why is to-day our Day of days?
    Why do we cherish and revere it?
Thus we preserve and keep ablaze
    Sparks of the old ancestral spirit—
That which undauntedly displays
    Contempt for swords
        Which despots wield—
For slavish hordes
        Their kingdoms yield—
That will not waver,
    That will not falter,
Nor cringe for favor,
    Nor weakly palter,
Nor tamely fall
    Before any assaulter.
But throw its all
    On sweet Liberty's altar!
Hence do we raise our gleesome lays—
Therefore is this our Day of days.!

Welcome!  All hail, blithe Day of days!
    Swell the gay song—the cannon's thunder!
Yonder bright sun with glowing rays
    Elsewhere glads not such land of wonder!

Never a breeze that gently plays—
    That disports—blandly sports—
        With yon Standard so rare,
Finds its peer, far or near,
6.          In the world anywhere!
Let it gleam—let it stream
        On the sweet Summer air!
Let it wave o'er the brave,
        Let it float o'er the fair!
Let it shimmer and shine
        As on gala-days vanished!
Let us all care resign—
        Let all sorrow be banished.
During this day of boundless praise—
During this peerless Day of days!

Greet we as ONE this Day of days!
    Strife's accurst demon can ne'er divide us:
O'er us shall gloom no war-cloud's haze:
    Naught shall dissever, whate'er betide us!
Trust we in God—to Him be praise
    From all our hearts
        For this Eden of ours—
    Its prosp'rous marts
        And its halcyon bowers!
Ev'rywhere —north and south—
7        Ev'rywhere—east and west—
From our grandest stream's mouth
    To its parent lake's breast—
Ev'rywhere—from our shore
    The globe's vastest deep beats.
To our strand where its roar
    That most storm-vexed repeats,
In peace our flags fly,
    And our huge cannons thunder.
United, we cry:—
    "Let no hand rend asunder
Ties the divinest Earth displays—
Ties that make blest this Day of days!"

Aye and for aye on this Day of days,
    Thus may each subsequent generation
Mingle with fittingly gaysome lays—
    Ev'ry due token of meet elation—
Rendering homage and soul-felt praise
    To that all-revered band
        Of the days of old,
    Who delivered our Land
        From Oppression's hold—
    Left a heritage grand—
        One of worth untold!
    May it aye expand
8.        As the years unfold!
    May the Flag we so love,
        O'er us witchingly gleaming,
    Evermore thus above
        In full glory be streaming!
    May its Stars never pale,
        Nor its Stripes become dim;
    May our love never fail,
        Nor the praises we hymn!
    Let it flow to and fro
        In the vale—on the height—
    Let it glow high and low
        In the loving sun's light,
Charming the whole world's rev'rent gaze!—
Ever be this our Day of days!

# WHY DO WE GATHER?

### FOR MEMORIAL DAY.

WHY do we gather from near and from far?
    Why seek we the mounds where departed ones slumber,
Strewing the ground where those still sleepers are
With flowers which none but the Most High can number?
We call to mind days that grow dim in the distance—
Dire days that imperilled our Country's existence—

# Odes Written for Patriotic Occasions.

Dark days ere oppression and discord were banished—
Yea, days of deep gloom that forever have vanished!
What visions arise in remembrance to-day,
As wreathe we the beautiful flowers of May!

2.

To-day we assemble in honor of those
　Who hazarded life to annihilate Treason—
Whose breasts formed a barrier firm between foes
　And all that we cherish—yes!—That is the reason
Why we to-day pluck from Nature's robe vernal
Floral gems glorious—almost Supernal—
Why we to-day twine in garlands of beauty
Flowers—bright flowers—we hold it high duty!
Therefore we gather together to-day—
Gather to scatter the blossoms of May.

3.

What a thrill went abroad through this fair Land of ours,
　When its Banner was torn by the guns of Secession!
Peerless heroes pressed forward to brave leaden showers.
　Who in private life graced ev'ry rank and profession!
The architect left the grand dome he was rearing,
The backwoodsman left his small cot in the clearing;
Mechanic and husbandman ceased from their labor,
To shoulder the musket or gird on the sabre.
How many of these sleep the last sleep to-day!
Their low beds we deck with the flowers of May.

4.

Who, who can depict stirring scenes that ensued—
　The commotion—the tumult of quick preparation
For war with its terrors?　What fervor endued
　Those who sacrificed all for the life of the nation!
Oh, who can portray half the sorrow—the anguish
Of those doomed in broken home-circles to languish?
How anxious the heart of the wife, mother, daughter,
For loved ones arrayed on the red fields of slaughter!
'Tis meet we assemble together to-day,
And scatter the blossoms of halcyon May.

What knowledge have they of the march or the camp,
　Who in prosperous homes are now peacefully thriving?

The heat of the conflict—the long weary tramp—
5.    Who so well can describe as the remnant surviving—
The remnant of those who so proudly stood under
The Flag that we love 'mid that civil strife's thunder—
Who manfully bore it till victory crowned it,
And now with their nobly-won laurels surround it?
Ah, gratefully come we together to-day,
To scatter the orient flowers of May!

Who can relate half the horrors endured
    By famishing hordes in the dread, noisome prison?
Only the few to those hardships inured,
6.    Who welcome this day, know what woes have arisen
From such inhumanity!   Bitter, O, bitter
The keen sabre's flash and the bayonet's glitter;
But bitterer still those long hours of repining,
To those who so longed for the cloud's silver lining!
Most thankfully come we together to-day,
And scatter the beautiful flowers of May!

How sadly we think, as our flowers we twine,
    Of those who on Southern savannas are lying!
Beneath the palmetto as well as the pine,
7.    O'er patriot graves are the gentle winds sighing!
Rest, Martyrs of Freedom!   Rest calmly and sweetly!
Oblivion ne'er shall enfold you completely!
Whether your names on proud shafts are recorded,
Or wholly unblazoned, Earth's praise is awarded!
The glory of gallant deeds cannot decay—
'Tis evermore fresh as these flowers of May!

Time, grim and remorseless,—the foeman of all—
    Your ranks, O, survivors, is steadily thinning!
The stoutest and bravest is certain to fall,
8.    Ere long, in the contest he surely is winning!
Year in and year out, you are one by one going
Across the wide River so noiselessly flowing;
Yes, one by one joining the silent procession
That ne'er shall return—which makes no retrogression!

Ah, many lie under the green-sward to-day,
Who one year ago scattered flowers of May!

Heroes departed!  We gratefully lay
  Our tribute of flow'rs on the verdant mounds o'er you!
Heroes surviving!  We greet you to-day!
9.      May comfort and peace fill the days yet before you!
Be ready whene'er the Great Captain shall call you,
To join the bright ranks where no ills can befall you.
Ah, when the great Roll-Call is heard over yonder,
May each answer "Here!" and in fragrant fields wander
'Mid flowers that never shall wither away—
Sweet flowers that bloom in perpetual May!

# HONOR THE BRAVE.

FOR MEMORIAL DAY.

HONOR our heroes—the brave who are lying
  In tombs that are scattered throughout the broad land
  Land which they saved when, proud Treason defying.
    They went forth to battle with stout heart and hand!
Honor the brave!  Cover deeply with flowers
Graves wherein slumber those heroes of ours;
Rain down the flowers in rainbow-hued showers.
    Transforming each mound to a pyramid grand!

Honor the brave, who 'mid horrors of battle—
  Dire sights and dire sounds that attend mortal strife—
Thunder of volleys and bayonets' rattle—
2.      Sustained the grand cause they held dearer than life!
Honor the brave, who unwav'ring, undaunted,
Rushed to the region the Death-Angel haunted—
Rushed to the Eden where Tyranny vaunted,
    That Liberty's joys in its bow'rs might be rife!

Honor the brave, who sans murmur forsaking
  Home scenes and home ties—friends and kindred—
    their all—

3.
Nobly went forth when our Commonwealth, shaking
Upon its foundation, seemed ready to fall!
Ah, what sad partings from fathers and mothers—
Tearful embraces from sisters and brothers—
Anguished—yea, heart-breaking farewells from others
Pledged—bound by such vows as 'tis bliss to recall!

4.
Honor the brave—those who gallantly perished
On far Southern fields 'neath the fire of the foe!
Honor the brave! Be their memory cherished
While floats the starred Banner they triumphed below!
Honor the brave who are dreamlessly sleeping
Where the soft gales of the South-land are sweeping,
O'er whose low beds the green mosses are creeping!
Our souls should with rev'rence and gratitude glow!

5.
Honor the brave—those who sleep under lonely
And dreary mounds marked by that sad word,
"Unknown!"
What was their history? Kind Heaven only
Has record entire of those slumberers lone.
Doubtless fond hearts that were bursting with yearning
Waited in vain their long looked-for returning—
Waited till naught save deep sorrow discerning,
They pined and were laid 'neath the cold churchyard stone.

6.
Honor the brave—those who stir not, nor waken,
At note of the bugle or beat of the drum!
Rock-rooted hills to their hearts might be shaken,
And still would they slumber, unheeding and dumb!
Calm be their rest! All their conflicts are ended!
Fame that is theirs shall through time be extended,
Shrined by the Nation their valor defended!
May each have a part in the glory to come!

7.
Honor our heroes—the thousands who slumber
In countless still cities, 'neath marble shafts white.
Years as they fly are fast swelling the number
Of those who within them are lost to our sight.
Honor our heroes, preserving in story
Marvels they wrought in that contest so gory:

Green keep their memory—sacred their glory!
In peace may they sleep—may their waking be bright!

Honor the brave—yea, in words fitly spoken,
Honor them proudly, our Land's gallant dead!
Render full tribute—withhold not a token—
8.    Homage their deeds—let their praises be said!
Stay not the tear that in gratitude started!
Honor them freely, the noble departed!
Honor the living, the loyal true-hearted—
Honor their Banner and ours overhead!

✳ ✳

# BEAUTIFUL
# FLAG OF OUR NATION.

O BEAUTIFUL Flag of our Nation!
The Banner of banners thou art,
Fair Standard! The world's admiration,
The pride of the patriot's heart!
Thou wearest the crimson of morning,
Heav'n's blue and the hue of the snow,
And stars of yon welkin adorning
Thy folds—how sublimely they glow!

Forever, O, Banner of Beauty,—
Forevermore wave, freely wave!
To love thee is life's sweetest duty—
2.    To bear thee the joy of the brave!
O'er land and o'er ocean victorious,
For aye, kissed by Heav'n's golden light,
Float, Standard of standards most glorious,
Float, Symbol of freedom and might!

O, beautiful Flag of our Nation
How bravely the noble and good,
Beneath thy divine Constellation,
3.    In strife for our Country have stood!

How brilliant thy triumphs on ocean,
　　Thy conquests on battle-swept field!
To thee our most loyal devotion,
　　Our hearts' deepest homage we yield!

Oh, when the wild battle is raging,
　　How sweet to behold thee above,
The rapture of vict'ry presaging,
4.　　Fair Flag of our hope and our love!
Like angel-eyes, tenderly beaming,
　　Thy stars shine o'er dying and dead:
Like iris-hued seraph-wing gleaming,
　　Thou flutterest softly o'erhead!

When traitors dared basely and madly
　　Thy orient fabric to rend,
What heroes sprang forward most gladly,
5.　　Thy Stars and thy Stripes to defend!
Love reigns where grim cannons roared loudly,
　　And hostile ranks bristled with steel,—
Thy colors fly gayly and proudly,
　　And all hearts are true to thy weal!

O, beautiful Flag of our Nation!
　　We pledge thee anew heart and hand!
Ah, yes! For thy leal preservation,
6.　　Till death we would dauntlessly stand!
Each enemy's ensign before thee
　　Shall vanish with meteor flight,
And Heav'n smile approvingly o'er thee
　　When foes are o'er-mastered in fight!

O, beautiful Flag of our Nation!
　　Bright Banner of peerless renown!
For aye may thy blest Constellation
7.　　Shine on—may its Stars ne'er go down!
In peace, or 'mid warfare most gory,
　　Stream ever in splendor above!
We tender forever, Old Glory!
　　Allegiance, reverence, love.

# A SONG
# OF THE
# KLONDIKE

# A Song of the Klondike.

A WAY to the Klondike! Away with the rush
Of throngs that move on with the Spring torrent's gush—
That sweep like the waters of ocean that urge
Their flight to the shore in vast surge upon surge—
That sweep like Niagara's current of might—
Like avalanche down from the Alps' dizzy height—
That sweep like the worlds as they hasten through space.
In God-given orbits revolving apace—
Throughout the wide Universe circling abroad,
Where none save the Infinite ever hath trod!

Away to the Klondike! Away with the mass
That speeds to the trail o'er the tempest-swept Pass!
Away to the new Eldorado that lies
Far under the arch of the bleak Northern skies!
Away to the Klondike! Away with the crowd
The poor and the affluent—humble and proud!
Away, noble youth with ambitions sublime!
Away, stalwart man in thy life's golden prime!
Away, thou on whom the slight first frosts of age
Are scarcely distinguished—away, silvered sage!

Away to the Klondike! Away from the scene
Where pearly streams wander through fields growing green;
Away from sequestered and calm rural spot,
Where, mantled by vines, stands the husbandman's cot!

# A Song of the Klondike.

3. Away from the spot where the bluff mountaineer
Has ventured aloft his rough cabin to rear!
Away from the balmy and fragrance-fraught South,
Where sweetest of fruits tempt the epicure's mouth!
Away from the East and away from the West—
Away from all points of the land we love best!

Away from the hamlet, the village, the town—
Away from the city, whose toil-noises drown
Our thoughts with their clamor—from avenues grand,
Where dwell in vast domes the elite of the land;—

4. Away from obscure and from widely-famed street—
From dark, squalid alleys where Crime's children meet
Away from the bustling—the overthronged mart,
Where pulses the busy metropolis' heart;—
Away from the Capital's boulevards fair—
Away from our vast country everywhere!

Away! Thousands echo that magical word,
And millions of hearts by its blithe sound are stirred!
Away from forge, factory, foundry and shop,
Where eager mechanics their implements drop—

5. From stores of all kinds, all descriptions, away!
Let ev'ry vocation its quota array!
Away! From all places of business men start—
From studios—galleries sacred to Art—
From temples of Science, anear and afar—
From press and from pulpit, from bench and from bar—
From ev'ry profession beneath the wide sky
They join the vast host and augment the wild cry!

"On, on to the wonderful gold-fields!" say they.
"What care we, although they are far, far away?
We know there is hardship and danger and cold,
But these we will gladly encounter—for gold!

6. All obstacles we will remove or surmount—
All arduous tasks as mere pastime account—
Esteem e'en as pleasure all trouble and toil,
If from that far land we may wrest precious spoil!

204

# A Song of the Klondike.

What reck we of peril on land or on wave?
On, on to the gold-fields!—'Tis gold that we crave!"

Away!—From all quarters—from all climes they come;—
From far Southern Pampas—from Afric's shores some—
From isles of the deep—Australasia—Japan—
From Asia:—from China—from Afghanistan—
7. Arabia—Persia.—From Europe they swarm:—
From Norway's cold hills to Italia's bow'rs warm.—
From dense Old-World cities they haste to be gone—
From London, Rome, Paris, Vienna anon—
From Bombay—Calcutta—from Pekin so old—
Ah, yes!  The whole world has gone mad after gold!

Away to the Klondike, where glitters the gold,
With all its enchantments—its charms manifold -
In all of its beauty, its lustre, its sheen!
Who would not possess it with spirit serene?
8. Gold!  Who does not seek it—at loss of it grieve?
And what can it not in our strange world achieve?
It rears gorgeous mansions, procures gay attire,
And myriad luxuries mortals desire.
Ah, what will it not in its plenitude buy?
And who that possesses it vainly may sigh?

Away to the Klondike!  There snatch from the earth
The sun-bright rich metal in all of its worth!
And when its pure sparkle thy vision descries,
Rejoice—ay, be glad, and give thanks for thy prize
9. To Him who vouchsafes ev'ry good gift to give—
Empowers thee daily to move and to live!
Away to the gold-fields with sanguineness press!
May Providence mete to thee ample success: -
There may you bask gladly in Fortune's rare beams,
And find grand fulfillment of all your high dreams!

Away with the blessings of those whom you love
Upon you—a benison down from above!
May Heaven your steps in your wanderings guide,
And good angels ever walk close by your side!

# A Song of the Klondike.

10. May demons ne'er lure you to evil intent—
To deeds that would make those who trust you lament—
To acts that would cast the least shadow of shame
Upon those who bear your as yet spotless name!
Away, and God speed you! Of perils beware!
I breathe for your safety a warm, heart-felt prayer!

Away to the Klondike, as songsters of Spring
Their northward hegira in joyousness wing,
From far-away regions of tropical flowers.
To nestle and warble amid the North's bowers;—
11. Away like the bird as he speeds to his goal—
Away to that realm which approaches the pole!
May He who directs through yon welkin so wide
The bird's roving pinions thy errant steps guide!
He will—yield Him only unfaltering trust—
More precious to Him than to you the bright dust!

Away, but be sure you will find where you go,
'Mid people of all kinds, the vile and the low.
But not of their vileness and lowness partake:
Strive those who are round you more noble to make;
12. Bear principles steadfast, by all understood,
And constantly overcome evil with good.
Amid wild environs, and clad in rough dress,
Remain a true gentleman, nevertheless.
Heed those who your help or your sympathy need:
Successful or not, you will gain a true meed.

Away to the Klondike; but take heed! 'Tis not.
As thoughtless ones dream. a luxurious spot.
'Mid trials. privations, with struggles untold,
Men wrest from earth's bosom the shimmering gold.
13. O, thou who dost dawdle away in gay ease
Thy days—so fastidious scarce aught can please
Thy taste or thy fancy,—dost thou, too, upstart.
And sigh for that Goal of all goals to depart?
There luxuries scarce even gold can procure:—
Much thou must forego—much perforce must endure.

# A Song of the Klondike.

Away to the Klondike, from hilltop and vale
And wide-spread savanna!   Board train and set sail!
But brace nerve and sinew, and strengthen thine heart,
O, thou who dost on that long pilgrimage start!
14. For ere thou may'st reach the bright shrine of thy hope,
With much must thou grapple—with much must thou cope:—
With hardships uncounted by land and by deep—
With perils that well make the faint-hearted weep!
Say, hast thou endurance and courage to last
Until the grand gauntlet, as 'twere, shall be passed?

Away—but how well have you counted the cost?
Though much may be gained, there is much may be lost!
Have you the full bloom and full vigor of health?
And would you exchange them, as some have, for wealth?
15. Have you the society, day after day,
Of dear ones around you, light- hearted and gay?
And would you exchange it, O, man, for the cold
And voiceless companionship even of gold?
Now life and the comforts of life are all yours;
And dare you to stake them for Fortune's wild lures?

Away to the Klondike!—For there is no dearth
Of what men so sigh for—the riches of earth !
But is there no dearth where those craved riches are
Of something more precious—more sacred by far?—
16. Of life's choicest blessings?—Of love's magic smile
And home's fond endearments?  Think!  Is it worth while
To leave spot where only one want you have known—
Of gold—and go where there is plenty alone
Of one thing—of gold?—You your pref'rence may take:
Are you all this sacrifice ready to make?

Away to the Klondike!   But pause ere you part .
From all that is dearest and nearest your heart'
Perhaps that fond wife you may never more see:
Perhaps that sweet babe may no more press your knee.
17. Perchance father, mother, or daughter, or son,
May sleep the last sleep ere your long quest be done'

# A Song of the Klondike.

Away to the Klondike!   But pause ere you go
From scenes emblematic of Heaven below!
Away to the Klondike!   But count the cost well,
Ere leaving the home where you peacefully dwell!

Away to the gold-fields!   But pause while you burn
With eagerness—while all restraint you would spurn:
Ah, many who pass o'er that long, dreary track
Shall over that desolate route ne'er come back!

18.   How many go out from their dwellings to-day,
No more to cross over their thresholds for aye!
So take a fond look ere you hasten to roam,
At scenes that surround the blest spot you call home!
Press close to your heart those most dear!   Men propose,
God only disposes—futurity knows!

Perhaps you may find, not vast wealth, but a tomb.
I seek not to burden your bosom with gloom:
I would not be curt, rude, uncivil, unkind,
But wish not that you should rush thitherward blind.

19.   Beneath those renowned but far, far away skies,
Alone you may slumber—strange hands close your eyes—
Strange hands may your own cross upon your still breast,
And shroud you and coffin you—lay you to rest.
'Mid scenes unfamiliar, with no loved one near,
In that lonely land you may close life's career.

As king who would forth go to conquering war,
As one who a dome would rear, none might abhor,
Hast thou all computed—well weighed—counted cost?
If so, by no wav'ring emotion be tossed!

20.   Away to the gold-fields!   Naught venture—naught gain!
Attempts must be made, if to aught men attain!
The weak only dream, while the strong boldly act!
Be earnest, be resolute, matter-of-fact!
Let reason and judgment have due scope and sway,
Approve they thy project?   Away, then, away!

Away to the Klondike!   For earth is no vain
Respecter of persons, and thou may'st obtain

# A Song of the Klondike.

As much—haply more than the proud millionaire:
For thou art as truly as he Nature's heir.

21. Away, nor depend upon fickle Dame Luck!
Depend on thine own individual pluck!
Rely on no talisman, token or charm,—
Rely on the might of thy good brawny arm!
Be manful—industrious, diligent be,
And Fortune, perchance, will smile sweetly on thee!

O, thou from whose hold a grand fortune has passed,
Like leaf wrenched from tree by rude whirl of mad blast!
Despond not, nor droop, nor with bitterness rife,
Declare there is nothing left worthy of life,—

22. Nor seek in a frenzy existence to end!
Thy broken designs thou may'st yet haply mend!
From honor, from rectitude suffer no lapse!
The wealth that was lost in a moment, perhaps.
May now be as quickly recovered!   Away
To regions where fortunes are found in a day!

Away!   But beware ere directing your feet
To land Hope makes brilliant—entrancingly sweet!
Perhaps disappointment may meet you—deny
All that for which now you with confidence sigh—

23. Yea, illness, misfortune, disaster and pain
May there cross your path in a shadowy train!
Prepare for the worst, though it may not appear:
Prepare for the worst, and then be of good cheer!
For sweet expectation must hearten the breast
Of those who attain to life's grandest and best!

And thou who air-castles Titanic dost build,
With boundless expectancy ravished and thrilled,
Who fondly dost dream of securing amain
What millions have striven for only in vain!

24. Let not thy heart break—let thy spirit not faint,
Should all the grand pictures thy fancy may paint
Prove wholly phantasmal—should Fate be unkind—
If thou should'st but failure inglorious find—
Reflect!—There are more ways than one to win gold—
More methods than this one so primitive, old.

# A Song of the Klondike.

By planning and toiling in many a sphere,
With far less of hazard—exertion severe—
What thousands on thousands have won fortunes vast-
What millions a competence nobly amassed!
25. And though, when compared to the mine's profuse spoil.
Slow seem the returns of all common-place toil,
More sure in proportion are they—oft more prized—
Than riches with suddenness thus realized.
And though you should lose in this race after gold.
Life's race is not lost—yet be hopefully bold!

And think!. Should you utterly fail in the strife,
You yet may be rich in the blessings of life!
The man without wealth may enjoy freedom's boon—
The sweet, balmy air—beam of star, sun and moon—
26. The marvellous treasure of health, without which
All life is insipid—as well as the rich.
And Oh! All of life's other treasures above,
The man without opulence yet may have love,
Without which existence has no pith or zest—
Without which a mortal can scarcely be blest.

Away to the Klondike—that spot so divine!
For you may its treasures in full glory shine,—
Its nuggets so fabulous dazzle your gaze;
And may you prove true tales that wake earth's amaze!
27. But what will those riches so coveted bring?
A residence meet for a nabob or king—
All palate craves—all the fastidious claim
By way of adornment—some flattery—fame—
And glances of envy from those round your way—
Society's butterflies, thoughtless and gay!
But say! Will these things bring you fullness of joy.
And give you exemption from ev'ry annoy?

Away to the Klondike! But know ere you go,
Complete satisfaction is found not below.
Though earth untold treasures should yield to your hand
Nay, could you possess *all* that marvellous land,
28 And heap the bright particles up mountain-high,
In peak that should pierce the cerulean sky,

# A Song of the Klondike.

Yet would your insatiable soul thirst for more—
Your ambition higher and yet higher soar,
Until the whole world would seem small to your eyes,
And you would crave others more splendid in size.

Away to the Klondike! But pause to reflect,
Nor pleasures proportioned to treasures expect.
The rich man gains not an additional sense
Wherewith to enjoy what his fortune immense
29. Endues him with privilege—power to possess:
And oft his capacity truly is less
For heart-felt enjoyment;—for harassing cares
Steal in until happiness flies unawares.
And splendor in all forms will soon or late pall—
Life's commonest pleasures are sweetest of all!

Away—but stop! What is your motive, my friend?
Much would you acquire on self to expend?
Seek you to lay up all this much-dreamed-of pelf
Alone for the gratification of self?
30. Or is it to help on your fellows, O, man?
Say, what is your purpose, and what is your plan?
Ah, better, far better the gold-dust should lie
In earth's bosom dark, never tempting the eye,
Than merely to pander to selfishness—greed—
And not to be minister to the world's need!

Away to the Klondike! Away to the mines,
Where gold in its virginal loveliness shines!
But idolize not—worship not as a god
The yellow earth Nature has placed in the clod!
31. Away to the Klondike! And gather your share
Of treasures so marvellous—treasures so rare!
But not that you may by Mankind be adored,
Those treasures so carefully gather and hoard!
For joy you may give—for the good you may do
With what you obtain, Fortune's smiles afar woo.

Away to the Klondike, and gather the gold!
If prospered, remember the hungry and cold.
Be not like the Rich Man who said to his soul,

"Take ease and be merry, enjoying the whole!"

32.   Be not like the niggard who holds ev'ry dime,
As if to disburse it were even a crime,—
Nor yet like the Prodigal, casting away
Thy portion in one brief, hilarious day.
Each tendency sordid, extravagant quell,
And what thou securest use wisely and well.

Away:—but remember life's triumphs are brief,
That ev'rything mundane must pass like the leaf;
That though all your hopes should prove loyal and true,
Ere long you must bid all you sigh for adieu.

33.   So while you seek gold in that cold Northern clime,
Be sure you possess Heaven's treasures sublime,
Which never misfortune may wrest from your grasp,
And never the hand of the pilferer clasp—
Those treasures which bring real joy and true peace,
And unalloyed pleasures which never shall cease!

Ah, many an argonaut ardent and bold
Who speeds to that far-away Country of Gold—
Who hastes to that region of wondrous renown,
To seek Fortune's smile, shall meet only her frown—

34.   Instead of her favors, repulses and spurns—
Mere tantalization in lieu of returns!
But he who seeks treasures by Heaven assigned
Shall seek not in vain—he that seeketh shall find—
Shall find and possess them long after this world
Shall have to nonentity duly been hurled.

Away to the Klondike! Its fame is unfurled—
The cry is resounding throughout the whole world!
From earth's farthest ports are men eagerly bound
To region where fortunes so splendid are found: —

35.   From every nation—from every shore
They hasten in quest of the magical ore!
Away to the Klondike! Away with the crowd—
The low and the lofty—the humble and proud—
The poor and the rich—small and great—young and old—
Away in the wild and mad scramble for gold!

# Psalms Of Hope and Good Cheer.

## BE A MAN!

HAVE you met repulse inglorious
  On some battle-field of life?
 Is the watchful world censorious?
 Is its laugh of scorn uproarious,
 Since you failed to be victorious
  In the weary, weary strife?
 Let no desperate mood steal o'er you!
 Men have suffered thus before you!
 Listen calmly, I implore you!
  Though beneath Misfortune's ban,
 Do not quaff Despair's dark cup!
 Let this motto brace you up—
                    *BE A MAN!*

 Are you slandered, wronged and slighted
  E'en by those you deemed your friends?
 Are good deeds with ill requited?
 Is your faith in mortals blighted?
 What is wrong will yet be righted!
  Justice soon will make amends!
 Though you meet mankind's displeasure,
 Bear opprobrium without measure,
 Keep your courage as a treasure!
  With fresh hope the future scan!
 Do not quaff Despair's dark cup!
 Let this motto brace you up—
                    *BE A MAN!*

215

To some lofty height aspiring,
    Of your aim have you come short?
Seems the goal you are desiring
Ever from your steps retiring?
Seem all things with Fate conspiring
    You to baffle, you to thwart?
Though your quest be fruitless purely,
Some prize you can grasp securely!
You were born for some good, surely!
    In life's march still seek the van!
Do not quaff Despair's dark cup!
Let this motto brace you up—
                    *BE A MAN!*

Has harsh criticism awed you?
    Human standards are not God's!
Be a man, though none applaud you,
Though no soul on earth should laud you!
Though of praise mankind defraud you,
    Manfully, despite all odds,
Strive no less to be deserving!
Do not cringe—be not time-serving!
Forward press with course unswerving,
    Resolute as you began!
Do not quaff Despair's dark cup!
Let this motto brace you up—
                    . *BE A MAN!*

Though all others underrate you,
    Do not value yourself less!
Grandest fortune may await you—
Where you long to be instate you!
Joys long dreamed of may elate you—
    All that waits on true success—
All you wish for, all you care for—
What you breathe your fondest prayer for!
Hearken! What do you despair for?
    Fill your place in God's great plan!
Do not quaff Despair's dark cup!
Let this motto brace you up—
                    *BE A MAN!*

# Psalms of Hope and Good Cheer.

Bravely face all trials! Never
  Cease to struggle, cease to hope!
Let the Past be past forever!
Banish dark forebodings! Sever
Chains that drag you down! Endeavor
  Nobly with life's ills to cope!
Know your worth and proper station
In the ranks of God's creation,
And, though missing approbation,
  Be as worthy as you can!
Do not quaff Despair's dark cup!
Let this motto brace you up—
                    *BE A MAN!*

Be a man! Ay, naught is grander
  Than true manhood here below!
Set at naught the breath of slander,
And all petty souls that pander
To the enemies of Candor—
  Ev'ry envious, jealous foe!
Live above earth's low derision!
Leave to Heav'n's supreme decision
Your achievements! Let your vision
  Soar away beyond life's span!
Do not quaff Despair's dark cup!
Let this motto brace you up—
                    *BE A MAN!*

Be a man! Whate'er may grieve you,
  Or disturb your life's career,
Let no whit of virtue leave you!
Of Truth's gem let naught bereave you!
Though the conscienceless deceive you,
  Still be earnest and sincere!
Though the world no meed accord you,
Though it may have scorned abhorred you,
Be a man! Heav'n will reward you!
  Hope's expiring embers fan!
Do not quaff Despair's dark cup!
Let this motto brace you up—
                    *BE A MAN!*

217

Have you sought wealth's regal splendor,
   Or the halo of renown,
And been deemed a mere pretender,
Or, perchance, a gross offender?
Do not abjectly surrender
   Self-respect, your manhood's crown!
There are better things than glory,
Gold or Fame's enchanting story!
Let regret be transitory,
   Though a losing race you ran!
Do not quaff Despair's dark cup!
Let this motto brace you up—
                              *BE A MAN!*

9.

Whatsoe'er your occupation,
   Be it honest, be it pure,
Bravely follow your vocation!
Heed no base insinuation
That your task brings degradation!
   Toil no stigma should endure—
Should no sense of shame awaken!
Let your spirit be unshaken,
Though you find yourself forsaken
   Be some set, or caste, or clan!
Do not quaff Despair's dark cup!
Let this motto brace you up—
                              *BE A MAN!*

10.

Every mortal has a mission
   In this wondrous world of ours,
Whatsoever his condition,
Whatsoever his position,
Whatsoever his ambition,
   Whether small or great his powers.
Find out what you were designed for,
Fitted, placed among mankind for,
What you long have yearned and pined for
   May not suit your Maker's plan.
Do not quaff Despair's dark cup!
Let this motto brace you up—
                              *BE A MAN!*

11.

Do not fall a prey to Folly;—
   Do not droop and pine and die!
Do not yield to Melancholy!
Better far a life most jolly
Than a bed 'neath yew or holly,
   Where the churchyard shadows lie!
Though disparaged, joyless, mirthless,
Do not view yourself as birthless;
Do not say your life is worthless—
   That your being is a ban!
Do not quaff Despair's dark cup!
Let this motto brace you up—
          *BE A MAN!*

12.

Be a man!  Say not existence
   Is a failure flat, entire,
Though you meet untold resistance,
Though you battle for subsistence,
Though clouds mutter in the distance,
   And you see them looming higher.
Be a man in deed and bearing,
Nobly prudent, wisely daring!
Calmly for the worst preparing,
   Blench not—do the best you can!
Do not quaff Despair's dark cup!
Let this motto brace you up—
          *BE A MAN!*

13.

By a moment's frenzy driven,
   Do not cast your life away!
Frowning barriers may be riven;
Foes may fly that long have striven:
Triumph may to you be given!
   Wait a more auspicious day!
Precious passing computation
Is life's hand-breadth of duration!
Dare you compass its cessation,
   And your soul forever ban?
Do not quaff Despair's dark cup!
Let this motto brace you up—
          *BE A MAN!*

14.

Be a man!  Has Love allured you
  With his subtle, magic art?
In his silken toils secured you,
Rapture unalloyed assured you,
Then remorselessly abjured you—
15.      Tantalized and torn your heart?
Has some soul that gave you gladness
Fickle proved—tinged life with sadness?
Let not sorrow, nursed to madness,
  Wreck your life-work's glorious plan!
Do not quaff Despair's dark cup!
Let this motto brace you up—
            *BE A MAN!*

Be a man!  Is there within you
  Some dread tendency to ill?
Inborn impulse that would win you
From Right's arrowy track, and pin you
Firmly down?  Faint not!  Continue
16.      To resist with all your skill!
Steel yourself against temptation!
Strengthen your determination
To defeat Sin's usurpation!
  Conquer!  Yea, you must—you can!
Do not quaff Despair's dark cup!
Let this motto brace you up—
            *BE A MAN!*

Be a man!  Be not a coward
  In the contest you must wage!
Be not lightly overpowered
By the blows upon you showered!
All who have as heroes towered
17.      O'er the mass in every age
Have been dauntless, persevering,
From their way obstructions clearing,
Naught save things unmanly fearing—
  Things ignoble—things that ban!
Do not quaff Despair's dark cup!
Let this motto brace you up—
            *BE A MAN!*

Be a man!   Waste not in fretting
   Priceless unreturning days,
Vainly cureless ills regretting,
All the good of life forgetting,
All at naught Heav'n's favors setting.
18.      And the mercy it displays,—
Puerile complaints out-pouring,
Weakly, childishly deploring
What can not be helped—ignoring
   What you should not fail to scan!
Do not quaff Despair's dark cup!
Let this motto brace you up—
             *BE A MAN!*

Let no headstrong passion sway you;
   O'er yourself hold staunch control!
Teach your spirit to obey you!
Let not, I entreat and pray you,
Some wild inclination slay you—
19.      Kill your body and your soul!
Weak, unreasoning submission
Has wrought untold demolition—
Hurled down myriads to Perdition
   Since earth's history began!
Do not quaff Despair's dark cup!
Let this motto brace you up—
             *BE A MAN!*

Do you sigh for vanished riches?
   Have you been at Luxury's court?—
Known the flattery that bewitches
All who reach Earth's loftiest niches?
Say you fickle Fortune pitches
20.      Things awry, as if for sport?—
That she joys to render sadder
Hearts that long to be made gladder?
Has she thrown you from her ladder?
   Start again where you began!
Do not quaff Despair's dark cup!
Let this motto brace you up—
             *BE A MAN!*

Rouse from hypochondriac dreaming!
That which causes you to cower
May be direful but in seeming!
Souls with dolesome forecasts teeming
Only shadows see 'mid gleaming
21.        Midday's unbeclouded hour.
Let not gloom upon you settle
Till your mind shall have no mettle!
For the rose, and not the nettle,
    Earth's fair fields around you scan!
Do not quaff Despair's dark cup!
Let this motto brace you up—
                *BE A MAN!*

Ne'er assever, and believe it,
    Life is not worth living!  Shame
On such tenet!  Ne'er receive it!
Live for something and achieve it!
'Twill not help your lot—retrieve it—
22.        Thus your Maker to defame!
Usefulness should be the measure
Of life's value—not its pleasure,
Not its quantity of treasure,
    Not its brief duration's span!
Do not quaff Despair's dark cup!
Let this motto brace you up—
                *BE A MAN!*

Be a man!  Ne'er blindly groping
    All your woes ascribe to Luck!
Discontinue listless moping!
Act!—Of what avail is hoping
Sans endeavor,—never coping
23.        With life's difficulties?  Pluck
You require—force, manly vigor!
If with these you meet earth's rigor.
More diminutive, not bigger,
    Will appear the ills you scan!
Do not quaff Despair's dark cup!
Let this motto brace you up—
                *BE A MAN!*

Be a man!   Be not dead-hearted,
  Although indigent your lot!
Has your soul in penury smarted?
Thousands of the great departed
From as low a level started!
    Not from palace, but from cot
Which Art never deigned to dizen,
Have the world's renowned arisen.
No conditions bind or prison
    Genius.   Form an aim—a plan!
Do not quaff Despair's dark cup!
Let this motto brace you up—
                    *BE A MAN!*

Be a man!   Your patience double!
  Temper—dominate your grief!
In the frenzy of your trouble,
Seem all things as chaff or stubble—
Unsubstantial as a bubble?
    Of all woes deem not yours chief!
There are other bosoms bleeding,
Other hearts for pity pleading;
Be not selfish and unheeding;
    Lend assistance when you can!
Do not quaff Despair's dark cup!
Let this motto brace you up—
                    *BE A MAN!*

Do not magnify your trials!
  Seem the prayers you waft above
All repulsed with cold denials?
Seems Heav'n pouring out its vials—
· Of its wrath the baleful phials—
    On you, and on all you love?
Seem impending miseries boundless—
Shoreless deeps whose depths are soundless?
You are filled with fancies groundless!
    Heav'n's wish is to bless, not ban!
Do not quaff Despair's dark cup!
Let this motto brace you up—
                    *BE A MAN!*

Be a man!   Do not be daunted
  By the arrogant and proud!
Let them vaunt as they have vaunted;
Let them flaunt as they have flaunted!
By no servile dread be haunted:
    By their hauteur be not cowed!
Both were by one God created,
Both are to one Judgment fated,—
Money-king with pride inflated,
  Artisan with cheek of tan!
Do not quaff Despair's dark cup!
Let this motto brace you up—
          *BE A MAN!*

Be a man!   Be self-reliant!
  Ne'er on others weakly lean!
Do not be the vine whose pliant
Tendrils wrap some sylvan giant;
Be the forest-king defiant,
    Calm in strength—'mid storms serene!
Be no spiritless dependent!
Culture manhood's traits resplendent;
Be in nobleness transcendent;
  For yourself think, judge and plan!
Do not quaff Despair's dark cup!
Let this motto brace you up—
          *BE A MAN!*

Be a man!   Be not a grumbler,
  Finding faults in all things rife!
Your estate might be far humbler!
Like a dark-bewildered fumbler—
An unseeing midnight stumbler—
    Do not pass along through life,
Treading only paths of roughness,
With a voice of bateless gruffness,
Charging Nature's self with bluffness,
  Nature's God with flawy plan!
Do not quaff Despair's dark cup!
Let this motto brace you up—
          *BE A MAN!*

27.

28.

29.

**224**

Does some secret anguish bitter
   That no other heart may share
Cause drops lachrymal to glitter
On your cheek, while gay souls fritter
Time away like birds that twitter,--
30.      As unthinking, free from care?
They will soon with grief be bending:
Mirth and woe have likewise ending:
Both in alternation blending
   Make up life's ephemeral span.
Do not quaff Despair's dark cup!
Let this motto brace you up--
        *BE A MAN!*

Be a man!   Black schemes eschewing,
   Ne'er your fellow-creatures wrong!
Think you profits are accruing
To that soul who, lightly viewing
His dishonor, is pursuing
31.      Ways of turpitude?  Ere long
Comes a day of retribution
For each misdeed's execution,--
For all baseness, fraud, pollution!
   Evil's consequences scan!
Do not quaff Despair's dark cup!
Let this motto brace you up—
        *BE A MAN!*

Be a man!   Do problems vex you?
   Seem the times all out of joint?
Do affairs perturb, perplex you?
Whatsoe'er bars, frustrates, checks you,
Let not aught unman, unsex you;
32.      Bear what Heaven may appoint!
Earth is full of fluctuations,
Agitations, innovations;
Constant be amid mutations;
   Trust the Highest's changeless plan!
Do not quaff Despair's dark cup!
Let this motto brace you up—
        *BE A MAN!*

Does your soul, forlorn and weary,
   Tend to brood on things abhorred?—
Things horrific, gruesome, eerie?
Do your lips propound the query,
Mournful as the Miserere
   With a quaver in each chord:—
When will fearful thoughts that haunt me,
With their spectral presence daunt me,
Cease to haunt me, daunt me, taunt me
   In an endless caravan?
Do not quaff Despair's dark cup!
Let this motto brace you up—
         *BE A MAN!*

33.

Pessimistic plaints contemning,
   Strive to view life at its best.
Only what is ill condemning!
Petulancy's cavils stemming,
Think of all the fair things gemming
   This most lovely planet's breast—
Of the songs that Nature sings you—
Of the good existence brings you!
Contemplate what tortures, stings you,
   Little—seldom as you can!
Do not quaff Despair's dark cup!
Let this motto brace you up—
         *BE A MAN!*

34.

Be a man! Do projects fail you,
   Dreams long harbored prove untrue.
Disappointments keen assail you,
Losses harass, wear and pale you,
All your efforts naught avail you,—
   Others with indifference view
All that causes you annoyance,
All that robs your soul of joyance.
Makes it wild as weird clairvoyance
   When your grievances you scan?
Do not quaff Despair's dark cup!
Let this motto brace you up—
         *BE A MAN!*

35.

Be a man!   Like blossoms vernal.
　Perish grandeur and display!
Choose between the husk and kernel·
Only goodness is eternal:
Live for that which is Supernal —
　Cannot change or pass away!
'Mid the ills your life invading,
'Mid Humanity's up'braiding.
Think!   From halcyon Realm unfading,
　Time withholds you scarce a span!
Do not quaff Despair's dark cup!
Let this motto brace you up—
　　　　*BE A MAN!*

# KEEP A BOLD FRONT!

IN the tumult of life's battle,
'Mid its hurry, bustle, rattle,
'Mid its idle, trivial tattle,
'Mid its gossip's frivolous prattle.
Whatsoe'er may fret or ail you,
Whatsoever may assail you,
Whatsoever hopes may fail you,
Whatsoever fears may pale you,
Heed advice blunt!
(This be your wont)
'Mid the strife's brunt,
Keep a bold front!

Do not vacillate or waver;
Never show the foe such favor!
Let your voice betray no quaver:
As your peril grows, be braver!
Sturdy as some ancient yeoman—
Some staunch mediæval bowman·

**227**

Some indomitable Roman—
Face the most intrepid foeman!
Heed advice blunt;
(This be your wont)
'Mid the strife's brunt,
Keep a bold front!

Still maintain a calm exterior,
To assaulting ills superior:
Though of earth-jars waxing wearier.
Cow not—be no base inferior!
In a valorous mien is ever
3.   Half the virtue of endeavor.
Brave the world, unskilled or clever!
Men contemn true courage never!
Heed advice blunt;
(This be your wont)
'Mid the strife's brunt,
Keep a bold front!

# BEYOND THE CLOUD.

### I.

GRIEVE not, O, child! Surcease repining!
   Though frowns yon cloud with thunders loud.
Beyond its gloom the sun is shining,
   And Heav'n is blue—beyond the cloud.

Thou look'st around—the world seems cheerless.
2.   The wind a knell—the sky a shroud;
But weep not—let thine eyes be tearless,
   For there is light—beyond the cloud.

Soon, soon—ah, soon will earth so dreary
3.   With Heav'nly glory be endowed—
The landscape dark grow bright and cheery
   With radiance from beyond the cloud.

Soon yon dense mass, so blackly rolling,
4.    Will shrink away like monster cowed;—
Soon brilliance gladdening, consoling,
    Will reach thee from beyond the cloud.

Lo, now—e'en now—'tis fleeing—fleeing!
5.    No longer be with sadness bowed;
Let joyousness pervade thy being!
    The sunshine smiles—departs the cloud!

## II.

O, thou whose life is overclouded
6.    By woes avowed or unavowed!
'Twill not be long thus darkly shrouded,
    For there is light—beyond the cloud.

'Tis ever thus—an alternation
7.    Of shade and shine—of woe and mirth:
Each soul must look for such mutation,
    While tabernacled here on earth.

Think not if adverse fate o'ertake thee
8.    It will forevermore remain;
Whate'er perturbs will soon forsake thee,
    And Peace will re-assert her reign.

So let thy step—thy look be firmer!
9.    With more implicit trust endowed,
Wait—bide thy time without a murmur;
    For soon will pass away the cloud.

Let this thought nerve thee to endeavor,
10.    Whatever ills upon thee crowd:—
They will not—cannot last forever—
    *Light lies beyond life's darkest cloud.*

# A BURST OF SUNSHINE.

I SAT within my study,
　　Alone with demon Doubt.
The sunshine warm and ruddy
　　Cheered not the world without:
My heart was full of sorrow,
　　My soul with fears was rife;
Hope of a better morrow
　　Forsook my drooping life:
Dread fancy-wrought creations,
1.　　Chimerical and vain,
Uncouth hallucinations
　　Besieged my throbbing brain,
When—sudden—transitory—
　　Soon gone beyond recall—
The sun burst forth in glory,
　　And shone upon my wall!
It to my heavy spirit
　　Restored the promise bright—
Aye since I joy to hear it—
　　"At eve it shall be light!"


It shone with smile Elysian,
　　As sped the clouds apart;
'Twas Heaven to my vision,
　　'Twas Heaven to my heart!
Like loving voice Supernal,
　　It bade my sorrow cease,
Like word from the Eternal,
　　It brought my bosom peace!
My future's prospect brightened
2.　　As I beheld its glow;
My fortitude was heightened,
　　No more I bent in woe;

The Tempter's charm evanished,
    No more I felt his thrall;
Fiend-visaged Doubt it banished—
    That sun-burst on the wall!
I looked to Him whose servant
    I am—unburdened quite—
Repeating with lips fervent,
    "At eve it shall be light!"

The glorious sun, descending
    'Mid hill-tops in the West,
His farewell beams was sending
    Abroad upon earth's breast;
His parting glance so tender,
    That through my lattice stole,
Presaged with its soft splendor
    A triumph for my soul!
With what emotions grateful
3.    I hailed that sun-burst's gleam,
To me sublimely fateful
    Beyond all pow'r to dream!
It seemed from Him a token
    To whom for aid I call,
Whose word is never broken—
    That sun-burst on the wall!
Strengthened to meet all trials,
    I firmly said:  "Despite
The carping world's denials,
    'At eve it *shall* be light!'"

O, thou whose soul is dreary,
    Who hast a wounded heart!
Leagured by fancies eerie,
    Let not thy faith depart!
Whate'er now thwarts endeavor,
    Or bids thee deeply grieve,
Will soon or late forever—
    Forevermore take leave!

Bravely endure thy sorrow!
4.     Nobly sustain the strife!
Trust for a fairer morrow
    Him who fore-knows thy life!
Remember, in thy sadness,
    Immortal Love rules all.
Into thy life shall gladness
    Like that sweet sun-burst fall.
Though sore be thy annoyance,
    Thy woes as dark as night,
Thou yet shalt know true joyance—
    "At eve it shall be light!"

# A PAEAN.

THERE is joy in the lucent sunlight
    That streameth over all,—
There is joy in the titillation
    Of yon pearl waterfall;—
There is joy in the wide-spread forest,
    'Mid oak-trees Titan tall,—
There is joy where the Nature-lover
    Gloats o'er yon vine-twined wall!

There is joy where the dancing lilies
    Dot yon blue-bosomed lake—
Where the boat that disports so swan-like
2.     Leaves sheeny argent wake;—
There is joy on its strand of saffron
    Where sapphire wavelets break,—
Where the cliffs, to the welkin soaring,
    Supernal echoes make!

There is joy where the lucid fountain
    Aspiringly leaps out,—
There is joy where the songful river
3.     Hastes on its sinuous route;—
There is joy in the wild-bird's warble,
    The playsome school-boy's shout,—

There is joy in the gaudy garden—
  Ay, joy all round about!

Stream adown and abroad, O, sunlight,
  With rapture in each ray!
Laugh, bewitchful, mellifluous torrent,—
4.      Laugh on for aye and aye!
Leap aloft—higher yet—O, fountain!
  Be gayer, all things gay!
For the clouds in my life have vanished!
  My heart exults to-day!

# OUR MOTTO.

ONWARD! Let this be our motto, and the burden of our
      song!
  With the word upon our Banners, let us bravely march along!
Onward! There are fields of glory we may win by noble strife!
Waste no time in idle dreaming! Onward in the march of life!

  Onward, onward! Ever onward! Look not back, nor stay
      thy feet!
2.  Loiter not 'mid morning's freshness, falter not 'mid noontide's
      heat!
  Ever onward, ever onward! There are treasures to be won!
  Haste to grasp them, lest they vanish ere shall rise to-morrow's
      sun!

  Onward! Brighter days are coming, O, ye weary ones who toil!
3.  Onward, laborer, grandly onward! From no worthy task recoil!
  Onward, brilliant Son of Genius! Honor waits thee—death-
      less fame!
  Onward, onward to achievement! Thine may be a lofty name!

  Onward! There are deeds of grandeur, deeds of wonder to
      perform!
4.  There are mighty hosts to vanquish, towering fortresses to
      storm!

**233**

# Psalms of Hope and Good Cheer.

There are vast, unfathomed problems in the boundless realm
of Thought!
Onward, onward! You may solve them! Onward! Toil
where none have wrought!

Onward in the ranks of Progress! O, let naught thy steps
impede!—
5   On with unremitting ardor! Never from the van recede! ·
All that makes Earth happier, better, all that elevates Mankind,
Strive with dauntless soul to forward! Not an instant fall
behind!

Onward—on! Though worn and weary, do not fail to render
aid
6.   To the struggling ones around you! Onward! Never be
dismayed!
Onward in life's glorious battle, though by foes most sorely
pressed!
Onward! There is naught like courage! Victory brings joy
and rest!

Onward ever, onward ever in the sacred cause of Right!
7.   Let not Error's threats alarm thee, though her arm is full of
might!
Onward! If thou be triumphant, thou shalt wear a peerless
crown!
Thou shalt share the bliss of angels! Onward! Heed not
scoff nor frown!

Onward, though the way be thorny!—On tow'rd Heaven— on
tow'rd God!
8.   Onward till you scale the Mountains that no mortal feet have
trod!
Onward till by Life's pure River you may rest—the bright
Goal won—
And the sweet voice of the Master shall repeat the words,
"*WELL DONE!*"

# Idyls Of Home

# Idyls of Home.

## Home.

SOME souls have a wonderful passion
 For distant scenes splendid or strange:
Some travel because 'tis the fashion,
 And seldom their route care to change.
But tell me, adventurous rover,
 Where'er, seeking marvels, you roam,—
Say, where, though you search the world over,
 Is aught half so lovely as home?

Some castle, old, ruinous, hoary,
 Or palace surpassingly fair,
Has charmed you in song or in story.
2. Till fondly you wished to be there.
But when you arrived and beheld it,
 Its grandeur seemed empty as foam.
The spell——what so quickly dispelled it?
 Remembrance of home-land and home!

Though famed foreign cities invite us
 'Mid wonders to bide for a time.
Not long they beguile and delight us:
3. We long for our own native clime.
The grandest attraction soon ceases
 To charm us, wherever we roam;
We crave with a strength that increases
 The beauties and duties of home!

Ah, yes! Though our home-walls be humble,
 Those walls over all else we prize!
Proud structures may crumble and tumble
4. To dust—we their glory despise.

With ennui we leave them behind us—
　　E'en relics of Greece or of Rome;
For strong chains invisibly bind us—
　　Insensibly draw us tow'rd home!

Home!　Blissful retreat—refuge cheery
　　For those who are anxious and worn.
For souls that are troubled and dreary,
5.　　For hearts that with anguish are torn,—
Where all that is nearest and dearest
　　Is gathered beneath the sky's dome!
We hail thee with rapture sincerest,
　　Earth's sweetest spot—Heaven's type— *HOME!*

# Down Upon The Old, Old Farm.

O THE lovely old, old farm
　　Where I passed my youthful days.
　Ere I knew the wide world's charm.
　Ere I trod the wide world's ways,—
Where I sported, blithesome, free
　As the bird that knows no harm!
Earth was Paradise to me,
　Down upon the old, old farm!

Every spot to me was dear—
　Every nook and quiet place.
As I muse, I feel a tear
2.　　Softly steal adown my face.
O, that I might rove once more
　Where the meadow holds its charm
Wander as in days of yore
　Down upon the old, old farm!

O, the bright dreams that I dreamed!
　O, those castles in the air,

How magnificent they seemed!
 Ah, but they were wondrous fair!
Honest, wholesome, healthful toil
 Stirred my blood and nerved my arm,
When I turned the fertile soil,
 Down upon the old, old farm.

3

When the waters are unbound,
 And the violets unfold,
And amid the fields around
 Busy workers I behold,—
Then I think of days long flown—
 Days that bore a wondrous charm—
Furrows drawn, seeds planted, sown,
 Down upon the old, old farm.

4.

When from ruby lips the rose
 Sends abroad its breath so sweet,
And along the wayside glows
 Witchingly the ripening wheat,—
Then I think of days of old,
 When, with bare and brawny arm,
Toilers gathered sheaves of gold,
 Down upon the old, old farm.

5.

When the heavens wear no gloom,
 And from meadows that abound
With sweet clover all abloom,
 Comes the mower's stirring sound,
Sweet to me as any chime,—
 Memory then recalls the charm
And the joys of haying-time
 Down upon the old, old farm.

6.

When the trees wear colors gay,
 And soft haze wraps hill and dale,
And I listen as I stray
 To the piping of the quail,—
Then I think, both night and morn,
 Of those days of sweetest charm,

7.

When we gathered in the corn,
  Down upon the old, old farm.

When the heav'ns beclouded frown,
  Shutting out the sunlight's ray,
And the rain comes pattering down
8.     Throughout all the livelong day,
Such days past I call to mind;—
  Even such days had a charm,
Real, though vague and undefined,
  Down upon the old, old farm.

In the quietude of night,
  When the world is hushed in sleep,
And I hear the breezes light
9.     Sigh as o'er the earth they sweep—
When in wakeful mood I lie,
  Slumber having lost its charm,
Oft I think of days gone by
  Down upon the old, old farm.

When the moon in splendor beams,
  When its argent light o'er all
In its soft effulgence streams,
10.     Nights long vanished I recall—
Nights as halcyon, clear and bland,
  That to Memory wed their charm—
O, those nights so witching, grand,
  Down upon the old, old farm!

O, the well-remembered haunts
  Of life's golden morning days!
Not a place the wide world vaunts,
11.     Or with aught of pride displays,
Howsoe'er renowned or rare,
  Has for me one-half the charm
Of those favorite spots so fair,
  Down upon the old, old farm!

O, the murm'ring tortuous stream
  That I strayed and played beside!

How majestic did it seem
12.    When I was a child—how wide!
I have been where streams far famed
    Roll their waves the eye to charm;
Deeper homage that one claimed
    Down upon the old, old farm.

O, the hill on whose high crown
    When a child so oft I stood,
And delightedly looked down—
13.    Gazed as far as e'er I could!
Mountain-like it seemed—how grand!
    Ever it possessed a charm;
What a joy thereon to stand,
    Down upon the old, old farm!

O, the fields I trod so oft!
    E'en the very atmosphere
Floating o'er them seemed more soft—
14.    Skies above more blue and clear—
Than elsewhere.   Each plot of ground
    Held for me a subtle charm
Only found within the bound
    Of the lovely, dear old farm!

O, the tree so huge and lone
    That so many years was seen
Rearing high its Titan cone,
15.    So imposing, so serene!
Like a sentry true and good,
    Ready to give forth alarm,
In the pleasant field it stood,
    Down upon the old, old farm.

O, that ancient, ancient tree!
    When most witheringly gleamed
Summer's sun o'er field and lea,—
16.    Heavenly its shelter seemed!
Waves it yet?   Or is it gone?
    Hath some axeman wrought it harm?

Would it could for aye live on,
　　Down upon the old, old farm!

O, the old barn 'neath whose roof,
　　On the hay so fragrant, soft,
When my childish heart seemed proof
17.　　'Gainst all woe, I romped so oft!
On its cross-beams, far above,
　　Where their nests were safe from harm,
Pigeons, cooing, told their love,
　　Down upon the old, old farm.

O, the old house where I dwelt
　　When a gay and careless boy,
Where with me kind Fortune dealt
18.　　Gently—gave me no annoy!—
O, each well-remembered room,
　　Which discomfort and alarm
Never entered, bringing bloom,
　　Down upon the old, old farm!

O, the well so deep and old!
　　How inspiring was each draught
Of its water clear and cold　　　.
19.　　That on sultry days was quaffed!
Borne to hands in harvest-field,
　　Heated men with weary arm,
What a solace did it yield,
　　Down upon the old, old farm!

O, the roses by the door,
　　White as snow-flakes undefiled!
Do they flourish as of yore—
20.　　As when bygone Summers smiled?
Free from stain as Angels' wings,
　　Free as they from blame and harm,
Were those types of all pure things
　　Down upon the old, old farm!

O, the lilacs by the walk!—
　　How I loved those beauteous flowers

244

# Idyls of Home.

And their fragrance! You may talk
Of Cathay's or Cashmere's bowers.
Nothing floral ever wreathed
In such regions wore the charm
Of those flowers whose breath I breathed
Down upon the old, old farm!

O, the orchard gnarled and old,
And the treasures that it bore!
Could I see the fruit that rolled
From its boughs to earth once more!
O, the blissful hours I knew—
Hours that had a lasting charm—
'Mid delicious things that grew
Down upon the old, old farm!

O, the bird-frequented grove
With its aged trees so tall!
What a joy it was to rove
In its depths I well recall!
How refreshing was its shade!
Hottest sun could wreak no harm
In the refuge that it made.
Down upon the old, old farm.

O, the willows by the lane!
They were dear—those wayside trees!
I can yet, with vision plain,
See them swaying in the breeze!
'Neath their leafy colonnade,
Hand in hand, or arm in arm,
With companions oft I strayed,
Down upon the old, old farm.

O, the paths I trod of yore—
Paths familiar, pleasant, sweet!
Are they grass-grown, used no more?
Are they trod by other feet?
O, those paths where to and fro,
With light step and swinging arm.

Oft I bounded long ago,
　　Down upon the old, old farm!

Oft I dream a gladsome dream,
　　And I seem returning then;
Throbs my heart with joy supreme!
26.　　I am coming home again—
Home to Mother, home to rest,
　　Home where naught can bring me harm,
Home to all that I love best,
　　Down upon the old, old farm!

Now, methinks, 'tis night.　Afar,
　　Shining on my darksome way,
Gleams the home-light like a star,
27.　　With its steady cheering ray!
Now I pass the threshold o'er—
　　O, let naught dissolve the charm!—
Let me be at home once more,
　　Down upon the old, old farm!

Let me be at home once more—
　　Home just as it used to be—
Shut the dear familiar door
28.　　'Twixt the outside world and me!
Let me say goodbye to woe,
　　Care, anxiety, alarm;
These I never used to know
　　Down upon the old, old farm.

Let me be at home once more,
　　From the ills that fret me free,
Life's best treasures all in store,
29.　　All its grandest scenes to be.
Let the witcheries of Hope
　　Glad me with their old-time charm,
Centered all within the scope
　　Of the farm—the dear old farm!

Let me be once more at home;
　　Let all things be as they were

# Idyls of Home.

Ere I ventured forth to roam—
30.    Made myself a wanderer!
Let me be at home again—
    Let me know once more the charm
That so strongly bound me then—
    Bound me to the old, old farm!

Ah, what days have gone for aye
    Since I from thy portal passed—
Since from thee I went away,
31.    Dear old home!—Beheld thee last
'Mid the stilly rural scene,
    Menaced by no hint of harm,
Smiling in the sunlight's sheen,
    Down upon the old, old farm.

I have wandered—wandered far—
    Gazed on many scenes renowned.
Scenes more marvellous there are,
32.    But none sweeter have I found
In my wanderings' ample range,
    Though not mindless of the charm
Of things fair in places strange;
    Lovelier seemed the old, old farm.

O, the countless cherished things
    Fancy brings before my eyes—
Things to which affection clings—
33.    Things I cannot cease to prize!
By fond Memory enshrined,
    They can never lose their charm,
Though they all are left behind,
    Down upon the old, old farm.

O, the myriad incidents
    That Remembrance conjures up,
And successively presents,
34.    Till o'erflows emotion's cup!
How my heart by them is stirred,
    Though all destitute of charm

Each one seemed as it occurred
　Down upon the old, old farm!

O, the voices that I hear!
　O, the faces that I see!
One by one they all appear—
35.　Those who smiled of yore on me!
I would clasp them to my breast
　With a true and loving arm,
As in vanished days so blest
　Down upon the old, old farm!

Of life's days could I restore
　Any that have taken flight,
Of its pleasures taste once more
36.　Any past and lost delight,
I would choose those days divine—
　Days that brought no woe, no harm,
And the sweet enjoyment mine
　Down upon the old, old farm!

# A Drink From the Old Well At Home.

HOW sultry, oppressive the weather!
　How welcome this spreading tree's shade!
No breeze that would waft e'en a feather
Since morn o'er the landscape has played.
Lo, a stream at the foot of the mountain
　Issues forth and falls downward in foam!
And I sigh, as I bend o'er the fountain,
　For a drink from the old well at home!

I have wandered afar, but I never
　Have drunk from a source so divine!
Fondest mem'ries, whose ties naught can sever,
2.　Around it for aye closely twine!

# Idyls of Home.

With affection akin to devotion,
  My heart thither turns as I roam!
With what tender, what soul-felt emotion
  I think of the old well at home!

Mortal lips ne'er a beverage tasted
  Sweet as that for whose drops I now pine!
Ev'ry siren enchantment is wasted
3.   That would lure me to sip the bright wine.
I fancy 'tis red with the slaughter
  Of millions allured by its foam.
O, give me the pure crystal water—
  A drink from the old well at home!

'Tis sacred—that old well—'tis holy!
  For in childhood, in youth's glowing days,
I slaked there my thirst.   Softly, slowly,
4.   As Remembrance her picture displays,
To the Past in a dream I am drifting!
  Yea, no longer in famed haunts I roam;—
To my lips the worn cup I am lifting,
  For a drink from the old well at home!

No water like that!   I am thirsting,
  Though again and again I have quaffed
This stream from the mossy rocks bursting.
5.   It refreshes me not like a draught
From the spot where Ambition—gay, golden
  Enchantress!—First reared her bright dome
In my soul.   O, that well deep and olden!—
  I sigh for the old well at home!

From scenes of celebrity turning,
  I long for the loved scenes of yore!
Within me arises a yearning
6.   To view the old homestead once more!
I behold it!   Fond Fancy discloses
  Its walls!—Yon huge pile with its dome
Is as naught to the house 'mid the roses,
  That stands by the old well at home!

There are springs far-renowned for their healing:
   Wondrous cures they are said to impart,
Heav'nly potency—almost—revealing.
7.     They relieve not my worn, homesick heart!
But a remedy sure and unfailing.
   Could I stand 'neath my native sky's dome,—
Balm of balms, o'er all heart-ills prevailing,
   I would draw from the old well at home!

Throng around me, ye memories tender.
   Ye visions that come without call!
To your magic my soul I surrender;
8.     Most precious to me are ye all!
Of what moment is Florence or Naples,
   Or London, or Paris, or Rome?
O, to stand once again 'neath the maples,
.   And drink from the old well at home!

# The Old Rocking-Chair.

T makes an odd sight in the parlor to-day,
   Drawn forth from its undisturbed nook:
It cuts but the sorriest figure, you say,
   As on it you carelessly look.
I place it alongside a mammoth affair—
   An ornate and new-fangled thing—
Ah, what a strange contrast you see 'twixt the pair—
   A peasant beside a proud king!
I need not dispute with you which is more fair,
But, given my choice, I prefer the old chair.

Its long paintless rockers are worn nearly through—
   In one I detect a slight crack;
Its arms, too, are loose—almost broken in two
2.     Some rounds in its old-fashioned back.
And yet 'tis a relic which no one could buy
   With all of the treasures of earth.

# Idyls of Home.

Surprised and nonplused, you may question me why
    I hold it of limitless worth.
Why is it so precious beyond all compare?
Ah, that is my dear mother's old rocking-chair!

That old rocking-chair! It calls up to my sight
    A face lying low in the tomb!
I see her with memory's vision so bright,
    In all of her womanhood's bloom!
3.    By fancy transported, I yet am a child,
    With childish illusions aglow!
Upon me she smiles, as upon me she smiled
    So long—O, so long, long ago,—
When foreign to me was all sorrow—all care!—
Serenely she sits in that old rocking-chair.

Ah, in it she sits as a queen on her throne!
    Leal subjects has she—loving hearts!
Not one will her sway disavow or disown,
    Whatever the world's crafty arts!
4.    Immovably fixed in my innermost soul
    Is each inculcation she gave:
She taught me to strive for a glorious goal—
    For things that defy the cold grave—
To live this life well—for the next to prepare;—
These lessons she taught from that old rocking-chair.

What magical wonders were wrought in that chair,
    In childhood's delectable hours!
Whatever arose hard for young hearts to bear—
    Appeared as a thorn in life's flowers—
5.    We flew to that throne of the queen of our home,
    And all was adjusted thereat!
O, never a ruler of Greece or of Rome
    Had potency equal to that!
With love's word and kiss, ev'ry ill vanished there,
Beneath mother's glance from the old rocking-chair!

What wonderful stories we heard on her knee,
    Ere drowsiness conquered our eyes—

What marvellous tales of strange lands—of the sea—
6.    What charming—what sweet lullabies!
And when we sore languished in illness—in pain—
    For childhood is oft-times distressed—
We found such relief as we ne'er could obtain
    Elsewhere—folded close to her breast!
Ah, never such shelter we found anywhere
As mother's arms gave in that old rocking-chair!

How sweet was repose, and how joyous each dream,
    As, clasped by her dear loving arm,
We sank into slumber—for well did we deem
7.    That nothing could there give us harm!
How soft each caress, and how soothing each tone,
    As backward and forward she rocked!
Ah, there we knew peace that we ne'er have since known,
    In fondest embrace tightly locked!
Small novices then, we were all unaware
That earth had no refuge like mother's old chair!

And often on midsummer long afternoons,
    When whispered no breeze anywhere—
When rest—complete rest—seemed the sweetest of boons,
8.    She sat in that sacred old chair:
By household tasks wearied—by cares that would rise—
    Yea, oft by anxieties deep,
She leaned her head backward, and, closing her eyes,
    Fell softly and sweetly asleep!
Ah, oft have I seen her, released from all care,
Ensconced thus within thee, thou dear rocking-chair!

I see her take down her old Bible once more,
    And, seating herself in that chair,
Peruse the worn Volume, the leaves turning o'er
9.    With thoughtful and reverent air.
Now laying it up in its place on the shelf,
    She tells us in grave, simple way,
Of Him who left Heaven—to death doomed Himself,
    That men might be happy for aye.

# Idyls of Home.

Our love for God's Truth had its origin there,
When gathered were we round that blessed old chair.

And when, the day's duties and labors complete,
   Our chairs to the fireside we drew,
And God's Word was read with solemnity meet—
10.   With care and with reverence due—
And all bowed in unison, kneeling around
   That family altar so blest,
And language of gratitude, true and profound,
   To Heaven's high Throne was addressed,—
How graciously then bent thy occupant there—
How humbly, devotedly, dear rocking-chair!

As vanished life's morn, and approached its broad day,
   And swiftly augmented our scope
Of action and view—when in serious way
11.   Began we with life's tasks to cope—
'Twas ever the same! Ay, whatever perplexed
   Our souls, or embittered our lot—
However our spirits were harassed or vexed,
   We hied to that halcyon spot
Where sat our consoler, so patient with care;—
To us she spoke peace from that old rocking-chair!

Made weary and sad by the burdens of life—
   The ills that I meet in its race—
Unquiet around me—unending mad strife
12.   And struggle for pelf and for place—
How often I yearn for the tender caress,
   The hopeful and comforting voice
Of her who was ready, whate'er my distress,
   To cheer me and bid me rejoice—
All trials with sympathy cordial to share—
How oft would I turn to that old rocking-chair!

But ah, it is vacant—that loved form is gone!
   The vision dissolveth apace!
Those eyes have beheld a more glorious dawn—
13.   Behold a more glorious place!

Her seat here is empty—no more to be filled;
  For far, far away in the skies
She bides.   Dazzling gleams from Jehovah's Throne gild
  The Mansion her soul occupies!
Ah, matchless memento!   I guard it with care—
My dear, sainted mother's old, worn rocking-chair!

Ah, this is a changeful—a mutable world!
  Not always may those whom we love
Be with us—their spirit-wings soon are unfurled,
14.     And join they the wing'd ones above!
How well I remember that saddest of days,
  When upward her soul took its flight!
A cloud seemed to shroud the October sun's rays,
  Although it was smilingly bright.
She tranquilly passed from earth's sorrow and care,
As oft she had fallen asleep in that chair.

Memorial cherished—forevermore dear!
  With sigh and with lingering look,
And—ay, I confess it, with many a tear,
15.     I place thee again in thy nook!
Amid keep-sakes sacred to home and its love
  Rest, heirloom of measureless worth!
Ah, when I shall go to those Regions above
  Forsaking all treasures of earth,
May others regard it—with deference spare
This Relic of relics—this old rocking-chair!

# The Old Door-Yard Tree.

BENEATH it merry children played,
    And workmen rested in its shade;
    Among its leaves blithe songsters sang,
  And gleefully their chorus rang
  Amid its canopy of boughs,
  When noon-dazed earth was fain to drowse.

# Idyls of Home.

Ah, long, long years the sun hath seen
Its branches bare, its branches green;
2. Long years the calm moon hath looked down
Upon it—silvered o'er its crown.
Uncounted storms have round it raved,
But each and all it well hath braved.

The children, grown, are far away,
Save him alone who writes this lay;
3. The birds that erstwhile sang—glad throng!—
Where, where are they?  I hear no song!
The lab'rers from earth's tasks are gone;
And still that old, old tree lives on!

It seems to welcome me once more,
As I approach it as of yore;
4. Yet sighs, methinks, for seasons flown,
For childhood's gay and careless tone,
For those once sheltered by its limbs—
For tranced wing'd singers' wordless hymns.

Lovely indeed art thou to me,
O, ancient and familiar tree!
5. What numberless sweet visions rise,
As thou dost greet again mine eyes!
For home—my old home—rears its walls
Hard by where thy broad shadow falls!

Ah, home, loved home—prized old-time home!
Though it has been my lot to roam
6. 'Mid various scenes well known to Fame
By lofty and historic name,
The sweetest spot of earth to me
Is here—beneath thy guardian Tree!

I stand within its shade again!
It is as sweet to me as when
7. In life's Spring I this refuge sought,
And gave myself to dreamful thought—
Revolved in soul the world so broad,
And yearned to tread where few have trod!

# Idyls of Home.

Why did I ever sigh to stray?
Why must I go once more away
8. From scenes where once I knew true joy,
And now find peace without alloy?
O, could my days have all been spent
Amid these scenes in calm content!

Long may'st thou flourish, olden Tree!
Sacred remembrancer to me
9. Of countless golden days gone by —
Of joy and sorrow—song and sigh!
While I go forth o'er earth to roam,
Guard, true, tried sentry, my old home!

Still prosperously wave, O, Tree!
Still spread abroad thy branches free—
10. Still rear aloft thy unbent form!
Tow'rd thee my heart is ever warm!
'Mid moonlight's shimmer, sunlight's glow.
Wave—thrive as thou did'st long ago!

O, Tree so venerably old!
Wave on 'mid all the manifold
11. Vicissitudes that come to all—
To ev'rything—whate'er befall!
'Mid peace, or elemental ire,
Still Heav'n-ward gracefully aspire!

Wave on in sheen, in pearly shower,
Wave on in balmy vernal hour,
12. In glorious Summer days wave on,
Serenely as in Summers gone;
Wave on when Autumn tints the leaves,
When melancholy Winter grieves!

Wave while mutation and decay
Are busy ev'ry passing day—
13. Busy with all things here below—
While men like shadows come and go—
While e'en familiar scenes grow strange,
To one who notes not ev'ry change!

I go, dear Tree! But ere I go,
My figure at full length I throw
14. Upon the sward, and thus, apart
From all, a song draw from my heart.
This tribute from a lover true
Deign to accept—'tis homage due.

Hail and farewell, O, aged Tree!
If I once more thy form may see
15. Some day amid the future years,
'Twill be with joy and grateful tears.
O, land-mark of the precious Past!
Thou shalt be cherished to the last!

# The Old Barn.

T stands by the roadside. 'Tis weather-stained, worn,
'Tis mossy, 'tis seamed and 'tis gray;
Its ruinous roof, here and there rent and torn.
Admits the full glare of the day.
Alas! It seems evermore mutely to mourn
For years that have long passed away!
Those years—ah, those years—with what fleetness they rolled,
'Mid changes—mutations untold, manifold!
O, structure breeze-shaken, forsaken and old.
To desuetude destined for ever and aye!
Thou victim art—helpless and succorless prey
To conscienceless, merciless, ruthless Decay!
Within thee the farm-hand no more whistles clear.
Nor in odd moments mirthfully spins his gay yarn.
Year in and year out, year succeeding to year.
Thou art silent—art voiceless and useless, old barn!

My soul well recalls how within its cracked walls
Stood steeds that were glossy and fine;
But now in its battered-up, shattered-up stalls,
Through which the winds dolesomely whine,

Save when some dull insect in sluggishness crawls,
2.    Of life exists never a sign!
No longer entrancingly flit to and fro,
So lightly and brightly, on pinions of snow,
The doves that in innocence long, long ago
Perched high on its beams—mammoth beams—overhead!
'Mid silence like that which abides with the dead,
The spider's gay gauze-work so flimsy is spread.
Its vane—its worn wavering, quavering vane—
    Points afar to a lonesome familiar broad tarn.
Ah me!   Wondrous phantasies wake in my brain,
    As I gaze on thy form so decrepit, old barn!


Of old in its loft—in its most spacious loft—
    Blithe children used often to play;
With laughter ecstatical, silvery, soft,
    Exhilarant, jubilant lay,
They clambered aloft—clambered thither full oft.
3.    To romp 'mid the sweet, fragrant hay;
But each sportive child, to maturity grown,
Departed as birdling when full-fledged has flown.
All empty, all dreary, all desolate, lone,—
Of all things most solemn—of all most forlorn—
Thou standest, old barn, 'mid broad acres of corn,
Wherein thou would'st shrink from the passer-by's scorn!
Still, still does thy quivering, shivering vane
    Point afar with gray bar to that old well-known tarn—
That lovely old lake which seemed wide as the main
    To the children who played 'neath thy rafters, old barn!


What memories centre—what fancies arise,
    Old barn, as thy form I behold!
What wonder if tears should well up in mine eyes,
    If sighs should escape uncontrolled?
Ah, though I have wandered 'neath far-distant skies,
4.    My heart to old scenes is not cold!
The view calls to mind long-past days of pure joy,
When I was a rollicking, frolicking boy—

When life had no burthen, no cark, no annoy—
Recalls youth's delightsomely glorious time,
When earth was to me so divine—so sublime—
And thou as a structure wast yet in thy prime!
No more wilt thou hear, as year fast follows year,
  The farm-boy's chirk whistle—his often-spun yarn.
Though all else contemn thee, to one thou art dear—
  To me thou art hallowed and precious, old barn!

# Haunts Of Boyhood.

WHEN the sun goes down in glory,
    And from distant Western hills,
    His last smile so transitory
Earth and Heav'n with brilliance fills,—
When the stars begin to shimmer
    In the welkin's arch above—
Shine with that serene, pure glimmer
    Which poetic eyes so love,—
Then, at close of span diurnal,
    Oft as in a dream I gaze,
With a joy almost Supernal,
    On the haunts of boy-hood days!

Ay, how pleasant to remember
    All loved scenes I used to know,—
Sweet in June—sweet in September—
    Sweet amid the Winter's snow—
Sweet, whatever season, weather!
    Where, each careless as an elf,
Roved young friends and I together,
    Mindless of earth's race for pelf.
Ah, because of incompleteness
    Of our knowledge of world's ways,
Scarce we knew or prized the sweetness
    Of those haunts of boy-hood days!

259

# Idyls of Home.

Fancy with sublime presentment
　Brings each precious scene to view!
O, what years of calm contentment
　'Mid those cherished scenes I knew!
Why did I, as those who squander
3.　Hoarded treasure, all forego?
Came a wild desire to wander
　Through the vast world to and fro.
Men were demi-gods in seeming,
　Earth was Eden to my gaze!
Ah, what hours I spent in dreaming,
　In those haunts of boy-hood days!


But illusions fleetly vanished
　As the dew touched by the sun;
Childhood's fancies soon were banished—
　Its enchantments all undone!
Though not doomed to mix or wallow
4.　With the basest of mankind,
I have met the false, the hollow,
　The ungrateful, unrefined;—
I have seen deceptive faces,
　Empty smiles have met my gaze.
Since I saw those old-time places—
　Stood in haunts of boy-hood days!


I have seen mankind so eager
　In its thirst for gold—its greed—
That its sympathies were meagre
　For a mortal's sorest need:
I have seen dissimulation,
5.　For the sake of social rank,
Or of civic elevation,
　Till my heart within me sank.
And my trust was sadly shaken,
　As this song of mine bewrays,
And I longed for scenes forsaken—
　Lone, sweet haunts of boy-hood days!

Of perplexities aweary—
Of vexations—trials sore—
I would turn from scenes grown dreary
To the halcyon scenes of yore—
From life's care and strain and anguish
6.     To those scenes so purely bright,
Where I knew no cause to languish,
Save for ills that now seem slight—
From each cankering annoyance
That on heart and spirit preys,
To those scenes of matchless joyance—
Peerless haunts of boy-hood days!

Sweeter seem to me the flowers
That around the old home spring
Than those elsewhere! In its bowers
Sweeter songsters, methinks, sing!
Seem the trees to wear more splendor.
7.     In their regal crowns of green,
Seem Heav'n's orbs with glance more tender
To survey the cherished scene
Where I dwelt in life's blest morning.
Ere I viewed its sober phase—
Of its real woes had warning!—
Blessed haunts of boy-hood days!

# The Old School-House.

RANK grasses wave where erst it stood:
The place is desolate and lone!
All who assembled here have grown
To manhood or to womanhood.

Once more I see, with mem'ry's eyes,
2.     The children as of yore at play;
In fancy I am young and gay,
With spirit cloudless as the skies!

261

Ah, vanished are those early days!
3.    Departed is life's golden morn!
    New pleasures and new hopes are born,
But cherished are youth's haunts and ways.

Some who with light feet pressed this spot
4.    Will tread the paths of earth no more:
    For them life's lessons all are o'er—
Its tasks and all its cares forgot.

The flowers blow, the grass is green,
5.    Around my childhood Idol's tomb:
    For her the flow'rs unfading bloom—
The flow'rs but by Immortals seen.

Not far away the brooklet flows,
6.    Where, with a fresh and wild delight,
    So oft we gathered lilies white
And stainless as untrodden snows.

Near by the willows stand, whose shade,
7.    When Summer noons poured down their rays.
    Gave shelter from the sun's fierce blaze.
What garlands of their boughs we made!

Lo, yonder is the well-loved slope,
8.    Where, when keen Winter piled his snow,
    We coasted—cheek and soul aglow—
Buoyant with peerless mirth and hope!

Still smiles invitingly the vale,
9.    In robe of verdure gayly dressed,
    Where we were wont to rove in quest
Of skyey violets meek and pale.

Ah, prized old structure! Thou art gone'
10.    Within thy faded walls no more
    Shall young souls gather earthly lore—
No more the needful lesson con!

Naught here attracts the stranger's gaze:
11.    Naught marvellous the eye can see;
Yet 'tis enchanted ground to me,
Hallowed by mem'ries of old days.

Still, as the swift years come and go,
12.    And Time on all things leaves his trace,
This aye shall seem a sacred place—
Yea, long as life shall last below!

# The Old Village Church.

THE old village church—O, the old village church!
    Aloft in its belfry the pigeons still perch;
With impudence woeful, irreverence dire,
The woodpecker still tunnels holes in its spire!
It stands as it stood on its site by the green,
With face to the sun-rise, sublimely serene;
Apart from all traffic, all bustle, all strife,
Suggestive for aye of a more peaceful life—
Of all for which mortals on earth vainly search,
Ah, dear to me yet is that old village church!

The old village church—O, the old village church!
On high, where the pigeons so airily perch,
The old bell still swings in its place to and fro,
And sends out such peals as I well used to know.
2.  Ah, yes!  It still rings as it rang in my youth,
To call weary souls to a fountain of truth!
How oft then, obeying its summons so sweet,
I hasted away to that sacred retreat,
And found pure delight—joy that guerdoned my search
In no other place—in that old village church!

That bell—ah, that bell of the old village church,
Around which the pigeons erst perched and yet perch!
How sweetly its tones stole o'er valley and hill,
On bright Sabbath morns when the landscape was still!

**263**

3.
How charming were they on serene Sabbath eves!
What glamor hangs round it—what spells Mem'ry weaves!
What genuine sympathy seemed in each knell!
What presage of joy in each wedding-call fell!
Its clear sound the innermost soul seemed to search
Of all who for worship approached that old church!

The old village church—O, the old village church!
None ever missed peace who sincerely made search
Before its loved altar!   At that holy spot,
How many have found what the world giveth not:--
4.
How many have there found the only true way
That leads to a Country unmarred by decay!
How many I long ago knew were there blest,
Who since have departed—have entered their rest—
Sleep now on yon hill-side, 'neath pine-tree or birch!
How many have well called thee blessed, old church!

That church—ah, that old-fashioned, quaint village church!
Its history amply repays all research!
How many therein have been mated for life--
By union made strong for existence's strife!
5.
How many have pallid and pulseless there lain,
For whom, 'mid rites solemn, descended grief's rain!
What anthems, what dirges have there been up-sent!
What praises impassioned—what wails of lament
Have startled the pigeons up there on their perch--
And yonder wing'd vandal who mars thee, O, church!

The old village church—O, the old village church,
Within whose high steeple the pigeons aye perch!
How many within its loved pulpit have stood—
God's own chosen servants—the noble— the good—
6.
Proclaiming His Word with unfaltering voice—
Beseeching men early to make a wise choice—
To choose the good part. as did Mary of old,
Which cannot be taken—Heav'n's joys manifold—
Entreating men ever their hearts well to search—
Thy flock has known zealous, true shepherds, old church!

The old village church—O, the old village church!
I watch as the pigeons fly up to their perch—
I watch as the woodpecker, wickedly gay,
Bores in his sharp dwelling a new entrance-way.
7.   And muse, while my vision is thus upward cast,
On days that for ever and ever are past!
Though Time all around thee vast changes hath wrought,
To thee hath his hand only few as yet brought:—
Ay, thou art less altered, I find in my search
'Mid prized olden scenes, than aught else, dear old church!

Still stand as thou standest, beloved old church!
Still yield the innocuous pigeon a perch;
But ne'er shouldst thou condescend refuge to yield
To long-billed despoiler thy spire's cone gives shield!
8.   Still, still as the years with their onward sweep glide,
Thy portal to world-weary souls open wide!
Still, still may the living within thee be blest,
And from thee the lifeless be carried to rest!
May tempest ne'er cause thee to topple or lurch—
May Time and Decay touch thee lightly, O, church!

# Home Dreams.

IN dreams—sweet dreams—I oft revisit thee,
  Dear home, ensconced 'mid trees so far away;
  And as in childhood's happy hours of play—
Ah, hours of pure, incomparable glee!—
I tread the old paths, buoyant, blithesome, free!
  Again earth seems a Paradise most gay—
  An Age of Gold each swiftly-passing day!
Cares, doubts and fears like sombre shadows flee.
I see the sunshine gild thee as of old,
  I feel the fragrant winds that round thee sigh;
    I wander 'mid the green fields as of yore!
I waken—other scenes mine eyes behold:
  Those fancies—blissful fancies!—Fade and die—
    Alas! I am a care-worn man once more.

# A

# PORTFOLIO

# OF

# LYRICS.

# A Portfolio Of Lyrics.

❖

## Vox Populi.

LONG Tyranny girdled the earth with her sway,
    And scoffed at the precepts of Justice and Duty;
But now shines a brilliant—a jubilant day,
    And Freedom enchants the broad world with her
    beauty!
The rod of Oppression no longer men kiss!
    For power despotic is there an aspirant?
The cry of our Era of Progress is this:—
    *"LONG LIFE TO THE PEOPLE, AND DEATH*
      *TO THE TYRANT!"*

*THE PEOPLE* shall reign from the north to the south,
    From east unto west, all the blue heavens under!
Who dares to say nay?  Let the cannon's black mouth
2.    Each adverse voice still with its terrible thunder!
Ah, straight let the tomb of Oppression be made!
    Down, down, O, presumptuous, haughty aspirant
To laurels secured but by tyrannous blade!
    *"LONG LIFE TO THE PEOPLE, AND DEATH*
      *TO THE TYRANT!"*

Away with the sceptre!  Away with the crown!
    And down with the throne!  Dissipate their false glory!
Flout, flout the gay robe!—Rend to shreds—cast it down!
3.    Let Royalty's glamor exist but in story!

Uphold not the monarch—the monarch will fall!
Discountenanced—aidless—soon fails the aspirant!
Let Liberty's pæan resound over all:—
  "*LONG LIFE TO THE PEOPLE, AND DEATH
    TO THE TYRANT!*"

# The Ruined Sea-Side Castle.

**M**ILDLY, yet wildly, ivy round it wreathes;
    To reeling walls brown mantling mosses cling;
    Apartments that once housed a loose old king
    Are vacuous—voiceless.   Shrilly round it breathes
The fretful wind.   Regretful ocean seethes
  Below.   The gloom of the swart raven's wing
  Is over all.   No banners gay folds fling
From tower—no fuddled warder sword unsheathes.
The "glory" is departed.   Nevermore
  Shall these halls' walls shake with outrageous mirth,
    Nor tameless, shameless Royalty's haunts be.
Thy revels Sodomitical are o'er;
    Thy titled lechers curse no more the earth.
    Lone—lorn art thou, O, Castle by the sea!

# The Fated City.

*Port Royal—June 7th, 1692.*

**D**WELLERS erudite and witty
    Had that celebrated city—
    It had bards who sang sublimely—
      Minstrels skillful with their lyres—
    Architectural marvels glorious,
      Meet to charm the most censorious—
Mansions of surprising grandeur—
    Welkin-piercing domes, towers, spires!

Ah, that city! It had riches!
It had beauties—very witches!
Versed were they in all enchantments—
All arch blandishments benign!
2.    But ill-gotten was its treasure,
And its belles lived but for pleasure:
Shirked its beauties all high duties,
And its gold had evil shine.

Vice was rampant in that city;
Bacchanalian shout and ditty
Issued aye from revel-haunted—
Truly devil-haunted halls;
3.    Virtue was for absence prominent;
Bold debauchery was dominant:
'Twas a duplicate Gomorrah!—
How its tale the soul appalls!

Came a day of cloudless brightness;
Scarce a breath-like breeze in lightness
Wantoned o'er the breast of ocean;
All was halcyon as could be—
4.    Naught above, below portended
That the day and sway were ended.
Of that city—haughty city—
Godless city by the sea.

All at once upon that city
Far too profligate for pity,
An astounding doom descended—
Haply judgment Heaven-sent—
5.    Nature, so reposeful seeming,
Suddenly ceased placid dreaming—
Trembled like a frenzied demon
Moved by untold wrath long pent!

Fiercely heaved earth's bosom under
That doomed town! With voice of thunder,
Ocean, like affamished monster,
Uttered a voracious roar!—

**273**

6.    Ah, with lightning land-ward motion,
      Wild—deliriously wild Ocean—
Forward sprang, and took that city
    To itself forevermore!

    Yea, upon that stately city,
    Meriting no drop of pity,
Where their nameless, shameless orgies
    Held voluptuaries bold,
7.    Leapt the deep in heedless madness—
    Boundless maniacal gladness—
In demoniacal rapture
    And undreamed-of fury rolled!

    Ah, the crying of the dying!
    Ah, the yelling of the flying,
As from lecherous embraces
    Rushed they forth to Death's embrace —
8.    With unrivalled trepidation,
    And unmeasured consternation,
Mad with troubles, sank 'mid bubbles
    To subaqueous resting-place!

    Ah, the blasphemy and cursing,
    As now thronging, now dispersing,
Pallid votaries of Venus,
    Bacchus' bloated devotees,
9.    Like mere pismires, hither, thither,
    Ran for refuge—none knew whither!
But one common wish—for safety—
    Had those quaking debauchees!

    It was vain! Creation spurned them!
    Wheresoever Terror turned them,
They were fronted by disaster—
    Gaping earth and hungry deep!
10.    Here they hurried—there they skurried—
    Baffled, worried—flustered, flurried—
Till apace—sole anæsthetic—
    Came the ultimate dread sleep!

# A Portfolio of Lyrics.

Yawned the sepulchres, and yielded
   Those their confines long had shielded—
Dead and perishing commingled
   In the raging, howling tide!
11.   Ah, what Pandemonium followed!
   Earth disgorged and Ocean swallowed,
Then in weird regurgitation
   Spewed them—strewed them far and wide!

Land and sea, fresh horrors wreaking,
   Smothered their frail victims' shrieking—
All anathemas and wailings
   With relentless rigor stilled!
12.   'Twas the hand of Vengeance, surely—
   Superhuman dealing purely—
Ay, 'twas righteous retribution,
   By Omnipotence fulfilled!

When the wave is stillest, clearest—
   No rude wind thou feelest—fearest—
Rowing out from shore brief distance,
   And intently gazing down,
13.   You may see that city sunken—
   See its turrets sway like drunken
Titans, as the waters, swelling,
   Move above that ill-starred town.

There its cross in mockery lifting,
   Ocean-monsters round it drifting,
You may see the old Cathedral,
   Standing in its watery tomb:
14.   And the halls where met to revel
   Those leal minions of the Devil—
Where Carnality in triumph
   Reigned until that day of doom.

In and out of hall and mansion,
   Through that sea-tombed town's expansion,
Finny wanderers glide ever
   'Mid those ghastly, ghostly forms—

275

15.    Bones of those who delectation
        Sought in deepest dissipation—
O'er two centuries have sported,
    In innumerable swarms.

    Ah, that buried city olden!
    Ah, those ill-got treasures golden!
Ah, those blushless, shameless beauties'
Ah, those works of Art so grand!
16.    Listless waters o'er them gleaming
        Lie in calmness, as if dreaming.
Ocean like a ruthless siren
    Guards its prey with aspect bland.

# Sonnet To The Stars.

HOW beautiful ye make the heav'ns at night,
    Ye countless hosts of Stars, when, serried there,
    Ye look on us! At times ye seem to share
    Our thoughts, desires, affections! When in might
Trials and woes have come my heart to smite—
    Its peace to mar—when menaced by Despair—
    I oft have found, in gazing at your fair,
Sweet beacons, hope, serenity—delight!
O, mystic orbs—worlds, suns beyond our reach!
    How glorious ye make that upper sea!
    What beings tread your globes we cannot know:
Yet unto me as clear as mortal speech
    Is your mute language! Ye reveal to me
    Lessons of Him who formed you thus to glow'

# The Enchantress.

ER eyes were like stars in their brightness,
  And made the beholder rejoice!
Her hands were like lilies in whiteness,
  Her feet were like fairies' in lightness,
And hers was a seraph-like voice!
O'er snowy keys her fingers strayed,
And rippling, witching music made;
I well recall the airs she played,
March, schottische, waltz and serenade,--
  Deferring in all to my choice!

My Queen Cleopatra!  Your glances
  Were fire to my soul and my heart!
They woke all the olden romances,
They lured me to make love's advances
2.    With far more of fervor than art!
Like him of old who cast aside
Crown, sceptre, purple, kingly pride,
For her sweet sake for whom he died,
I followed thee, O, siren guide!
  What passion thy smile could impart!

I wander and ponder in sadness
  Where oft-times together we trod,
In days of rare beauty and gladness,
When I, in strange folly and madness,
3.    Was slave to your beck and your nod!
But ah, the dream, thank Heav'n, is past!
The viewless chain that bound me fast
· Is broken, thrown aside at last—
From my soul's fane its Idol cast!—
  Henceforth I will kneel but to God!

# After Long Years.

HERE 'neath this tree, where long ago we parted.
    Amid the glorious Summer night I stand!
    Here last I lingeringly clasped thy hand.
    While from mine eyes impetuous tear-drops started.
By every token, I was broken-hearted.
    Not so wast thou —thyself thou couldst command;
    Affection bound thee but with silken band—
Only a fleet pang through thy bosom darted.
After long years! This spot is still romantic—
    Both sweet and sad; for love was buried here--
    Love pure as ever reigned in mortal breast!
But Time heals all. Emotions, howe'er frantic,
    Subside. Although Fate's fiat seemed severe,
    False one! 'Tis well that we thus walk apart!

# The Song She Sang.

I DREAM I hear the song she sang—
    A lay divinely sweet!
    That silver strain—ah, how it rang!—
    With pathos how replete!
'Twas rendered with such flawless art
It thrilled my inmost soul and heart;
It made the diamond tear-drop start—
    That song for angels meet!

What potent magic had that song!
    'Twas at the gloaming hour—
The time when tend'rest mem'ries throng.
    And music hath such power!
Old hopes with all their pristine glow,
Old joys and griefs with flood tide flow.

Returned—and scenes of long ago—
   Thronged street and shady bower!

How calm those vesper moments were!
   Reposeful Nature seemed
A rapt and breathless listener,
   Or so I fondly deemed.
3. The ling'ring fires of sunset blazed,
And on them absently I gazed,
While that bright nymph her voice upraised—
   I listened, gazed and dreamed.

Yes! I recall the song she sang,
   The singer, too, as well:
And though *that* mem'ry costs a pang
4.    Whereof I scarce need tell.
That song—no fragment, but the whole—
Shall hold its place, shrined in my soul,—
While eviternal æons roll,
   Within me throb and dwell.

# A Rhapsody.

*H*, what a form! Ah, what a face!
What matchless symmetry and grace,
Young maid, are thine! I hope thou art
As beautiful of soul and heart!

2. For, void of virtue,—to be terse—
Beauty hath only power to curse.
With this, her sway o'er heart and mind,
To please and bless, is unconfined.

3. If thou as flawless art within
As outwardly—pure—free from sin—
Angels scarce more Supernal are,
Amid their holy Realm afar!

279

# Our Meeting.

*A LOVER'S REMINISCENCE.*

### I.

WITH smile supremely tender,
    Shone Autumn's skies above,
That day of mellow splendor,
    When first I met my love!

2.
Amid a convocation—
    A multitudinous throng—
One woke my admiration—
    One held my vision long.

3.
Yet 'twas not merely beauty
    Or grace that charmed my gaze,
But sweet regard for duty
    In all her looks and ways.

4.
O, sweetest of romances!
    How throbbed my wakened heart,
Beneath those bright, pure glances,
    Made magic by love's art!

5.
How pleasant was our meeting!
    How sweet each interview
That followed our first greeting,
    Until we bade adieu!

### II.

6.
We parted wond'ring whether
    We e'er should meet again,
And walk and talk together
    As happily as then;—

7.
We parted marv'ling whether
    We e'er again should meet,
And thus enjoy together
    Companionship so sweet:

And as apart we wandered,
8.    Each of the other dreamed,
And life seemed sorely squandered.
    However Fortune beamed.

While severed thus, we wondered
9.    Each of the other's fate;
While we were thus dissundered,
    The world seemed desolate!

We craved each other's presence
10.    As home-sick ones at sea
Long for the home-scene's pleasance—
    Yearn 'mid its joys to be!

## III.

We met again, and sweetly
11.    Acquaintanceship renewed—
We met once more, and meetly
    The golden Past reviewed.

Soft-murmured words were spoken,
12.    Heard but by One on high—
Vows that could but foretoken
    Bliss such as hath the Sky—

Vows that shall never, never
13.    Be riven e'en by Death—
Vows that shall not dissever
    When shall surcease this breath—

Vows that in Realm Supernal,
    Which peerless pæans thrill,
'Mid bowers sempiternal,
    Shall link our spirits still!

'Twas in the sweet September,
15.    And skies were bland above; —
Ah, well do I remember
    When first I met my love!

# The Ship And The Iceberg.

*A* STREAM of ice flowed through a polar land—
With muggish, sluggish current sought the sea,
Whose waves upheaved it till a part set free
Departed from the frigid Arctic strand,
And southward sailed where vaster seas expand.
A ghostly Titan, scorning tempest's glee,—
Disdaining from the storm's fierce hosts to flee—
Slowly it voyaged to regions balmy, bland.
A ship sailed from a sunny Southern shore—
A gallant ship with gallant souls aboard—
Destined afar; where Northern waters lie.
The mist-robed, cloud-crowned Ice-king downward bore
Ah! Cruelly his bark that fair ship gored.
And bright eyes weep beneath the South's bright sky!

# Entree Of March.

*B* LOW, loud-voiced, proud-voiced Winds—heralds of
March!
Come forth. O, first-born Offspring of the Spring!
O, Nature's orchestra—tranced warblers—sing!
Smile, gold-eyed Sol, from firmamental arch!
Scatter thy life-charged beams!—not such as parch
Earth's bosom—rays of bland, soft warmness fling!
Release the streams—we miss their murmuring—
Scoff—doff—hurl off the shroud that wraps the larch!
Lo, icy Winter hath relaxed his clasp!
The heav'ns assume more fresh, more vivid blue,
And Nature smiles in calmy, palmy gladness!
Ah, soon will flow'rs spring up to woo our grasp!
Soon will the landscape don porraceous hue,
And joy-fraught hours atone for hours of sadness!

# A Spring Rhapsody.

THE gray birds of Winter have flown from our bowers,
    The gay-plumaged songsters are coming again;
    Now rise in their charmingness sweet early flowers.
        And green grasses garnish the brook-threaded glen!
Again the warm fragrance-fraught south-winds are blowing;
    The sun smiles on high like a conquest-proud king;
The waters unbound are with gaysome sounds flowing—
    All things wear new life in the freshness of Spring!

Ah, welcome the riddance of days dark and dreary—
    The season investing the earth with a pall—
Converting each breeze to a weird miserere!
2.     A reign of pure loveliness spreads over all!
List! Music, rich music is ev'rywhere ringing—
    Rapt birds in the wood-land—tranced birds on the wing—
Blithe Nature's own minstrels bravuras are singing,
    In hail to bewitchful and halcyon Spring!

What joy to breathe in the pure air in its sweetness,
    To look up to heavens so blue and so clear,
To view the bright streams as they run on in fleetness,
3.     The bright, charmful flow'rs as again they appear!
Ah, yes! 'Tis delight verging on the Supernal
    To witness the pleasure of ev'ry live thing
That creeps, walks or flies, in this period vernal—
    This advent of beautiful, bountiful Spring!

# April Phantasy.

APRIL, like some most passionate nymph art thou—
    Half smiles —half tears! Gayly thou trip'st along,
    Witchingly beauteous, thy lips in song.
        And exquisitely garlanded thy brow!
Poets behold and high delight avow;
    But grieved that some amid the rushing throng
    Adore thee not, thou weepest at the wrong—
In fits of violent woe, meseems, dost bow!
Ah, Life! Thy symbol is an April day,
    Half sun, half shower! Yet truly not in vain
    We see thy brightness oft-times fade away;—
We learn to prize it. I have seen it wane.
    Of all my days, the goldenest—most gay—
    Was April's—when the sun shone after rain!

# Dawn-Song.

A HINT of light is in the East;
        The darker shades of night are gone:
    Swiftly yon radiance is increased;—
        Hail, beauteous Dawn!

2.  Yon hoary peak grows roseate now;
        No longer it stands cold and wan:
    A crown of gold bedecks its brow,—
        Thy gift, O, Dawn!

3.  But, though thou showest tints most fair,
        And charmest all thou smilest on,
    Thou wakest Man to toil and care.
        O, witching Dawn!

4.  Soft slumber came with shadowy Night,
        Whose curtains thou aside hast drawn;
    Labor returneth with the light;
        Yet hail, sweet Dawn!

# O, The Beauty Of The Sky!

*THE* beauty of the sky,
When the clouds are out of sight,
And the golden sunbeams fly
From the chariot of Light,
Making all the azure bright,
In their sally from on high—
Making gaysome vale and height—
All the scenes that round us lie—
Whatsoe'er our eyes descry!

But anon dark clouds arise,
Bidding sunlight's glow depart;
And the red keen lightning flies,
Rending Heav'n with zig-zag dart;
And from rolling nimbus' heart
Black, impervious to our eyes,
Devastating torrents start;
And the tempest raves and cries,
And deep thunder's voice replies!

Yet if never paled the skies,
Never ceased the sun to shine,
Never cloud of Titan size
Came with visage saturnine,
Came with aspect mad, malign,
In demoniacal guise,
To obscure Heav'n's face divine—
If no cloud came on this wise,
How could we the sunshine prize?

# The Thunder-Shower.

MID-DAY was bright, but soon a cloud uprose
 Far in the West—O, ebon was its frown!
 Not long the sun in smilingness looked down:
  Anon gloom gathered as at daylight's close-
Fell an untimely twilight. Night's repose
 Not quieter makes wood-land, field and town
 Than grew they then. From vale to mountain crown,
Reigned silence deep as earth at midnight knows.
A few huge drops from out the welkin rushed
 Swift vanguard of a host decillions strong:
  A crash horrific burst Heav'n's raven dome!
Fierce torrents poured. Scarce e'en an instant hushed,
 The thunder's voice re-echoed loud and long.
  'Tis past. Wide rivers o'er their high banks roam!

# Rhapsodic Sonnet To An Errant Cloud.

BEWITCHFUL Cloud, that softly floatest by,
 Unsoiled as Heav'n's own flakes, high overhead!
 Thou seem'st an isle formed but for Seraph tread
  'Mid amethystine ocean of yon sky
A drifting isle! No other cloud is nigh
 No cloudlet e'en doth gauzy mass outspread
 Anigh thy snow-hued marge. Whence hast thou fled?
Whither dost glide in sinuous course on high?
Emblem of pureness—type of truth and love—
 Of all things noble, tranquil, winsome, sweet!
  I would my soul were stainless as thou art!
Still traverse yon cerulean deep above!
 Thine is a ministry with power replete:
  Thou hast refreshed my sad world-wearied heart!

# A June Sonnet.

NYMPH crowned with roses most divinely fair!—
    Gay roses of the garden—roses wild—
    Red roses—roses snowy, undefiled—
  Roses diffusing fragrance ev'rywhere!
Thy beauty is, meseems, beyond compare!
    Ah, June! More sweetly radiant days ne'er smiled
    Than these of thine, so songful, cloudless, mild—
Free from cold wind and from oppressive glare!
O, Month Belov'd! Thou dost recall my youth,
  Whose hopes, unfolding like thy blowing roses,
    Made earth a boundless garden to my sight!
Though some have false, ephemerous proved, in truth,
  On some my heart with fondness still reposes,
    And thou dost bring me, as of old, delight!

# Sundown Musings.

THE sun is down! How brilliant the day's close!
    How fair the West with hues gold, Tyrian, red!
    Anon the coyish stars peep forth o'erhead,—
  More bold beseem as twilight's deepness grows!
Lo, Venus in sereneness yonder glows!
    Softly the shades of gloaming overspread
    The halcyon earth. I rove with hasteless tread,
Semi-oblivious of life's tasks, cares, woes.
O, Vesper Hour! Thy fairhood I much prize!—
  Thy stilly scenes most passionately love!
    A world of poesy I find in thee,
O, Even!—In thy iridescent skies—
  In thy Supernal calm, below, above!
    What grateful thoughts thou dost suggest to me!

287

# The Mountain Spring.

O LANDSCAPE almost overcome with heat!—
  Grasses that curl—declining, pining flowers—
  A wood with leaves adroop for want of showers—
  A tideless brooklet coursing once most sweet,
Now dried-up meads! Where Earth and Heaven meet—
  Lo, on yon peak, which welkin-ward so towers,
  A tuft of foliaceous trees embowers
A font, whose stream hastes down my steps to greet!
Ah, how it sparkles as it hither leaps,
  Like laughing childhood when in joyous play
  It chases some craved glorious winged thing!
O'er rocks and ferns it runs and flies and creeps,
  Freshening, brightening all about its way!
  Gush forth for aye, O, gaysome, playsome spring!

# When The Year Is In Its Prime.

I N the golden Summer-time,
  When the year is in its prime,
  Ah, existence is sublime!
  When the trees and fields are green,
And the skies deep-blue, serene,
Bearing not a hint of gloom,
And the roses are in bloom,
Seems the world like Heav'n's own clime—
When the year is in its prime!

In the golden Summer-time,
When the year is in its prime,
How the Poet's numbers chime!
Ah, what charms doth he descry,
2.    Round, beneath him, and on high!

Scenes harmonious are—complete
Sounds euphonious are—most sweet!
All his soul is full of rhyme,
When the year is in its prime!

In the golden Summer-time,
When the year is in its prime,
What a joy the hills to climb—
'Mid the heary mountains roam,
3.   Or to stroll where sea-waves foam,
Viewing Nature at her best,
With the fullest sense of rest,
On bright sands, or 'mid sweet thyme,
When the year is in its prime!

In the golden Summer-time,
When the year is in its prime,
Feast our eyes on scenes sublime,
Typical of those above,
4.   Where are perfect peace and love,
Perfect knowledge, perfect bliss,
Where there comes not aught amiss—
Loss or sorrow, want or crime!—
Ah, the year's delightsome prime!

# The Outlaw's Fate.

HE lurks amid the forest black:
Unceasingly he must beware;
Death seeks him hourly ev'rywhere
Is evermore upon his track!

That reckless hand is stained with blood!
2.   Why should the Messenger so grim
Seem dread—seem hideous to him
Who oft hath viewed life's gushing flood?

He knoweth not the joys of home:
3.      Within his soul is Love no guest:
      Peace is a stranger to that breast:
He will not—cannot cease to roam.

He is by all that breathe abhorred!
4.      An outraged world he hath defied,
      And striveth from its wrath to hide;
With Earth—with Heav'n he long hath warred.

He hath sent many to the tomb
5.      With no compunction—no regret!
      A price upon his head is set;
Hath he not merited such doom?

Even at midnight's silent hour
6.      In dreams he stands 'mid scenes of strife;
      His days with countless fears are rife;
To soothe his spirit naught hath power.

There is a movement of the boughs!
7.      They come—the vassals of the Law!
      He starts, but is not whelmed with awe:
The sight doth all his fury rouse!

He shrinks with oath and glance of ire—
8.      A weapon bright gleams in his grasp!
      He holds it with a faltering clasp.
His foes but wait the word to fire.

"Hands up!" Is their bold leader's cry.
9.      Hands up, O, man of crimes untold—
      Of deeds abhorrent manifold!
Hands up, red-handed man,—or die!

Hands up! Ah, will his vaunt prove true,
10.      Whose lips so often have declared
      That ne'er would he who ne'er man spared
Ask life of those who might pursue?

Hands up! Aloft he will not throw
11.      Those guilty members—will not live!
      His captor thus is forced to give
The fateful mandate:—"Lay him low!"

An instant deadly volley sped!
12.   One wild, weird curse was heard—no more.
      The gruesome tragedy is o'er:
A prone form lies 'mid ferns made red.

"Tis done! He who made many fall
13.   Himself is victim now and prey;
      He died as some fell beast at bay,
With one anathema for all!

Godless—relentless to the last!
14.   Who knows?—Perchance a mother's tears
      And prayers pursued him years on years!
Who knows that wayward mortal's past?

Alas for him who bleeding lies!
15.   For he was once a sinless child.
      Like those on whom the Master smiled—
Type of the Pure Ones of the skies!

Alas for him whose corse lies there!
16.   Why will men turn from paths of right
      To paths that lead to darkest night,
To deepest anguish and despair?

# The Fate Of The Lilies.

No longer they bloom on the hill, in the valley,
      No longer the breeze wafts their fragrancy on:
No longer they nod where the pure waters dally
      In Summer's soft kisses—the lilies are gone!

No longer they shine in their wonderful splendor,
2.    To lighten my heart when with care I am wan;
The sky may be cloud-free, the golden light tender,
      I long for their grandeur—those flow'rs dead and gone!

At morn and at even I lonesomely wander,
3.     Since vanished their forms from the hem of the lawn:
And driven to moralize deeply, I ponder
    The fate of the beautiful lilies now gone!

Thus ev'rything lovely we give happy greeting
4.     Enchants us, and lo! From our gaze 'tis withdrawn!
Like yours, perished lilies, Man's life is but fleeting—
    Like you he blooms briefly, and soon he is gone!

# September's Advent.

SEPTEMBER! Most majestic is thy mien!
    In chariot of gairishness untold,
      Thou comest, scattering abroad thy gold!
    The stately maples, late arrayed in green,
Are clad in robes of Phoebus' hue and sheen!
    The lake, like some blue banner wide unrolled,
      Lies glistering and gorgeous to behold,
Befringed with forests saffrony, serene!
September reigns o'er earth and sea and sky,
    And, though the bloom of Summer days is gone,
      Fresh glories Nature spreads below, above!
O, when life's August shall have glided by,
    May its September come as grandly on,
      Golden with wisdom, friendship, faith and love!

# Golden Leaves Among The Green.

IN the early Autumn days,
    When the hills are wrapt in haze,
    When in multitudinous ways
    Her decline the year betrays,
    Then it is that they are seen
    Golden leaves among the green.

Then in groves and woodlands wide,
Where before our gaze descried
2.    But one hue on every side,
Here and there they are espied.
How they change the sylvan scene—
Golden leaves among the green!

We behold them and we sigh,
Thinking of bright days gone by,
3    Of the chill, bleak season nigh—
Dreary earth and eerie sky.
But their look is all serene—
Golden leaves among the green.

All must bow to Nature's sway:
Loveliest moments cannot stay;
4.    Swiftly day glides after day;
Bloom is followed by decay.
Potent symbols these, I ween,—
Golden leaves among the green.

Life is passing like the year:
Fast its glories disappear;
5.    Autumn all too soon draws near.
There are hints of days more drear—
Waning freshness, changing mien—
*Golden leaves among the green.*

# "Where The Leaves Are Never Brown."

O THE sunny days are past..
    And the darksome days have come!
Heav'ns are thickly overcast,
    Woods are voiceless—lorn and dumb!
Winds by no means fragrant. bland.
    Shake the forest's frost-touched crown!

I am thinking of a Land
  Where the leaves are never brown—
Where the roses aye are grand,
  And the leaves are never brown.

2.

Not some region of the South,
  Where but mundane flowers smile,
By some tropic river's mouth,
  Or on some far tropic isle,—
But a Country far more blest
  Than those spots which win renown
From the Winter-shunning guest—
  One where leaves are never brown—
One by steps immortal pressed,
  Where the leaves are never brown.

3.

There is all for which we yearn—
  All we sigh for evermore!
Here gay Summer will return—
  Brilliant days will come once more—
But ere long will clouds appear,
  And perchance dread tempest's frown;
And the skies are *always* clear
  Where the leaves are never brown—
In that Land without a tear,
  Where the leaves are never brown.

4.

Never there are dolesome days:
  Never there is storm or strife—
Aught we loathe, abhor, dispraise
  In this changeful world and life!
There our loved ones for us wait—
  Those in earth's bleak breast laid down—
Far beyond all adverse fate,
  Where the leaves are never brown—
Just beyond the shining Gate,
  Where the leaves are never brown.

# The Old, Old Story-- Life.

*IFE!* 'Tis an old, old story,
   The story of a day—
The sunrise with its glory,
   The noontide's dazzling ray,
The sunset's transitory,
   And Titianesque display—
Rehearsed till Time makes hoary
   The sprightly and the gay.

Yea, 'tis a story olden,
   With variations new;
To souls with fancies golden
   Its beauties are not few:
Souls whom high hopes embolden
   It thrills with rapture true;
Its grandeur is beholden
   To each one's point of view.

Earth's hosts are coming, going;
   The tale glides swiftly on,
Most ravishingly flowing
   To those in youth's bright dawn;
Less fascinating, glowing,
   To those whom cares make wan:
Scarce worthy heeding, knowing,
   To those whose hopes are gone.

Life's story is most glorious
   To those who form and hold
A purpose meritorious;
   To such, the true and bold,
The careful and laborious,
   Who their designs well mould,
And strive until victorious,
   Life is a tale well told.

# Day After Day.

D *A Y* after day we wake and view
The ambient landscape—Heav'n so blue—
Things that are old—things that are new—
Day after day;—
Things that abide, and things that range—
Things that are constant—things that change—
Familiar things—things that are strange—
Day after day.

2.

Day after day refreshed we rise,
When morning's roses deck the skies;
Fresh zest repose to life supplies,
Day after day;
Day after day to toil we go,
And in our tasks aweary grow;
And sweet were rest ere sunset's glow.
Day after day.

3.

Day after day we pass along,
Now lonely, now in busy throng,
With now a sigh and now a song,
Day after day;
Day after day experience brings
Its alternating joys and stings—
Peace and annoy, like swift-wing'd things,
Day after day.

4.

Day after day, as flies the year,
The grass grows green, the grass grows sere,
The flow'rs appear and disappear,
Day after day;
Day after day these frames of ours
Change like the herbage or the flowers—
So flourish or decline their powers,
Day after day.

# A Portfolio of Lyrics.

Departing hopes leave us forlorn;
To take their place, are new ones born,
And we await a brighter morn,

5.                         Day after day:
Reverse is met and triumph won,
Now smiles break forth, now tear-drops run,
And shadow alternates with sun,
                        Day after day.

Day after day draws yet more near
The close of our existence here:
Yet why should we be slaves to fear

6.                         Day after day?
If we but live here as we should,
Howe'er reviled—misunderstood—
We march tow'rd Heaven with the good,
                        Day after day.

# The Approach Of Winter.

SWEET Summer—fleet Summer—is crownless—dead!
Gay Autumn—gray Autumn—will soon be dying—
Eftsoon Winter's boon countless flakes be flying—
He stealthfully comes, though we note no tread!

Bewitchful, in sooth, were those by-gone days!
2.    Supernal, in truth, seemed those by-past hours,
When passionate south-winds kissed am'rous flowers.
And Phœbus looked down with a lover's gaze!

The leaves, quickly turning from gold to brown,
3.    Are falling!  The songsters have ceased their numbers—
Their dwellings are empty!  The forest slumbers:
The heavens wear daily a sullen frown!

But why should we pine for evanished joy?
4.    Bright Fancy will yield us her fairest treasures,
Fond Hope will entrance us with rarest measures—
Chill Winter our comfort need not destroy!

297

# December Ruminations.

COLD winds are raving, and wild flakes are flying'
The fields lie wrapt in burial-robes of snow,
And with funereal voice in notes of woe,
The fitful gusts are with each other vying'
I gaze without, and cannot keep from sighing!
For memories come of bright days long ago,
When life like Summer-time was all aglow!
How changed the prospect now before me lying!
Hopes like the flowers that lately bloomed and smiled
Like them have perished and been swept away,
E'en as their petals by December's blast!
O, Faith! Beam on me with thine eyes so mild!
Vouchsafe assurance of a brighter day—
Relume the heav'ns so darkly overcast!

# Christmas, Jovial Christmas!

TIS Christmas, jovial Christmas!
What music charms the air!
Notes tintinnabulary
Wake gayness ev'rywhere!
What makes the world so wildly glad?
Why are men's souls aglow?
Incarnate Deity was born
On this day, long ago!

# A Portfolio of Lyrics.

How sweetly Seraph-voices
    Divulged—promulged to men
The tidings!  Ah, what splendor
2.    Gilt awe-struck herdsmen then!
"Glory be unto God most high!
    Peace and good-will below!"
So sang that scintillant Orchestra,
    So long, so long ago!

How halcyon was the night-time,
    When o'er that town afar—
Town olden—hovered golden
3.    And supernatural star—
When Magi from the East drew nigh,
    Rare treasures to bestow
Upon the infant Son of Man,
    So long, so long ago!  .

Tell, tell to all the story
    Of Shiloh's wondrous birth;—
To lands most sore benighted
4.    In utmost parts of earth
Tell how the Son of God came down.
    Redemption to bestow
Upon a lost—a forfeit world,
    So long, so long ago!

Ring out, O, bells of Christmas!
    More madly glad become!
Ring, ring in jubilation,
5.    Throughout all Christendom!
For peace on earth, good-will to men,
    Are regnant now below,
As when the Holy One was born,
    On this day, long ago!

O, Christmas, jocund Christmas!
    With gush of hallowed mirth,
We hail thy annual advent,
6.    Day of our Saviour's birth!

For we are grateful that He came
To vanquish human woe,—
Messias, born at Bethlehem
Long centuries ago!

✦

# Old Year And New.

*T*HE Old Year died with moan disconsolate—
Like one remorseful for a life of guile.
The New is born—behold his joyful smile!
Farewell, Old Year! Thy joy, grief, love and hate,
Gains, losses, triumphs, failures, small or great,
For aye are past! Adieu to thy spent while!
Thou hast for us no longer charm or wile!
Welcome, O, New Year! Make us fortunate!
Yea, welcome, sweetly-smiling bright New Year!
Bring us fresh benisons from the hand of Him
Who bids the years with their mutations roll!
Some tears I drop upon the dead Year's bier,
But greet thee with a hope which naught can dim—
With resolute heart and with undaunted soul.

✦

# A Cold-Weather Pic-
# ture.

*T*HE maples of the Common's row—
Its margent—argent lustre wear:
With frost and ice and sleet and snow,
Beneath the morning sunlight's glow,
Bediamonded both high and low,
Earth teems with brilliance ev'rywhere!

# Pictures On The Pane.

O, there are pictures on my window-pane!—
      Castles with turrets soaring grandly high,
      Cities whose bright spires, tapering to the sky,
   Like angel fingers point tow'rd Heav'n's Domain—
Rivers that wend through vastitude of plain
      To seas where white-sailed vessels anchored lie—
      Savannas—mountains—glens that charm the eye—
Paintings no connoiseur could well disdain!
Ye pictures marvellous! I love you well!
   In childhood, waking from my childish dreams,
      I saw such scenes depicted o'er and o'er
Upon the nursery-window. None can tell
   The joy I felt, enchanted with their gleams!
      O, skilled Frost-Artist! Come and paint once more!

# Good-Bye.

H, saddest of words is the word good-bye,
      When, parting from those whom we fondly love,
   We utter it—hear it! Grows moist the eye,
      And darkens the landscape—the sky above!
The shimmering leaves and the flow'rs that blow,
   Though bright, appear tinged with a sombrous dye:
The river seems murmurously to flow;
      The breeze has a dreary—an eerie sigh—
      All things seem to echo that word—"Good-bye!"

Ah, sad—doubly sad is the word good-bye
   When spoken at last by the pallid lips
Of dear ones we watch as the end draws nigh—
2.      As life slowly passes 'neath death's eclipse!
The eyes, brimming over, are dimmed and blurred,

The torn bosom quivers with sob and sigh;
The acme of anguish is in that word—
That word which in mem'ry can never die—
That word —ah, that bitter-sweet word, "Good-bye"

It stirs the same chord in each loyal breast,
Whatever the language 'tis uttered in—
Whatever the clime—be it East or West—
For men are all brothers—all races kin.
3.
Ah, yes, 'tis the same to both old and young,
To rich and to poor—to both low and high:
And sadly it falls from each mortal tongue!
'Tis mournful alike to both ear and eye—
Oh, sorrowful, sorrowful word good-bye!

Ah, this is a world where we meet to part!
Wherever we mingle upon the earth,
The thought we must sever perturbs the heart,
And snatches the zest from life's hours of mirth'
4.
The moment of parting must come we know,
We cannot evade it, howe'er we try;
It comes unto each—unto all below;
To every one 'neath the broad, broad sky,
There cometh a time for that word good-bye'

Good-bye! Ev'ry moment that word is said
By some one—and will be while Time's sands run.
To hear it and say it, howe'er we dread
Its sound, we are fated till life be done.
5.
Ah, well! A far different world awaits
All true and leal souls that in this world sigh.
When softly behind us shall swing pearl gates,
No more shall we speak it up there on high—
No more shall we hear it—that word good-bye'

# The Last Look.

*I* LOOKED back at the mansion I dwelt in of yore,
I looked back at the lake with its bright pebbly shore,
I looked back at the stream with its moss-bordered bank,
I looked back at the pines as they rose rank on rank;
I looked back at the mountain which towered on high,
Till its purple cone pierced the cerulean sky;
I looked back at the friends I had bidden farewell,
And my breast heaved with ocean's tumultuous swell!
What could hinder the sigh— what prevent the tear's starting?
There is nothing so sad as the last look at parting!

A friend I had known from my earliest youth,
Whose soul was the temple of honor and truth,
Came to bid me adieu and to proffer his hand.
Ere he journeyed away to a far-distant land.
2.   Ah, well I remember the words that he said,
And well I remember my heart inly bled;
But the bitterest pang that my bosom then bore
Came when from me he turned, as he passed from my door!
What could hinder the sigh—what prevent the tear's starting?
There is nothing so sad as the last look at parting!

A loved one had passed from this earth-life away,
Her cold, silent form in its shroud calmly lay;
Sad rites were performed— the last solemn words said—
And forth she was borne to her last narrow bed.
3.   But though sad was my soul in the presence of Death,
When that one so adored yielded up her last breath,
Yet a far keener woe came my spirit to smite,
When I last viewed that face which the dust hid from sight!
What could hinder the sigh—what prevent the tear's starting?
There is nothing so sad as the last look at parting!

303

# Gone.

*(In Memory of my Mother.)*

SEEMS Aurora's robe less pearled—
Nature's loveliness withdrawn:
Strangely altered is the world,
Since she's gone.

Changed is ev'rything around,
2.    Field and meadow, lake and lawn:
Half their charms no more abound,
Since she's gone.

Dimmer seems the noontide's glow,
3.    Sunset's halo, glint of dawn;
Moanful seem the winds that blow,
Since she's gone.

Since she's gone—Oh! Is it true?
4.    Eerie dream!—'Twill fade ere dawn—
I shall yet those features view—
Nay, she's gone.

Bitter 'tis to realize;
5.    Hard grief's lesson is to con:
But within her grave she lies,
Dead and gone.

Not till life's tasks shall be o'er—
6.    Till a deathless day shall dawn—
Shall these eyes behold her more:
Yes—she's gone.

Yet I seem to hear her speak,—
7.    See the smile that, sweet as dawn,
Played upon that pallid cheek,
    Though she's gone.

Still she seems to linger near,
8.    Hopefully to cheer me on
When life's trials grow severe;
    But—she's gone.

Ne'er from Memory's Room of Gold
9.    Shall her presence be withdrawn;
There she bides, fair as of old,
    Although gone.

All her words of trust and love,
10.    All her counsels shall live on,
Prized all else beyond, above,
    Since she's gone.

Gone—yes—only gone before
11.    Whither we shall follow on;
For we seek that tombless shore
    Where she's gone.

We shall sometime clasp her hand,
12.    See that face no longer wan,
In the blessed Morning Land
    Where she's gone.

# Across The Bridgeless River.

*(In Memory of W——— S———.)*

ACROSS the Bridgeless River
   His soul has taken flight—
Across the mist-hid River,
   Whose spray so made us shiver,
To Shore where no lips quiver
   With grief—where all is bright;
Beyond the faintest, farthest star,
The stainless spirit soared afar,
Where all the holy Ransomed are,
Where Angel hands Pearl Gates unbar.

Vain, vain was each endeavor
   The Messenger to spurn—
Each anguished fond endeavor
Death's viewless grasp to sever,
And he has gone forever
   To Realm whence none return.
But God in love has called him home,
Beyond yon sun-lit, star-lit dome,
In ever-vernal fields to roam,
Where Life's mellifluent Fountains foam.

Although we droop in sadness,
   We have a peerless hope—
A hope that in our sadness
Can cheer and give us gladness,
And guard us from the madness
   Of those who blindly grope.
We lift our eyes from earth's cold sod
To yonder Paradise of God,
Whose paths ere now his feet have trod.
And meekly bow beneath the rod.

# God's Silence.

GOD'S silence seals those sweet lips! They will never
  Unfold the mysteries of that Shore beyond
  The rayless tide. Death waved his mystic wand,
And she, earth's fairest, passed from earth forever.
Why did the fearful Angel haste to sever
  The cord of being, that frail, marvellous bond?
  But sorrow not too wildly! She hath donned
White robe, gold crown, guerdons of soul-endeavor.
O, World! To her your pleasures seemed not sweet:
  Your sinfulness that saintly one abhorred!
  Ah, once sore grieved, but now enraptured soul!
To God's own bosom thou on pinions fleet
  Hast sped away! Loosed is the Silver Cord,
  And broken, broken is the Golden Bowl!

⊞

# Baby In Heaven.

*(To some Friends on the Death of their Infant Son.)*

AS leaflet in the forest
      That withers ere its time.
  While yet the vernal season
      Is regnant in its prime:—

2.  As flow'ret in the garden
      That only sees the light
    To droop and pale and vanish
      From our enchanted sight;—

3.  E'en so your precious darling
      Is taken from your view,
    And you with soul-felt sadness
      Have breathed a last adieu.

But far beyond the fading
4.     Of this most changeful sphere,
An angel on its bosom
    Has borne that one so dear;—

Has borne it to that Kingdom
5.     Unutterably pure—
Land of Life's Tree—Life's River—
    From chance and change secure—

Land of the Many Mansions,
6.     Transcendent in their sheen,—
Of God's own Home eternal,
    Which knoweth no sad scene,—

Where leaflets never wither,
7.     And flow'rets ne'er decay,—
Where all is never-fading
    And shadowless for aye.

Be this your consolation
8.     Henceforth, from day to day,
While here through life you journey—
    While here on earth you stay:—

Safe is the one you cherished—
9.     Safe from all lures of sin—
From all the countless perils
    That rise without, within,—

Safe from unnumbered trials
10.     To which all men are heirs—
From all the world's distractions—
    From all its untold snares;—

Safe now and safe forever,
11.     Kept by Immortal Love:—
A star to light you upward
    To Paradise above.

Be this your constant solace
12.      Until life's tasks be o'er:—
Your treasure waits your coming
    On Seraph-trodden Shore.

# In The Gloaming.

*I*N the gloaming, in the gloaming,
   We were roaming—I and she—
Idly roaming by the foaming
   Ever murmurous, restless sea.

In the gloaming, in the gloaming,
2.     By the bounding, sounding sea,
Ever foaming, sweet was roaming!
    Happy lovers then were we.

In the gloaming, in the gloaming
3.     Seemed a voice to say to me:
"Why alone in life be roaming
    Till its gloaming come to thee?"

In the gloaming, in the gloaming
4     Soft eyes said the same to me—
Spake to mine as we were roaming
    By the foaming, foaming sea.

In the gloaming, in the gloaming,
5.     By the glimmering, shimmering sea,
Heart met heart, no longer roaming.
    One were our two lives to be.

In the gloaming, in the gloaming
6.     Joy as great as joy could be
Thrilled our hearts as we were roaming
    Side by side beside the sea.

In the gloaming, in the gloaming
    7.    All our dreams were grand and gay.
As, while roaming by the foaming
    Sea, we planned our future way.

But the waking—ah, the waking—
    8.    The rude breaking of those dreams!
'Twas of Marah's fount partaking,
    No thirst slaking with its streams!

All the castles that we builded,
    9.    In that gloaming by the sea,
By the lingering sunset gilded,
    Could not, could not, could not be.

For amid another gloaming
    10.    Came an angel none could see,
Whispering in her ear: "Cease roaming:
    Come with me—O, come with me!"

So we parted—sadly parted—
    11.    In that gloaming—I and she—
Heavy-hearted—broken-hearted—
    By a soundless, boundless sea.

In that gloaming—that sad gloaming—
    12.    By that hueless, viewless deep,
I, alone in anguish roaming,
    Felt that foaming ocean's sweep—

Saw my earthly angel vanish,
    13.    With Heav'n's angels to abide;
And the mists that naught could banish
    Rose that spirit-bark to hide.

Gloom that there was no dispelling—
    14.    Gloom that naught has since dispelled—
Lingering, dwelling by that swelling
    Main, dimmed all mine eyes beheld.

But not hopelessly we parted,
    Though tears started,—I and she—
No despairing frenzy darted
    Piercingly through her or me.

25.

For despite that weird deep's foaming,
    Faith more strong, more sure than sight.
Saw a Land where falls no gloaming—
    Where the parted reunite—

26.

Where there is no sickening, dying.
    Not a jot or whit of loss,
No more trying ills, no sighing,
    No more crying, no more cross.

27.

So she left me in the gloaming,
    Whispering softly: "Bye and bye,
Where the Blessed Ones are roaming,
    We shall wander—you and I."

28.

Weakly shivering, with lips quivering,
    By that eerie dreary sea,
Love's last message thus delivering.
    Soared her soul away from me—

29.

Soared to Regions sempiternal,
    Where Life's River, bright and broad,
Rolls through vernal fields Supernal—
    To the golden House of God.

30.

www.ingramcontent.com/pod-product-compliance
Lightning Source LLC
Chambersburg PA
CBHW020946030726
47496CB00005B/1380